Rise, Rise, Dark Horses of American Noir

A POSTMODERN MYSTERY

Konrad Ventana

iUniverse LLC
Bloomington

RISE, RISE, DARK HORSES OF AMERICAN NOIR
A POSTMODERN MYSTERY

iUniverse books may be ordered through booksellers or by contacting:

iUniverse
1663 Liberty Drive
Bloomington, IN 47403
www.iuniverse.com
1-800-Authors (1-800-288-4677)

ISBN: 978-1-4917-0808-8 (sc)
ISBN: 978-1-4917-0809-5 (hc)
ISBN: 978-1-4917-0810-1 (e)

Library of Congress Control Number: 2013916859

Printed in the United States of America.

iUniverse rev. date: 11/8/2013

This novel is dedicated to Maria,
in memory of all the shining times we shared.

Contents

1. Hast Thou Eyes of Flesh? 1
2. First Recollections of a Crime Scene 7
3. Where Angels and Dreams Depart 25
4. Poet Laureate of the Inner Dark 47
5. No Time to Be Asleep 57
6. A Filthy, Ill-Lighted Place 69
7. Night of the Corpora Delicti 81
8. *Mis Pasos Resuenan en Otra Calle* 91
9. They'll Never Get to Hollywood 105
10. More Than Lamps Symmetrically Arranged 113
11. A Thousand Unblinking Eyes 125
12. Clutching a Handful of Smoke 137
13. My Lady in the Lake 155
14. Looking Deeply into Indifference 165
15. With a Finger to Your Lips 177
16. Chilling Moments of Uncertainty 191
17. Who's That Lounging in Those Chairs? 205
18. Cry Out into the Night 219
19. Rendezvous in Shadows 227
20. Where Only the Mist Is Real 233

1 Hast Thou Eyes of Flesh?

A poet told me something a while back that seems rather strange to say.

She said, "The luminous world is a nearly invisible world that we do not often see."

She said, "Our eyes of flesh, being human, view the colors of the night only in diminishing levels of darkness and shadows, in the likeness of film noir."

I didn't think much about it at the time. Back then, I was used to viewing things from a safe and dispassionate distance, looking upon every man, woman, and child in Los Angeles with the same judgmental disposition to discern their faults, the same uncharitable inclination to construe everything in the severest possible manner. Back then, I was accustomed to examining outward appearances and visible objects with a bitterness and vexation befitting a man of my profession, becoming hardened by the extreme violence of the postmodern underworld as it rages on in this dark city, and tempered by witnessing firsthand the unmitigated wrath of too many cruel and steely deeds. Back then, I was a promising forensic scientist with a brand-new diploma and a California license plate—that is to say, an apprentice crime scene investigator in need of a steady job.

Back then, before everything changed—before I changed—things were exactly as they appeared to the observant eye and the physical ear. There was nothing of value to be found behind the curtain, no unjustified beliefs to be held dear, and certainly no intuitive processes or "gut feelings" that I considered relevant to the rational examination and scientific analysis of postmortem artifacts. When, for example, an attractive female client leaned close to me and whispered softly in my ear, "There are spirits in the darkness riding horses of the wind," I would have smiled sardonically and—barring any extenuating sexual and/or financial circumstances—I might have excused myself gracefully from the case.

That, however, is not what happened.

You see, I was deeply in debt at the time and too insecure about my future prospects for employment to ignore this tantalizing client. If you must know, these two equally exquisite forms of extenuating circumstances (that is, *sexual* and *financial*) punctuated, if not defined entirely, my apprenticeship and consequent transformation into a private investigator in the City of Angels. And thus, I found myself embracing both my circumstances and my client that night beneath the covers and the shadows, hoping against hope that the beautiful, affluent creature lying there beside me, warm and wanting in the darkness, was neither violent nor insane, hoping against hope that her soft whisper of foreshadowing referred solely to the thunderous hoof beats of a corporeal passion that rises up from the loins of feminine desire.

Back then, I was a younger man; I'm older than that now.

• • •

It all started with a phone call from a friend of mine who said that the Los Angeles Police Department was offering me a position, if I could start right away—which seemed rather curious to me, since I was recently drummed out of a prestigious local university and its forensic research laboratory for blowing the whistle on, shall I say, the inauspicious behaviors of some *soi-disant* "pillars of the community," figuring, at the time, that this whistleblower might have to get used to waiting tables, performing occasional paternity DNA tests, and working odd jobs just to pay the rent.

It started out as *The Tragic Case of the Dangling Children*, but it didn't end there. That was just the beginning of my apprenticeship with Detective Dash Brogan, LAPD, and my long and perilous descent into the inner darkness and depravity of the criminal mind. It was a case that I, or rather we, should have been able to solve fairly quickly but couldn't. We were not yet properly equipped, not yet fully prepared for the task of discerning the elusive modus operandi, the subtle, maniacal leitmotif that binds a succession of increasingly horrific spectacles into a coherent whole. Yet this maniacal leitmotif, this guiding *thème noir,* would turn out to be as crucial to solving this emerging mystery as, say, *The Fire Sermon* might be to an aesthetic monk attempting to grasp the basic tenets of Buddhism, or *The Allegory of the Cave* might be to those incredulous "prisoners-in-chains" attempting to understand the illuminating philosophy of Plato.

But let's get back to those little children, lest we leave them dangling forever. Let's get back to those unfortunate children, where the criminal investigation begins ...

2 First Recollections of a Crime Scene

They appeared to me, at first, like large dolls with patterned shirts and colorful party dresses, hanging there from thick, knotted ropes strung high up in the branches of the majestic oak trees, lifeless, dripping wet with the slackening rain, twisting in the gathering brume—eight little children hanging frightfully still.

I can still see them as clearly as if it had happened just yesterday. Like a recurring nightmare that comes and stays with you too long, evoking the enduring horror of some inescapable reality, it galls and vexes me to this very day. They were only children: too young to be either cynical or jaded; too young to know the predatory darkness that lies at the heart of such a crime; too young to know anything about devious plots of murder, or to have heard the revealing exclamations of an old Shakespearian king who thunders through the ages, "*O, heinous, strong, and bold conspiracy!*" They were only children: innocent of the wicked ways of the world they were born into; innocent of the extreme cruelty of their fates, which were now so vividly, so ruthlessly displayed for all to see. They were only children: barely flowering in the emergent pageantry of youth, completely unaware of the treacherous world that swirled so violently around them. They were found dangling that frightful, objectionable afternoon in the arboreal canopy of the well-manicured Descanso Gardens arboretum, languishing on the chains of failed expectations at the darkening end of the line.

It started to rain again, and the ground was slippery as a coterie of sheriff's men took hold of the dangling children, one by one, and lowered them onto the sodden turf.

Moving closer, I suddenly stopped, froze. I could hear a distinctive creaking sound—that terrible creaking sound that winds its way into your mind as you stand breathless and still, staring in astonished silence at a childlike form suspended eerily before you, twisting in the vaporous twilight. You dare not move, or breathe, or look away as the tiny dancer slowly turns with the wind in an eerie, lifeless pirouette that revolves to a point of no return, and you stare into the gruesome face of death incarnate. Your mind reels at the sight of the tiny, skinless face, denuded of all recognizable human features, and those eyes, those wide-open, soul-piercing eyes, those perspicuous eyes that stare directly at you for a brief, stupefying moment—a moment that finally passes with the awful creaking rotation, yet it leaves an indelible tincture of horror among your most vivid memories and a primal sense of loathing for the flagrant villainy of the perpetrator, indeed, the vehement monstrosity of such a crime.

I steeled myself as I advanced upon the scene of the reposed bodies to investigate the missing faces of the children on the ground, but even cold-tempered steel was no match for the brutality of this particular crime. I stumbled in the mud, clutching at the bark of a live oak tree to avoid complete prostration. "Get out of my way, please!" I shouted to no one in particular, crashing forward to the ground as my mind burst into flames and I attempted to fathom what appeared to me to be one of the worst catastrophes in the world. I found myself clawing, climbing inside my mind this time, where I heard myself rambling in the manner of an aghast radio commentator witnessing the Hindenburg disaster: *Oh, the humanity!* I thought to myself. *And all these faceless little victims staring wide-eyed all around me ... I can't even talk to anyone ... Ahhh! I can't talk, ladies and gentlemen ... Honest, they're just lying there ... tiny masses of human wreckage ... and I can't stop their silent screaming ... and I can hardly breathe ... I'm going to climb further inside my head where I cannot see it. Listen, folks, I'm going to have to stop for a minute, because I'm losing my innermost voice. This is the worst thing I've ever witnessed ...*

I was knee-deep in the midst of my incoherent ramblings when Detective Dash Brogan grabbed me by the collar of my brand-new designer trench coat and hauled me to my feet.

"So this is the future of forensic science!" barked Brogan, sizing me up with more than a modicum of contempt. "I ask for new-school expertise, and they send me an idiot!"

"I'm terribly sorry," I muttered. "Really, I am. It's just that I have never seen, or even imagined, anything as horrible as this."

"If you can't stand the gore, you're not going to last long in this business," said Brogan with a faraway look that suggested a dark world of unspeakable crimes, leaving me with the uncomfortable feeling that there would be more appalling acts to come. A stream of rainwater fell from the ledge of his gray snap-brim fedora as he hunched forward to light an unfiltered cigarette. The dripping stopped, burning embers glowed brightly, and I was surrounded by a dense plume of tobacco smoke that rose and mingled with the volatile indoles of decaying oak leaves and the newly fallen winter bloom of camellia blossoms, adding a distinctive blend of oxidized carotenoids to the aromatic turpentines of the damp woodland bark. "I'm Detective Dash Brogan from the LAPD, and I can tell from your bearing and the mud on your knees that you've never been out of the crime lab."

"Actually, sir, I'm a postdoctoral research fellow with a concentration in forensic biology, biochemistry, and genetics. I admit that I don't have any experience—"

"Don't call me sir!" barked Brogan through clenched teeth. "It makes me nervous. It makes me suspicious. It makes me wonder how long it will be before some overly ambitious young punk from the bureau—with no real-world experience whatsoever—will come and place the sharp end of a stiletto into the center of my back."

Rainwater soaking into the darkened creases of Brogan's rumpled overcoat added a picturesque impression of credibility to the detective's ominous fatalism.

"I would never do such a thing," I protested, attempting to muster whatever fragile threads of dignity might have remained unsullied by my initial responses to the crime scene. "I was only sent here to help you in any way that I can. They asked for someone with expertise in DNA extraction and analysis, and I volunteered for the job."

"Well, all right then. Pull yourself together, college boy, 'cause we've got a serious job to do." As he spoke, he motioned with his head to the direction of the tiny victims now lined up on the ground. Walking over to the lurid scene together, Brogan waxed downright philosophical. "I'm old-school, college boy. In my time, high technology was fingerprints and gunshot residue—the physics of bullet trajectories and forensic ballistics—that's what solved cases in my day. See that fellow over there—the one with the camera bag and the crime scene tape? That's Clive. He's an expert in blood spatter, for what little it's worth in this case. You see, college boy, the problem with this here crime scene investigation is that there is no smoking gun, no fingerprints, and no blood spatter of any kind—not even a trace of blood in the rain, running thin."

"How can that be?" I queried, as much to myself as to Brogan. "It looks to me that their faces have been literally torn off."

"Not just the faces, but the skin of the hands and the feet, and even the teeth that might have revealed any kind of telltale dental work," said Brogan as we approached the man with the camera bag. "What's the word, Clive? Got anything new and interesting to report?"

"We got nothing, boss," said Clive. "We can get a luminol signal directly from the bodies, but nothing from the surroundings. Nothing on the ground and nothing seeping out—it's like they're petrified or something."

"This here's—"

"My name is Cornell Westerly," I quickly interjected, extending my hand and attempting to stifle the repetition of the unappealing nickname—alas, to no avail.

Clive only nodded. I noticed that he was wearing latex gloves.

"Okay, college boy," said Brogan with a smirk, "let's see what you can do to crack this case."

I stepped over the yellow tape and approached the lineup of tiny victims with trepidation, thinking that someone in a position of responsibility should cover up these poor dead bodies with some kind of blankets, at the very least, yet knowing full well that nothing under this setting sun could ever cover up the magnitude of the atrocity that was now laid to rest at my feet. Moreover, I knew from my studies at the university that *official cover-ups* do little to improve the forensic search for truth, including revelations of cause and effect that can only be discerned by the integrity of science and the meticulous application of modern investigative methodologies.

The rain had slackened up again, and though the twilight was fading to dusk, I bent down on my haunches and examined one faceless corpse and then another: each with a ghastly expanse of sinuous muscle where a human face should have been, each with an unremitting, unforgiving stare that grabs you and holds your attention with a pair of those same glaring, perspicuous eyes. I immediately noticed something strange when I palpated the limbs: there was much more stiffness, or rigor, in each of these little corpses than could be accounted for by the predictable processes of mere rigor mortis. There was something far more diabolical afoot. I was thankful when Clive handed me a pair of medical gloves, and I began to probe the overhardened tissues and the margins of the wounds with my thinly protected fingers.

"These bodies are already embalmed!" I shouted up at the solemn onlookers as I continued my examination. "But it's much more than that!" I added. "They're fixed and embedded, like tissue specimens on a glass slide. Only they're not just specimens. They were once living, breathing human beings, no different from you and me."

"Well, that's good enough for now," said Brogan. "Let's wrap them up, boys! And put them gently to bed!" he shouted to the sheriff's men who had gathered at the perimeters of the yellow crime scene tape. Turning to Clive, he said, "Maybe you can still make it home for dinner, Clive. You know, tomorrow's another day."

"Okay, Dash, if you say so," said Clive. Then he turned and began to walk away, but as he passed close by my side, he stopped briefly and said, "Good luck, kid—I think you're gonna need it." Clive paused for a lingering moment, as though thinking, and then he added, "But

13

I want you to know, we're all rooting for you to finger this perp."
And then he turned and walked down the gravel road, through the
crepuscular haze of the woods, and disappeared into the shadows.

"What do you mean that's good enough for now?" I queried,
facing Detective Brogan. "We still don't have a clue as to how this
terrible crime was committed."

"What we *do* know, college boy, thanks to your forensic analysis,
is that it didn't happen here. And that's enough for me to close down
this public hanging as a primary crime scene and send everyone
home for the night. Besides, I don't want to encourage the perpetrator
by allowing this nasty travesty to become the public spectacle that it
was obviously intended to be."

I retrieved my leather briefcase—which contained my scientific
tools of the trade, and which was now thoroughly soaked by the
rain—and prepared to exit the scene. "And so, where and when
should I meet you tomorrow to continue the investigation?"

"Not so fast, college boy. Since you trashed so much physical
evidence while you were stumbling around the area of interest like a
lunatic, the least you can do is help me get a bead on the secondary
players."

"I thought you said you were closing down this crime scene?"

"I said I was closing down this ghoulish piñata party as a *primary*
crime scene. And I have done just that. What we have left here—if
you can manage to keep your muddy shoes, knees, and elbows out of
it—is the makings of a *secondary* crime scene … as an extravagant
dump site."

I looked around the clearing for clues that might be separable
from the present activities of the sheriff's men. "You mean you want
me to help you make some castings of these tire tracks?" I bent down
to investigate the soggy indentations. "It looks to me like a medium-
size truck with four tires on the rear axle."

"That's about as useful as an igloo in this town, young man.
Without a license plate or a nametag to go on, we're dead in the
water. This is Los Angeles, for Pete's sake. There are more nondescript
medium-size trucks in this town than stars you can count in the sky."

"What then do you suggest we do next?"

"Watch and learn, young man! There is always useful information to be found, and nearer at hand than you think—that is, if you know how to reach for it. You see, someone in charge of this dandified botanical garden knows something about the son-of-a-somebody who strung up these kids, and I'm aiming to find that out pronto. It's what we call an old-school investigative style, college boy. It may not be pretty, but it *is* effective, and I want you to keep me company to make damn sure the hard-core conduct of my traditional police interrogation procedures doesn't get out of hand."

"Okay, you can count on me to watch your back," I said, without the faintest idea of what I was in for. "However, if I am about to go out on some kind of a limb for you, for the sake of these tragic kids and this criminal investigation … would it be too much for me to ask you to call me by my real name?"

"We'll see," was all he said. And then his eyes turned hard and rather scary, and I followed him through the dripping canopy of the old oaken woods to the Descanso Gardens headquarters.

On the Richter scale of hard-boiled interrogations, Detective Dash Brogan was a thirty-minute egg. No sooner had we found who was in charge of the park facilities and operations than Dash Brogan had him suspended by his neck, held up off the floor against a bulletin board of seasonal blooms and cuttings with a burly, adamantine hand gripped firmly around the man's neck. After such a personal and impassioned introduction, the park manager seemed quite amenable to reveal everything he knew in rapid fire, and I, for one, breathed a lot easier.

It turned out that the entire woodland quadrant of the arboretum was cordoned off from public view that morning, ostensibly by a Hollywood movie production company—which was not by itself unusual in this particular town. What was unusual, however, was the inability of anyone to produce any physical records of such a contractual arrangement, or even to have seen more than a glimpse of the production truck or trucks that apparently came and went without so much as a trace. One more trip to the bulletin board, and the red-faced park manager admitted that the missing contractual arrangement was made under the table, in cash, by courier, off the record—which was also not unusual in this town—and the only thing he could remember was the name *Art House Creations*, which was mentioned only once, over the phone.

Walking out of the Descanso Gardens headquarters and into the rain-soaked parking lot, Detective Dash Brogan must have determined that I had passed some kind of litmus test, for he finally cut me some slack, as it were.

"Well, that's a damned dead end," admitted Brogan, lighting an unfiltered cigarette he had planted in the side of his mouth. "I guess it's up to Cornell Westerly, after all." His exhalation engulfed me yet again in a great plume of tobacco smoke as he looked me up and down, like I was being fumigated and deloused at my inauguration to the venerable institution of true crime. "You and I both know that you didn't really volunteer for this job," said Brogan with a hardened blue-gray gaze that looked right through me and stifled all my pretenses. "What you don't know, *Cornell*, is that I'm the one who pulled your lame-ass name and your new career out of the hat."

"I … I don't know what to say," I said, offering sincerity in lieu of pretense. "You seem to know more about me and my current situation than I might have expected."

"You don't need to say anything to impress me, son," said Brogan reassuringly. "And it's my job to know more about my prospective operatives than they might have suspected."

"So, am I an *operative* or a *suspect* from the point of view of Detective Dash Brogan?"

"What you are, from my point of view, is a freak of nature—and that's not necessarily a bad thing," he said, turning up his collar against the wind and the creeping chill of the evening. "From my professional point of view, you are a freak of nature whose forensic capability is clear enough, but whose usefulness to me remains to be determined."

Brogan's eyes were calm and steady, neither challenging nor accusing, simply disarming. Though nightfall would soon be upon us, I could still see well enough in the remaining twilight to know that there was something one might refer to as *genuine* in his steadfast gaze. Again, I found myself at a loss for words.

"Come on, Cornell, you look like you could use a drink … I know I could." Brogan flipped the cigarette out in front of him, and we watched it arc and wink out on the wet pavement with a final discernable hiss. "Follow me in that imported jalopy of yours to Hillhurst Avenue in Los Feliz. I've got some important questions I need to ask you."

Brogan turned and walked over to a vintage Pontiac Catalina 2+2, circa 1967, in Starlight Black, which summarily growled and then roared to life, chastening me and my beat-up BMW, circa 1987, in Alpine White and primer gray, to hurry up and follow.

• • •

The sun plunged unseen beyond the vanishing edge of the Pacific Ocean. Two disparate vehicles motored into East Hollywood in an incipient darkness that seemed to be melding with thick layers of maritime fog and drizzle, smearing the headlights, taillights, and streetlights into surrealistic bokeh circles lacking in either clear definition or discernable boundaries, or both. We descended Hillhurst Avenue in a threatening rain squall that crept up into the Hollywood Hills and drenched the overcast village like a cold, gray curtain falling down in pieces.

The blurred taillights of the Pontiac Catalina flashed off and on again, signaling me to park on the street. We walked in the rain to a corner restaurant/bar called Little Dom's, a reference to its big brother, Dominick's, which was once a favorite watering hole for Frank Sinatra and the so-called Rat Pack. On a night like this, the sidewalk tables stood empty and dripping beneath the windblown awnings. Diehard customers were crowded inside, appearing from the street like a lineup of pale, ghostly masks—vague, pallid faces locked up and leering behind the steamed-up windows.

Inside the pub, the ambiance was warm and dry and aromatic, simply oozing with old-world charm, the redolence of wood-fired pizzas, handmade pasta sauces, and homemade bread. The décor was decidedly retro, salvaged from another place and time: a row of deep railroad-style dining booths trimmed in black leather, antique leaded-glass windows gleaned from demolitions in New York, and a 1930s wood-and-marble bar yanked from a saloon that once stood in Eaton, Pennsylvania. Above the bar with its beveled mirrors, vintage low-key lighting fixtures, and orderly arrays of bottles and glasses was a large hand-painted mural of Yosemite National Park. The grand mural had *allegedly* been appropriated from the Props Department of the Warner Brothers Studios.

It might have been the inescapable lure of those majestic mountains of Yosemite—one never knows—for Detective Dash Brogan eschewed the company of the local hipsters ensconced in conversation in the leather dining booths and the drool-inducing allure of the sumptuous Italian cuisine that was served up on white linen tablecloths; instead, Brogan headed directly to the bar, which was populated by a number of characters of remarkable alcoholic authenticity, some who looked like they might have been seated there since before the Prohibition—yet they all moved decidedly out of the way and out the door when Detective Brogan approached the base of those majestic Yosemite mountains in silence. I took an empty seat on a barstool beside him.

"You gotta stop doing that, Dash," said the barkeeper as he began to clear away the half-empty mugs and glasses. "It's bad for business." The man had the swollen face of a prizefighter in the later rounds of a hard life and a losing fight. In contrast, his black tie, vest, and period-correct sleeve garters gave him an elevated air of a mixologist who formulates his own bitters.

I hadn't seen anything that Detective Brogan might have actually done to encourage the barkeeper to ask him to stop doing it—short of flashing his badge in a subliminal manner that had somehow exceeded the speed of light—so I had to assume that it was Brogan's reputation that preceded him and precluded such quaint formalities as badge-flashing. However, this particular deduction made the bartender's dictum to cease and desist that much more curious.

Brogan didn't respond; he just sat there staring up at the scenic backdrop of the Yosemite Valley. His eyes appeared to be focused somewhere between El Capitan and Cathedral Rocks viewed from the level of the Merced River. The bartender returned with two glasses and a bottle of Old Forester. Brogan filled both glasses, slid one over to me, and fed himself an impressive slug of the bourbon whiskey. He shook his head sideways with a half smile, the way a man does when that badly needed drink is just right, and the first swallow is like a peek into a cleaner, brighter, loftier world than the one he has gotten used to living in. His steady gaze returned to Yosemite Valley for a brief moment, and then it turned back to me.

"I'm going to ask you a few questions, son … and I want you to answer me straight up!" Brogan slowly filled his empty glass, and then he gave me a piercing look that I'll never forget. It was a look of such directness and discernment that I suddenly felt like some kind of insect caught up in a specimen bottle, an insect that was being scrutinized to the extent of being systematically classified in accordance with the bimodal determinants of Brogan's personal taxonomic ranking system—liar or truth teller; poisonous or nonpoisonous; degenerate scumbag or decent citizen. There was no way out.

"I'll answer you as honestly as I can," said the captive insect that was me—caught up in an inquisition I could neither avoid nor escape, squirming against the reality, which was obviously transparent to Brogan, and the anonymity of a perfect nobody with half a brain who was simply at the wrong university—with the right kind of knowledge—at a crucial time in history.

The glare of Brogan's systematic taxonomy continued: "I don't want the kind of honesty that comes from the mouths of lawyers or district attorneys, son. I don't have time or patience for the *cuteness* of any nondisparagement clauses you might have memorized by now." Brogan emptied his glass again. "I'm going to ask you a few direct questions, and I want you to answer me straight up!"

I sloshed the glass of bourbon down my throat and swallowed hard, fighting against the violent shivers that coursed through my body from end to end. "Ask away!" I said.

"How in the wide world did you, of all people, manage to bring down the infamous Stem Cell King?" His knowing gaze was unrelenting. "With all that international hoopla and political pressures, it couldn't have been easy."

"I don't want to talk about that."

"I know what they did to you, son," said Brogan as he refilled both of our glasses to the brim. "Believe you me—I know how it feels to be the only man standing in our nasty little world where most people crawl." He deftly slid my glass back to me without spilling a drop.

"Thank you for that," I said, not knowing whether my appreciation was for the first real sympathy I had received in a very long while or for the generous serving of Old Forester, which went down a lot easier this time.

"I know it must have been hard on you," Brogan said sternly, narrowing his eyes as he spoke, "but I'm still waiting for an honest answer."

The detective's dark gaze pinned me to my seat, and squirm as I might, with no other exit in sight, I blurted out the truth: "Actually, it wasn't that hard. The so-called Stem Cell King was a charlatan, a deceiver, and a fraud!"

Brogan slammed his big fist on the table, rattling my nerves. "We all know that *now*, after the facts have been laid out on the table. I want to know how you, Cornell Westerly, managed to figure out the scam—that is, before anyone else was able to!"

"You give me too much credit, Detective Brogan." I gulped, attempting to explain the gist of a subject that had so consumed and shaped my recent life. "It's not as if I brought down the entire evil empire and the international drug cartel singlehandedly. I simply exposed the fraud in the notebooks," I paused, and when Brogan said nothing, I continued, as if filling in the blanks in some macabre game, "which exposed the scientific misconduct of the academic community," I flicked a piece of lint from my suit, keenly aware of the spotlight of Brogan's attention, "which exposed the administration of the university and its conflicts of interest with crony capitalists and its secretive collusions with big pharma," here I waited again, and

Brogan stared me down, "which exposed the whole house of cards to legal action and eventually to public scrutiny. It was the public scrutiny, not me, that brought down the infamous Stem Cell King."

"Fraud in the notebooks, you say? I don't remember anyone saying anything about fraud in the notebooks."

"Ha!" I shouted, happy to be free from the specimen jar for a moment, happy to have finally spoken a truth that was hitherto forbidden, at risk of legal action, or worse. "It's always the cover-up that does the real damage. Don't you know, the Stem Cell King had to go down to protect the interests of the real villains behind the charlatanism and the clandestine medical fraud!" I slammed my glass down hard on the counter in front of Brogan, as though I needed a refill, but something told me that I might have had enough whiskey already—perhaps too much!

"Look here, Cornell, I don't give a tinker's damn about the corrupt politics of medical schools and petty universities. I'm not interested in the dirty laundry of presidents, princes, or kings, for that matter." Brogan slowly filled both our glasses again and continued: "What I really want to know, what I need to hear from you right now, is how in the hell did you figure out the scam while every other clever son of a bitch was still in the dark?"

"Actually, it was easy for me—the results were clear as day!" I heard myself saying, obviously bolstered by the bourbon. "I am a man of science, first and foremost, with a keen sense of awe and wonder, a healthy respect for the intricate fabric of nature, and a fondness for the exquisite beauty of the physicochemical world around me. I simply reported the biochemical facts, as they were. The last thing I would allow anyone to do—the one thing I could not tolerate—would be to pervert the scientific method and subvert the findings of a scientific investigation. It would violate my belief in science, my sense of decency, and my love of nature precisely as she is!"

"Like I said before, you're a freak of nature! A geeky freak of nature! But your usefulness to me as a forensic investigator has yet to be determined!" Brogan emptied his glass and continued. "I don't want your highfalutin high fives for Mother Nature, Aristotle, or

21

Betty Crocker. I want to know exactly how you did it! Can you tell me that, or can't you?"

"Of course I can, but I'm not sure you would be interested in hearing all the grisly molecular-genetic details." I was feeling the effects of the whiskey pretty strong by now, and I wasn't too sure I could communicate the intricate details even if I wanted to.

Brogan was not satisfied in the least. "I may look to you like someone who's too dumb to understand the marvelous complexities of the molecular-genetic world you live in," he said as he rolled his right hand into an intimidating fist, "but I can assure you that these here knuckles are more than capable of beating the living daylights out of any wise guy who is foolish enough to insult my brutish intelligence!"

"Since you put it that way, Detective," I said, trying to sound firm in response to Brogan's menacing gesture, "it was right there in the chromosomes! The truth of the matter was right there in the chromosomes, if anyone bothered to look for it! The genetic signature of a cloned human stem cell is entirely different from a fraudulent cell culture that has been tripped into replication by parthenogenesis or otherwise artificial means."

"You mean you read the genetic signature like some kind of handwriting analysis?"

"Yes, exactly, just as one is able to read the genetic signatures of a number of troublesome physical traits such as hemophilia, cystic fibrosis, Down syndrome, and certain types of cancer."

"Is that what you've been doing for hire lately, in addition to DNA paternity tests?" Brogan looked me up and down like I was lower than an insect, lower than the lowest life form.

"Unfortunately, yes," I said, feeling myself squirm. "You'd be surprised how many requests I get to scientifically determine the suitability of mating partners for Hollywood big shots and celebrities."

"And you're happy with that! Given your advanced training in forensics, DNA analysis, and genetics, that's all you plan to do with your life?" Brogan shook his head.

"No, sir ... I mean, Detective ... I mean, I've been banished from my laboratory and the ivory towers of the academics. It's all that there is left for me ... to live ... to pay the rent!"

Brogan smiled and extended his great, battle-scarred hand to me as he offered me the job. "Congratulations, Dr. Cornell Westerly, you have just graduated from degenerate scumbag to apprentice investigator at Dash Brogan's Benevolent Institute of Crime Scene Investigations.

3 Where Angels and Dreams Depart

The next day, I drove the length of the Santa Monica Freeway into Los Angeles, where I met Detective Dash Brogan outside the LA County Morgue. He looked like a man that had, in the Western vernacular, been *"rode hard and put away wet."* He was wearing pretty much the same wrinkled suit that seemed at least one size too small, the same weathered trench coat that seemed at least one size too large, and the same snap-brim fedora that looked as though it had been bashed and battered and straightened out one too many times. He was smoking another unfiltered cigarette, facing down a sharp-dressed fellow with a red silk tie and an expensive pinstripe suit, fumigating the fashionable dandy only slightly less abundantly than he had fumigated me the day before.

From the sound of it, he was having a philosophical discussion with the LA County coroner over what, exactly, constitutes a *crime against nature.* The coroner—whose duty it is to inquire into and determine the circumstances, manner, and causes of all violent, sudden, or unusual deaths, particularly deaths that are known or suspected to be homicides, and deaths that are whole or in part occasioned by criminal means—was not pleased. Apparently, deaths associated with a known or alleged *crime against nature* are considered to be categorically distinct, leaving considerable room for Brogan's unique style of Socratic questioning.

"How the hell do you expect me to investigate this crime properly if I can't remove any of the physical evidence I need from the bodies?" snapped Brogan amid a cloud of cigarette smoke. Judging from the general redness of Brogan's face as he spat this question toward the coroner, there was a history and a significant amount of friction between the LAPD and the Coroner's Office over issues of jurisdiction.

"Look here, Brogan," said the sharply dressed coroner, waving the smoke from his face. "You either play by my rules, or I'll have you thrown off the case. There's real pressure coming from the top for me to keep this nasty business under wraps. The last thing I need is a high-profile homicide detective and his hired hands conducting their own criminal investigation on the front pages of the *Los Angeles Times*!"

"You don't want to go there with me, Chauncey! Not with your record! Not on this case!" Brogan dropped the cigarette onto the sidewalk in the space between them and slowly ground it out with the sole of his shoe. "I'll put my seniority and the privilege of carrying this LAPD detective badge on the line for those victimized kids, which is more than you're bound to do."

I approached the conversation with caution for several reasons: First, in addition to my forensic briefcase, I was gingerly wielding a paper cup filled with scalding-hot Starbucks coffee, which was burning the tips of my fingers. Second, the walkway leading up to the entrance of the imposing, red-brick building was still slick from last night's rain. And third, I was interested in hearing more of the heated conversation from a perspective of relative safety, as an observer.

"I'm warning you, Brogan … you're on thin ice! I'm not about to let you, your shadowy dragon ladies, and your unreliable team of scientific vigilantes ruin my day!"

Shadowy dragon ladies? I wondered what the county coroner was referring to. Although I was pretty sure that the *unreliable* part of the narrative was referring negatively to me.

"If we don't get to the bottom of this business—and quick," warned Brogan, "it will ruin a whole lot more than just one of your days!"

"What do you mean by that, Brogan? You think it's likely there will be more victims than these! Tell me, on what rational basis are you making this outrageous conclusion?"

"The same rational basis I can tell you that the sun is likely to rise and set tomorrow."

At this point, I decided to insert myself into the conversation, come what may.

"Good morning, Detective Brogan. I'm ready to start whenever you are."

The coroner looked me over with a critical, jaundiced eye. Noticing that my hands were full, he did not proffer a formal greeting. Instead, he turned back to Brogan, who was lighting another cigarette, and he stood firm against the fresh onslaught of Brogan's fumigating smoke. "Look here, Brogan, we have accredited standards for *investigator trainees*. I don't care how technically good you think or say he is." The coroner looked me up and down as if he was about to attach an official toe tag to my apprenticeship before it had even begun.

"This here's no physician's assistant, Chauncey ... no coroner's investigator trainee of any kind you're familiar with. This here's Dr. Cornell Westerly. He's a top scientist and a biochemist of the first rank, and he's an official member of my *independent* investigative team," said Brogan.

"Do you mind if I ask him a few simple questions about forensic science, genetics, and molecular biology?"

"Certainly, Chauncey, by all means, feel free to voir dire your *competition*," said Brogan, with a wink to me. "I'd say, your *superior*, but I think I'll let you find that out all by yourself."

The coroner crossed his arms in front of his chest and thrust his chin in the air. It was an air of haughtiness that held his head aloft in such a manner, a face of arrogance and pomp without circumstance that is all too common, all too familiar in hospitals and academic circles. It was a supercilious face that was just begging to be slapped—a notion that I struggled to resist.

The coroner spat out the first question as one would spit out an insult: "It's easy enough to *start* a criminal investigation, young man, as is the translation of a fragment of genetic code, but are you certain that you are wise enough to know exactly when and where to *stop*?"

Sensing a note of indignation in the coroner's clever double entendre, I responded appropriately, in kind. "To ensure that the mutable stopping point of said transcript is not lost in translation, I will be succinct: of the three triplets of fatal determination, I prefer ocher for its earthy iron oxide finality and opal for its rare gem-like qualities. However, if I had to choose at precisely which point to terminate the sequence of any progressive chain of events in the City of Angels, it would have to be at the first sign of a yellow light—that is, a change in the determinate complexion of the mater, which is known as *amber*."

The county coroner did not ask another question. He looked angrily at me, and then at Brogan, and finally at his watch. "You deserve each other," he said as he speed-dialed a number and held the cell phone to his ear. "Listen, Danny, Brogan's coming with his geneticist to collect some tissue samples. I want you to watch them carefully, making sure they don't take any organs of any kind. Do you hear me, Danny? Nothing larger than a match head!" When he finished the call, making sure we overheard his instructions, the county coroner rapidly departed from the premises in the direction of the parking lot, leaving the two of us to our business.

As we made our way up the steps of the imposing red-brick building ornamented with horizontal slabs of pale cement, Brogan turned to me and smiled. "I'm not even going to ask."

"It's just shoptalk, Detective, nothing serious," I said, blushing faintly and feeling a bit clever. "By the way, what did the coroner mean by the term *shadowy dragon ladies*?"

"You'll find out soon enough," was all he said.

We stopped at a covered landing at the top of the steps, and Brogan extinguished his smoke. I took a final sip of the hot coffee through the slit of the plastic cover and was just about to toss the remainder into a trash receptacle when Brogan interrupted me. "Better bring that coffee inside—you never know when it might come in handy."

• • •

The Los Angeles County Morgue is just like any other morgue in any other metropolis, only it is considerably larger in terms of inventory at any given time. It is also unusual in terms of the outlandish boundaries of its rather dubious taste—or should I say tastelessness—in that the LA Coroner's Office operates a macabre gift shop and novelty store that shares the same interior lobby with the assemblies of grieving, fainting, often crying people who have just identified the last remains of their loved ones.

"Someday I'm going to kick Chauncey's teeth in and make key chains out of the broken pieces," remarked Brogan as we entered the lobby and passed by an open door stenciled with the moniker, *Skeletons in the Closet*: the official retail store of the Los Angeles County Coroner. "This kind of vulgar nonsense and official pandering has no business in a place like this!"

I glanced inside at the morbid merchandise arrayed in the ill-illumined gift shop: life-size skulls were lined up on shelves, along with an absurd cachet of coffee mugs, cutting boards, mouse pads, T-shirts, barbeque aprons, garment body bags, toe-tag key chains, beach towels, and doormats emblazoned with chalk-outlined corpses. The artificial light from the Victorian lobby passed faintly through the angled slits of the venetian blinds that spanned the storefront windows, creating a dim, tomb-like atmosphere within the gift shop as if to accentuate the abject weirdness of the demented coroner's humor.

"It appears that there is no end to the depths that government bureaucrats will sink these days to balance their budget deficits," I offered in alliance. "It reminds me of Hollywood Boulevard, where everyone is trying to make a buck on dead celebrities, morbid landmarks, and mysterious unsolved murders."

Brogan only shrugged as he issued a grim reminder: "Now that we're in agreement with the social cost of incompetence, let's try not to forget what we came here for." He walked solemnly across the empty lobby—past an unoccupied ensemble of red-leather Craftsman chairs and an art nouveau staircase that led up to the coroner's office—toward a grim elevator platform that would lower us downward to the basement and the dreaded autopsy rooms of the county morgue.

I hurried to catch up with Brogan, and as we entered the elevator, I remarked, "If you ever go into the business of kicking in teeth to make key-chain trinkets, there are a few administrators at a local university that I would gladly add to your list of prospective donors."

We were greeted underground by Dr. Daniel Grist, a tall, lean broomstick of a man wearing surgical scrubs, surgical gloves, and a surgical mask over his nose and mouth. He made no effort at formal introductions, other than a brief nod to Brogan and a long, hard squint aimed directly at me. He silently turned around, and we followed him along an underground labyrinth of dim and dripping hallways, passing rows of parallel-parked gurneys and a series of cold rooms with milky condensation on the viewing windows. The dank air of the subterranean cellar was thick with the unmentionable issuances of morbidity.

"They have been weighed and measured and found wanting, Detective Brogan. Just like the writing on the wall at King Belshazzar's feast!" Daniel Grist spoke without stopping or even turning his head, and his irksome words were muffled to remoteness by the surgical mask.

"Wanting for what, Danny?" asked Brogan. "You boys wouldn't be having difficulties coming up with an official cause of death, would you?"

"The cause of death is officially *inconclusive* until further notice—coroner's orders." Daniel Grist was apparently not happy with the executive proclamation of his boss; it seemed to me that he was bridled by bureaucratic red tape and left chomping at the drill bit. "I'm not even allowed to open them up and take a peek until some purported experts from out of town fly in to hold an official conference with the coroner."

"What kind of experts, and from what sort of towns, are we talking about, Danny?" asked Brogan, with a hint of actual sympathy lurking amid the detective's frank interrogative.

Danny stopped in front of an autopsy room and turned around to face us. Though it was hard to tell with his surgical mask still on, there appeared a glimmer of indignation in his eyes. "Let's see," he said, "the powers that be are flying in a number of experts in wildlife taxidermy from the Smithsonian Institute in Washington, DC, a famous histologist from the University of Heidelberg, and a slew of experts in polymer chemistries and plastics from the East Coast."

"Plastics, you say," quipped Brogan as we entered the crowded autopsy suite. The room was a white-tiled crypt with fluorescent lighting overhead. It was jammed wall-to-wall with stainless steel sinks, autopsy tables, instrument trays, mechanical hoists, scales, wheeled lamps, and exactly eight rolling gurneys—each one supporting the last remains of a nameless, faceless child peering glaringly upward from the disconsolate grasp of an unzipped body bag.

"Yes, Detective Brogan, plastics! These little people were not just drained of all bodily fluids and embalmed and dressed for their last tango in the trees, as you found them; these poor unfortunate children have been plasticized like a class of grade-school Barbie and Ken dolls."

"That explains a lot," I asserted, trying to break the ice. "The lack of blood, the absence of smell, and the rigidity of the limbs." I tried to formulate a collegial smile but failed in my attempt and had to settle for a matter-of-fact sort of grimace. "Can we assume that the faces and the handprints were removed postmortem … after the actual deaths and embalming?"

"Yeah, you can tell the dissection by the margins *here*," he said, pointing a thin, bony finger along the perimeter of one of the grimly denuded faces. "And *here*."

I gloved my hands and examined the missing friction ridges on the tips of a child's tiny hand. "Are they all like this?" I queried. I was impressed by the delicacy of the dissection that was obviously made to obfuscate the fingerprints.

"Every one of them," he said. "Eighty painstaking dissections: each one removing the epidermis; each one down to the basal layers." Daniel Grist held up the opposite hand of the faceless child, turning the index finger sideways to reveal the dissection. Then he dropped the hand, which fell in an eerie slow motion, and then he lifted the child's leg. "Don't forget the toes," he added. Eighty little piggies that will never go to market or cry 'Wee! Wee! Wee!' all the way home."

I cringed at the gallows humor and looked away. I noticed

Detective Brogan was also looking away, intent on studying the orderly layout of an instrument tray. Brogan then began to survey the horizontal lineup of little bodies with the resolve of a general inspecting his troops. "These eyes don't look right to me," he said, bending forward, peering closely at one of the appalling faces. "Not like any dead man's eyes I ever looked into before."

I couldn't help but agree. Although my limited experience with cadavers in an academic setting may not be nearly as extensive as that of Detective Dash Brogan's, or in any way equivalent to his direct observations on the mean streets of Los Angeles, I could readily discern—from the striking degree of optical clarity, the persistence of an uncanny lifelike vivacity, and the resulting impression of intelligence that attended each outwardly leering expression—that something was definitely not right with these bright eyes. Something about these perspicuous eyes was totally incongruent with the prevailing framework of death.

"That's because the eyes are pure glass," said Daniel Grist. "Everything else is perfectly preserved and embedded with a silicone-based plastic, but these shining eyes are made of glass."

"What the hell!" said Brogan with a start. "What the hell do we have here, Danny?"

"What we have here is a failure to impregnate," explained Danny with a wry, though surgically masked, expression. "You see, this particular process of plastic imbedding is capable of preserving almost all of the anatomical and cytological features. Even the fine structures and the smallest capillaries are well preserved. However, the preservation of such lifelike qualities of a child's eyes must have been extremely difficult, so the eyes were replaced by replicas."

I watched in amazement as Detective Brogan—who was not amused or satisfied in the least—proceeded to back Daniel Gist into a dark corner: "With no fingerprints, faces, teeth, or eyeballs, we're going to have considerable difficulty identifying even one of these tiny victims. Hell's bells, Danny, without any blood or bodily fluids to go on, you and Chauncey are going to be hard-pressed to come up with a plausible cause of death with your routine toxicology."

"You're right about that, Detective, but what's a lowly pathologist to do?" Without waiting for an answer, Daniel Grist exclaimed, "My hands are tied when it comes to this matter! The coroner calls the shots around here, whether he knows what he's doing … or not!"

"And you know darn well, when it comes to this particular case," asserted Brogan, "the answer is definitely *not!*"

"Right," said Danny, with a passing glare that betrayed his slighted professional pride.

I looked on in a gathering fog of situational confusion as Brogan began to inspect the troops again, carefully examining each lifeless, plasticized corpse with a stern look of concentration. He paused briefly in his inspection, and then Brogan announced that this was Danny's "lucky day" and that all the necessary expertise—in the form of yours truly, Cornell Westerly—had already arrived on the scene, and just in time to save the lowly pathologist's standing in the community.

"You know that Chauncey will have my hide if I let you take anything larger than a match head from these premises," warned Dr. Daniel Grist.

"There's no need to worry about that, Danny boy," said Brogan. "Dr. Westerly won't need even that much material to accomplish his laboratory investigations. In fact, I want you to watch him real close as he takes his tissue samples. He's new in the field, and I want you to make sure that he follows all the specified departmental SOPs to the letter—I don't want any problems with the DA when it comes to establishing a chain of custody and preserving the hard evidence for DNA testing." Brogan flashed me a barely discernable wink as he relieved me of my coffee cup, signaling for me to proceed immediately with the specimen collection.

"Are you sure that you can extract sufficient DNA from these samples, even though they have been completely dehydrated and thoroughly plasticized?" asked Danny. "I understand that the analysis of ancient insect DNA extracted from fossilized amber was always considered to be somewhat ambiguous."

"Not to worry, Dr. Grist," I said, opening my leather evidence briefcase with the lofty confidence of a Zen master. "Analytical ambiguity is my business."

It took more than an hour, with Daniel Grist at my elbow, Dash Brogan following closely behind as a self-appointed quality-control monitor, and all the painstaking dissections, labeling, and cataloguing required for me to complete the routine task seven times over. Feeling cramped, I stood up straight to stretch my back—and as I did, I caught a glimpse of Brogan hunched over one of the plasticized bodies. He was holding my coffee cup in one hand and was reaching into his coat pocket with the other.

I quickly returned to the job of collecting the last tissue specimens, lest Dr. Daniel Grist become suspicious. Still, I couldn't help wondering what Brogan was up to, and I couldn't help noticing that a large bone chisel was conspicuously missing from one of the instrument trays.

When the job was finally completed, and Dash Brogan had inspected the bodies and zipped up each of the body bags, he said with a grin, "Nice work, men. Your mothers would be proud!"

Brogan handed me the coffee cup as I closed my leather attaché. Daniel Grist started to say something, but Brogan interrupted him. "Don't worry, Danny. I'll make sure you're the first to know when we find out something interesting and important. Then you can tell the coroner and his convocation of out-o'-town experts to stuff their opinions where the sun don't shine!"

I couldn't help but notice the glimmer of a smile emerging from the masked face of Dr. Daniel Grist when we left him at the elevator. And I couldn't help but notice that the unfinished cup of Starbucks coffee I was holding was considerably heavier than it was when I first handed it to Detective Dash Brogan.

We descended the front steps of the county morgue, and I looked up into a clouded sky still roiling with the somber shades of doubt and uncertainty, yet beginning to show signs of color and luminosity around the fringes. As we made our way to the parking lot, Brogan made a perplexing announcement: "The next thing we need to do is to set you up in a proper crime lab deep in the heart of this city."

"You're not going to establish my lab within the LAPD Scientific Investigation Division?" I protested. "The politics at the state university may not be ideal—and I may be persona non grata at the School of Justice and Criminalistics—but the new Forensic Science Center has all the modern research facilities I need to carry out my investigations. I don't understand."

"I said a *proper* crime lab, Cornell, my boy—not a *modern* one." Brogan ushered me to his Pontiac Catalina, standing there proudly as though it had been washed clean by the February rain and buffed to a fine luster by the prevailing sea breezes. Unlocking the driver's-side door, he added, "You and I both know that the university is often the last place you want to be if you're on a serious quest for truth or justice."

I couldn't argue with that, and I wasn't about to. I just stood there with my briefcase in one hand and a cold cup of Starbucks coffee and who knows what in the other—staring at the aging old-school detective, staring at the vintage American muscle car with its bucket seats and rugged sports car platform, and back again at the detective—trying to decide which one I admired more.

"I'll take that," said Brogan, unlocking the passenger door and relieving me of the mysteriously refilled coffee cup.

I hopped in the bucket seat and glanced at the elegant Catalina dashboard fitted out with full functional gauges. Stifling my impulse to grill Detective Brogan about the added contents of the coffee cup, I simply inquired, over the roar of the engine, "Where are we headed to next?"

Brogan smiled and said, "We're headed to the station where angels and dreams depart!"

• • •

We motored west on Mission Road, leaving the antiquated Coroner's Office building and the bleak concrete sarcophagus of the LA Medical Center in the rearview mirror, passing from one gruesome wrecking yard into another—one where used auto glass, mufflers, refurbished radiators, transmissions, catalytic converters, tires, and body parts are harvested from the rusting hulks of mankind's ruined chariots. A linear wall of whitewashed trailers stacked end-to-end along the sprawling rail yards of the Southern Pacific formed a continuous billboard barricade, upon which the blaring colors of urban graffiti were festooned in big block letters, spelling out doom with cryptic pledges of dire portent. Beyond the rail yards and the vast, expressionless spans of steel cargo containers stacked up like cordwood, there loomed the scant pinnacles of the Los Angeles city skyline, emerging like a congregation of solemn specters huddled together beneath the low-hanging clouds. Tires chirped and burned when Brogan downshifted abruptly and powered into a hard right turn to make the light at Caesar Chavez Avenue.

We hung a left on Broadway, and two gilded serpentine dragons flashed by my side window. They appeared to be fighting over an unlit glow ball of a globe at the imaginative Gateway to Chinatown. Approaching Temple Street and the antiquated Hall of Justice—which had been severely damaged in the last big earthquake—I noticed that the classical pillars of justice were still largely intact, but there was a lot of nasty plywood obscuring the lower galleries and the upper echelons of recessed window openings where the transparency of glass had once been. *Surely, we're not stopping here*, I thought as we passed by the damaged Hall of Justice.

"If it's not Union Station or Chinatown," I surmised, "it must be Civic Center or Pershing Square you have in mind. Seriously, Detective, can't you give me a hint where we're going?"

"I already did," responded Brogan with an icy grin as we rumbled by the myriad of courthouses, the iconic Town Hall, the cloistered Law Library, and headed up the hill on First Street. "You weren't listening carefully enough," he added.

"I heard you," I insisted. "Tell me where—in heaven's name—do *angels and dreams depart from* anyway?"

"Only one place in the whole wide world, son," responded Brogan rather matter-of-factly. "And that's exactly where we're headed."

With that, Brogan angled the Pontiac Catalina into the left turning lane on Olive Street, rounded the corner briskly, and gunned the engine, thundering past the surrealistic metal spans of the Walt Disney Concert Hall that was gleaming and glaring loudly, while rising curvaceously skyward from behind the dull gray bulwarks of a massive public parking structure that had been poured at its feet. Brogan braked hard and veered left into a smaller parking lot. The man at the parking shed waved us by, remarkably without any payment and without further ado.

Brogan Parked the Catalina at a point overlooking the Town Hall and the *LA Times* Building, and I followed him along the Olive Street sidewalk and into a tunnel that led under the foundations of the massive California Plaza: an urban complex comprised of two towering blue-glass office buildings, the luxurious Omni Hotel, and the Museum of Contemporary Art. A short ways into the tunnel, Brogan strode left onto a tree-encrusted park that formed the very crest of Bunker Hill, and I followed him in silence up a series of stairs that led to an enormous floating platform.

It was there, at the leading edge of the concrete-steel-and-granite platform, among the vast arrays of elegant outdoor amphitheaters, water features, and sitting areas, where I spied the incongruent architecture of a quaint Victorian railway station standing atop the immense concrete platform—standing there alone, in startling contrast to the ultramodern urban setting, floating high above and beyond the earthen reaches of the historic Bunker Hill.

Just then, a bell clanged, followed by a distinctive metallic rumbling and a grating of steel wheels on iron rails—and then, as if it had appeared from out of nowhere, a single railway cable car emerged from below the platform at a seemingly impossible angle. Atop the single railway car, bedecked in burnt-orange paint, was a black-and-white sign with two words that solved the immediate mystery. The sign said: Angels Flight.

"So this is Angels Flight—the place where angels and dreams depart," I said, as much to myself as to Brogan. I had heard the name mentioned once or twice before—as a nostalgic aside, at another place in the city, or a mention of times gone by—but I had never seen such a thing as this outside of an amusement park.

I leaned out over the handrail of the platform and looked down upon the steepest railroad tracks I have ever seen. There at the bottom of the hill was another singular cable car at another Victorian railway station. This station landing was smaller than the upper station, comprised of an ornate beaux-arts arch supported by two stately Doric columns that appeared to be out of place in the twenty-first century, but nonetheless these columns seemed to disappear into the discordant conglomeration of sights and sounds and architectural styles that spanned the LA city streetscape.

"Nice view, isn't it?" remarked Brogan, looking off into the distance.

"You can say that again, but I still don't understand why you brought me here today."

"This is where you catch the train for your daily commute to your new crime lab."

"What crime lab?"

"The one you're going to set up."

"When and where is this going to happen?" I asked.

"Now, and right down there," said Brogan, pointing downward, "just beyond that parking lot at the bottom of the hill."

"What do you mean?" At this point, I was pretty confused. "Can you please tell me why?" I asked, with rising indignation. "Why are we standing up here, marveling at this view, when we have detective work to be doing way down there?"

Brogan lit an unfiltered cigarette and took a deep prolonged drag, which he exhaled into the breeze after a moment of hesitation. He leaned back against the handrail, flicked the ashes off the glowing ember, and surveyed our surroundings. "Look here, Cornell," he said finally. "I know you have a pretty good head on your shoulders, and I'm beginning to believe you have a pretty good heart. However, when it comes right down to it, you haven't a clue about what's happening right now, or at any other moment, on the chronically mean streets of this dark city or any other metropolis." He took another long drag on the unfiltered cigarette and dropped the unfinished butt onto the cement. "You don't know who's watching; you don't know who's coming or going; you don't even know who could be taking aim at us as we speak—and that could be a problem."

I was about to muster a word of protest, but I decided against it.

Brogan ground the cigarette butt down to nothing, and then he looked directly into my eyes with a terribly hard glare that alarmed me, yet it expressed a decidedly steady gleam of real-world experience. "You see, Cornell, I figure this here Angels Flight Station is the only place that an innocent guy like you would be able to tell whether or not he's being followed."

He wasn't wrong about me. I just didn't like the sound of it; I didn't like the assumption that my so-called innocence, in the context of Brogan's mean streets, was so easily equated with cluelessness. I looked around me, casually at first and then more perceptibly. I looked high up at the shining sea-blue towers of the California Plaza: the surrounding spectacle of the courtyard, the city beyond, and the overcast sky above were all reflected in the mirrored glass spires like a shimmering pixilated panorama. I lowered my gaze slowly down to earth, and I immediately noticed two couples sipping coffee under a cluster of outdoor umbrellas. One Hispanic couple was clearly visible in the foreground while the second party was partially obscured by the fabric of an umbrella. *Wait, is that second couple alone, or is there a third person sitting there with them? What else am I missing?* I wondered.

A group of tourists was attempting to catch the action of the dynamic water feature with their cameras as bright sprits of water shot high into the air before splashing and cascading down upon the granite steps into shallow pools and canals that wound around the outdoor amphitheaters in a series of meticulously landscaped islands and moats. *Are they really tourists? And what about those people standing in line at that storefront … and those guys over there, behind the glass … are they looking this way? Are they dangerous?*

"Now, let's not go and hurt ourselves, Cornell—by trying to develop your professional *Private Eye* overnight or trying to make up for the lost time you spent in the learning library."

Brogan's sarcasm was brutal, but I knew that I deserved it. From this point on, I was determined to learn from Brogan more quickly, more astutely, to study my immediate surroundings in greater detail and to avoid, at all costs, appearing so clueless.

"Let's say, for example, if I was to hand you a pile of money in broad daylight, like this—" Brogan pulled five stacks of yellow-banded one-hundred-dollar bills out of his pockets, and he handed me what appeared to be $50,000 in cold, hard cash. "How else could I be sure that you would be able to get down this hill safely, all by yourself, and take this here rent money across the street, past all those people down there on the sidewalks … and those guys on the cement benches over there … across that parking lot over there," he said, pointing, "and into the alley beyond it … all the way to that dingy five-story building over yonder—the one with the painted-up windows—where you would find an unlocked gate to go through, and you would make your way up the fire escape to the top floor … where you would knock on the door and meet your new landlord, Señor Basilio Oxidado, better known as Rusty Beams."

Brogan smiled. He lit another unfiltered. And then, as I hastily stuffed the stacks of cash into the pockets of my trench coat, he held up a shiny new quarter.

"What's with the quarter?" I asked.

"It's for your first fare on the world's shortest railway," said Brogan, snuffing out my side of the conversation with a massive plume of secondhand tobacco smoke.

It was all I could do to keep my wits about me as I held my breath, grabbed the quarter, ran to the quaint Victorian station house, and purchased a paper one-way ticket for my first brief and plummeting journey on the Angels Flight Railway—departing from the very brink of Bunker Hill and soon to be arriving at the ominous sidewalks below.

Stepping cautiously into the vintage downward-tilted railway car, I felt like I was stepping off a cliff and into a vastly different world from the one I was accustomed to. It was a strange, surrealistic world where everything was tilted unnaturally, stepped and canted against the onset of a sharply downward trajectory, a trajectory from which there could be no exit, no hope of escape. I made my way along a series of iron bars that ran from the floor to the ceiling of the cable car, and I swung my frame into a hard wooden seat.

An alarm sounded, and the cable car jerked harshly when the brakes were released, forcing me to hold on tightly and to draw my briefcase up into my lap. I looked around and noticed that I was alone in the railway car. There were no other passengers onboard. There was no conductor, no brakeman. There was only the herky-jerky clambering of one conspicuous down-bound commuter—one who was clearly carrying far too much cash for his own comfort. I felt a looming wave of terror descending along with me, as real as the muffled rumblings I could feel beneath my feet, as alarming as that metallic shrieking sound that suddenly filled my ears.

I found myself running for the pedestrian crosswalk that would take me across Hill Street and away from the mulling sidewalk crowd, which suddenly looked far too suspicious for my liking. Feigning nonchalance, I slowed to a brisk walk, looking down as I advanced along the walkway, but all I could see was the outline of my own dead body surrounded by chalk marks—not unlike those freakish bath towels I saw in the coroner's damnable gift shop. All I could feel was the penetrating gaze of a thousand unblinking eyes that were following me—each one as glaring and perspicuous as the glass eyes of those ill-fated children we found dangling in the woods and whose petrified little bodies were now lying cold and stiff in the county morgue.

I realized that I was sweating now in my trench coat, but I dared not take it off, lest I distance myself from the contents of its pockets, lest I lose all control in the growing chaos of my surroundings. I spun around to see if I was being followed: if I was, no one was letting on. I turned into the aforementioned parking lot and ran past the lines of empty cars like a man possessed, scrambling into the adjacent alley, through an unlocked gate, up to the dingy five-story building with the fire escape, where I began to climb as if my life itself depended on it.

I knocked six times on the drab, windowless door and waited … There was no answer—just a man feeling entirely out of place, out of his element, out on an iron ledge in a cold sweat. There was no escape, except back down: down into that alleyway I had just managed to transit on the run. I glanced quickly around me—trying and failing to look casual; trying to look as if I belonged up here, alone, standing out like a sore thumb on the top level of this flimsy fire escape, overlooking the moving, seething masses of ferment and humanity that lived and lurked and hunted at will in the spaces between Angels Knoll and South Broadway on any given day or night.

I tried to breathe more slowly and deeply to relieve the creeping terror that now engulfed me, but somehow the thickness of the air, which smelled like fried onions and car exhaust, stuck in my throat. It was as though my windpipe was being held fiercely in the grasp of a thousand greedy hands; it was as though the interiors of my coat pockets were being entered and emptied out by ten thousand creeping fingers.

I pounded on the door again: harder this time, and thus louder. There was still no response!

By now I was certain that those eyes, those hands, those fingers, were fully aware of my predicament. I knew that I was still sweating profusely—I could tell that from the wet handprints I was smearing on the front of my trench coat. Still, I refused to reach into my coat pockets, for that would be a dead giveaway, duly informing every predatory soul in this degenerate City of Angels that this outstanding newcomer, trapped up here alone on this fire escape, sweating madly and struggling to breathe, was carrying a lot more baggage than he could safely handle. I looked across the parking lot and the seething streetscape to the Angels Flight platform in the distance, squinting hard, trying to see if Dash Brogan was still up there, hoping that the cavalry in the form of the LAPD would soon be coming to my rescue. Alas, no Dash, no dice.

I was about to pound on the door again—this time with all of my panic-stricken might—when the door itself disappeared from view, and the face of a man I'll never forget appeared like a haunting out of a midnight mausoleum of darkness.

"You're late!" said the face as a hunched figure of a man came vaguely into view. The words startled me at first, but not nearly as much as the face itself, which would find its material likeness nowhere but the netherworld of the imagination: somewhere between the native disfigurements of Victor Hugo's Quasimodo and the post-debauchery portrait of Oscar Wilde's Dorian Gray. The inescapable horror of that snarling face upon my overwrought nerves was matched only by the viciousness of the gaping mouth that opened and closed and growled within the context of that face. *You're late!* It had spoken directly at me, and possibly beyond me, in second-person singular.

"Brogan sent me," was all I could manage to say.

The face in the doorway moved closer to me, became clearer, became a man. And then the mouth moved again, exposing a set of clenched, gold-encrusted teeth that looked to me like moldy cheese. "You're not what I expected," said the man in a strong Mexican accent, adding an uncanny echo to his declarative statement. *"No es lo que yo esperada."*

Feeling relieved to have the darn door opened at last, no matter what emerged, I simply stood there silently, and most likely, I was grinning.

He looked me up and down with small, dark, mean-spirited eyes like one would find on a mole or a shrew, and then he said, "You don't look like no stinking laboratory rat ... *no apestosos rata de laboratorio!"*

Ignoring the double negative, which I assumed to be a compliment, I parried the thrust with a cryptic compliment of my own. "And you don't look like Rusty Beams to me."

"No one calls me that! Only Brogan!" he said, speaking through tightly clenched teeth. "You call me Señor Basilio Oxidado—or I break your legs. You have no permission, rat boy ... *no tienes permiso!"*

I noticed that the man was favoring one leg, as if he was sporting a badly broken kneecap, and I decided not to dispute the proposed nomenclature any further.

"I don't care if your name is Señor Basilio Oxidado or King Rust; it's all the same to me." It took me a moment to mind my Spanish, and then I added, *"Es todo lo mismo me."*

The challenge seemed to invigorate the man, as if the requisite machismo of trading insults, like the requisite haggling at a flea market, had served to satisfy some time-honored tradition. However enticing, I could feel the weight of the fifty grand in my pockets, and I didn't want to press my luck. I glanced into the relative darkness of the unlit interior space, where I could see only floating dust and cardboard boxes in the immediate foreground. I nodded and attempted to enter the building to complete the transaction, but Basilio Oxidado blocked my way.

"Do you want the money or don't you?" I said. "I don't have all day to get acquainted. I'm here on urgent police business!"

"No, *ese*. You are here on Brogan's business. *Los negocios de Brogan no es lo mismo como negocio de policía*. You think I am born yesterday, *ese*?" he added.

Señor Basilio Oxidado held out both of his hands and lowered his atrocious head as if he were expecting me to bless him with the Holy Communion. Instead, I unloaded the five stacks of cold, hard cash into the palms of his cupped hands. After the ceremony, he looked up at me like a man renewed—*un hombre renovado*. He clenched his teeth in an awful approximation of a smile as he deftly fanned the stacks of bills near his right ear—it was as if he were listening to the delicate sounds of angels' wings that would carry him to a greater level of avarice. I noticed, in the gilded gleam of his cheesy smile, that his teeth were the same gray-green color as the hundred-dollar bills.

"You're going to need a lot more to stay in business around here, *ese*. *Vas a necesitar mucho mas!*"

And then he turned abruptly and entered into the darkness, slamming the door in my face.

4 Poet Laureate of the Inner Dark

ater that evening, I got a call from Detective Dash Brogan on my cell phone.

"Did you make it to the delivery point?"

"Yeah, but—"

"Did you give Rusty the money?"

"Yeah, but—"

"Then you got yourself a proper crime lab."

I resisted the temptation to complete a trifecta of losing bets.

Sensing my reluctance in the silence that followed, if not my total chagrin, Brogan filled the lull with another question. "Any difficulties?"

"None worth mentioning," I lied, straining to keep my composure.

Brogan said nothing in response. I found myself squirming with the near certainty that the old-school detective was simply giving me sufficient rope to hang myself with, so to speak.

"Good," said Brogan, finally breaking the ice out of kindness. He continued with the following instructions: "I want you to meet me tonight at ten o'clock sharp at the Bordello Bar on East First Street— and be sure to wear a jacket and tie."

I clicked off my cell phone, feeling better.

Earlier in the afternoon, I had taken a Yellow Cab from the storefront/sweatshop/warehouse that Brogan determined would serve as my new crime lab, and I retrieved my BMW from the coroner's parking lot, so it was easy for me to cruise into Little Tokyo around nine thirty to try to find the place. The Bordello Bar used to be called Little Pedro's Cantina but was more recently transformed back to its nineteenth-century roots, when it was originally operated as a brothel. Tonight, as I rounded the historic corner that had, at one time or another, served as a downtown hangout for the thirsty, the hungry, the lustful, and the depraved late-night zombies of every denomination, I could hear the sound of sexually charged music that entices one to lowlife.

I parked on the street across from the gates of a Buddhist temple and made my way to the source of the music—it was soft, sultry jazz. Brogan's black Catalina 2+2 was parked at the curb. Inside the Bordello, the sexual ambiance of scarlet-red walls, provocative paintings, and gilded woodwork immediately struck me as a Victorian cabaret that served up spirits and burlesque as the main course. I was beginning to realize that Brogan was drawing me into something ancient and dark and yet strangely compelling, like the sensual allure of these black chandeliers with pink light bulbs that led me in, past a fanciful setting of plush velvet chairs and perfumed pillows that spoke to me in hushed and heady tones, past an ornate bar scene where an accommodating bevy of female bartenders wearing lace-and-satin lingerie piqued my curiosity.

I followed the sultry jazz music and the surrealistic chandeliers into another room: a more expansive arena arrayed in scarlet red with high ceilings and intimate tables arranged around an elevated theatrical stage. It was a thrust-type stage where three expressionless musicians were finessing live jazz with practiced nonchalance, accompanied by a nearly naked Asian woman with a crown of gold and peacock feathers on her head. The woman was moving suggestively, seductively, to the lively improvisations of the cool jazz riffs.

Beyond the lighted stage, with its lively characters in the foreground and its painted columns, ornate carvings, and gilded figurines behind them, the room was bathed in darkness. Only the tenuous pink lights from the black chandeliers gleamed faintly overhead like sleeping stars in a distant dreamlike sky. Only the dull yellow light of the votive candles on the tables shown sufficiently upward as to illuminate the shapes and faces of the onlookers in the audience.

"Down in front!" barked a familiar voice from the foreground. It was a hard-boiled, nicotine-soaked voice that could only belong to Detective Dash Brogan.

I bent clumsily forward and made my way to the table where I found Brogan fondling an unlit cigarette to the point where the tobacco was falling out from both ends. The empty glass of ice cubes suggested to me that he was drinking whiskey on the rocks. I shuddered at the thought of drinking straight whiskey again so soon.

"Hey, boss!" I said as I joined him at the table, not knowing whether to use his real name or his official position at such a time and place as this.

"Glad you made it, Cornell," said Brogan, confirming that I had, indeed, graduated from the depreciative label, *college boy*. "Let's get you and me a drink before the next act."

"Sounds good to me," I said, somewhat distracted by the Asian dancer and her feathers.

I wasn't sure how Brogan could operate so effectively in the dark, but he managed to summon a stunning blonde waitress who appeared before us in fishnet stockings, a tight, mouth-watering corset, and a rather generous smile. Brogan simply held up his glass, as if to order a refill, while I struggled to decide among the various specialty drinks that the waitress was patiently enumerating for my benefit. Finally resolving the issue by allowing the waitress to bring me *her* favorite drink, I ordered a dirty martini.

"Smooth move," said Brogan.

The musical jazz number meandered on to a conclusion, and a red-velvet curtain descended downward obscuring the stage. When the velvet curtain was raised again, there was a different burlesque dancer on the stage. This time it was a hugely buxom Marilyn Monroe lookalike with pinkish-blonde hair and a white, chiffon halter dress. Clearly, there were differences to a discerning eye, but whatever this Marilyn lookalike lacked in verisimilitude, she more than made up for in female pulchritude. Nevertheless, she was exceedingly vivacious and easy on the eyes.

Our drinks arrived, and I sipped the briny vodka and vermouth to the risqué strains of a provocative jazz number in which the white halter dress was flourished in an ostentatious manner and gradually divested to the point where large, star-shaped pasties dominated the performance. Still, this Marilyn lookalike continued to strut with dramatic sound and fury upon the thrust stage, and she basked in the glow of the spotlights to the fullest extent while the vibrant drums, the double bass, and the tenor sax of the accompanying jazz ensemble played on.

"So this is how you spend your free time." I chuckled playfully, somewhat bewildered by the bawdy spectacle so near at hand.

"When you get to know me better, son, you'll come to realize that I'm pretty much all business." Brogan drained his glass and leaned close to me, ensuring that no one else could hear what he said. "I invited you here tonight to meet someone special."

"Special?" I wondered out loud.

"And beautiful," responded Brogan.

"Beautiful?" I repeated.

"Beautiful … in every possible way."

"Beautiful with or without her clothes on?"

"That, you damn fool, is something you're going to have to find out for yourself."

The serious tone of Brogan's voice immediately wiped all traces of a smile from my face, as if I had been slapped hard by every decent person and kneed in the groin at the same time.

"I'm sorry, boss. I didn't mean anything, really," I said in embarrassment. "I don't understand what you're getting at. Is this where the shadowy dragon ladies come in?"

The red curtain went down and then up again. Only the musicians remained on stage. It appeared that the burlesque show was over. It was just as well, for I was now as confused as I was aroused and intrigued. We ordered another round of drinks, and Brogan began to explain.

"Look here, Cornell, there is only so much that I can teach you," said Brogan benevolently, "only so much that I can show you. But that's not all you need to learn. There are some things that cannot be gleaned by the eye alone—not even a meticulous private eye. There are some things that need to be *heard* or *read* carefully to be fully understood."

I sipped my dirty martini and wondered what was coming next. The band took a break, and we sat in silence for quite a while, nursing our drinks. Suddenly, the stage lights went dark. And then a single spotlight went on, and *she* was standing there. I couldn't believe my eyes.

Here was a pale, ethereal beauty of a woman with raven hair, the face of an angel, and skin that belonged on a priceless cameo. She was standing perfectly still, neither prancing nor gyrating nor breathing the same air as you and me. She was a raving beauty who had not yet spoken a word: a vision of a woman in a black evening gown that fell gracefully from her shoulders and draped down along the contours of her body with such feminine cultivation and nobility that the silken threads of the fabric itself seemed reluctant to ever, as in ever, release her from its grasp.

Brogan leaned in close to me again and said, "Listen carefully, Cornell. Tonight Lauriana Noire, *Poet Laureate of the Inner Dark*, is speaking just for you."

The saxophone player walked silently over to the center of the stage, placed a microphone stand in front of the poet, and returned to stage right. A moment passed, and the poet began to speak—expressively, poetically, with a voice that might as well have come from heaven itself.

"Have you ever watched a child die? I hope you never have to. It isn't a good thing to see. When you watch a man or woman die, you see only yourself, not someone who looked up to you for everything as you opened your heart and offered your benevolent love in return. A dying child falls from a higher realm than an adult; elevated by inexperience, they soar like little flags over the heads of men and women, whether they are sisters or brothers, daughters or sons. And regardless of whether he or she was good or bad, whatever a child's badness is, they fall in a flash with a fiery trace, like a disintegrating star that plunges into the depths of the ocean."

A pause in the poet's delivery must have been a signal for the jazz band to join in, for they filled the intervening silence with soft brushes applied to the taut skin of the snare drum, a tasteful riff of pizzicato thumps from the upright bassist, and a series of hushed and measured issuances from the tenor saxophone that breathed and whispered the soulful side of jazz.

"Seen from afar, it is just a tiny drop in the ocean, and as they disappear into the darkness, one by one, you can be absolved of any and all responsibilities. But standing close is a much more difficult undertaking—the shutting away of that defenseless heart nearly impossible. That face you see before you, the one that has just finished dying, will come back to you time and time again: ashen, sickly, sallow, palely haunting into every night's sleep for the rest of your life, no matter how much you attempt to justify or excuse the manner of its dying, no matter how tough your mind becomes. That scene, that inexcusable scene you saw before you that just ended, will come back meshed and melting into every dream that you ever dream again, so that you don't just watch it happen once, you watch it one and one thousand times. Unlike the child who once looked up to you for everything, those dreams you dream, they will not die, and all the liquor and all the sleeping pills can't make them go away."

Once again, the soft issuances of soulful jazz music filled the intervening silence. I looked over at Brogan, who was busy worrying the unlit cigarette to bits, and then I looked back again to the beautiful, ethereal Poet Laureate of the Inner Dark.

"Those eyes of a child that once glittered with bright reflections of love and laughter in your fondest memories will no longer glitter even faintly in your palely haunted dreams; they will glare knowingly into your mind's eye where everything that once was bright and shining is now no longer even close to innocence, having yourself become resigned to the inconsiderate ways of a world benighted, devastated, distorted, and unrestrained in death. The sun itself will eventually lose its luster; it will become cold and baleful, portending an even darker journey into a darker night. Whoever is so unfortunate as to allow even one child to die without objection ... allows the whole world to do the same."

The prose poem ended with some extended moments of unmitigated silence, after which the soulful jazz music rose up to a shimmering climax and then fell away as the spotlight went dark, and the Poet Laureate of the Inner Dark disappeared from my sight.

Hardly a minute later, I noticed that she was standing right next to our table. I rubbed my eyes as if to help them adjust to the prevailing darkness while Brogan stood politely and ushered this raving beauty into an empty chair beside me.

"Lauriana Noire, I would like you to meet Cornell, the promising new forensic investigator I told you about."

"It's nice to finally meet you, Cornell. Dash speaks so highly of you that I could hardly wait to find out for myself."

"Really, I can't imagine … I mean, I can't imagine Dash feeling that way … I mean, I'm really glad you feel that way, but I can't imagine how you knew … about me … about Dash and me … and about those tragic kids we found in the trees and all those things you talked about."

"Calm down, Cornell," said Brogan with a telling smirk and a wink. "You'll have to excuse my young apprentice, Lauriana. He's spent most of his adult life in a research laboratory, and he's not accustomed to *cherchez la belle femme*—if you'll pardon my French."

"Oh, Dash," said Lauriana Noire as she patted his hand. "You always were a charmer." Then Lauriana turned to me and said, "Now don't you mind his teasing in the least, Cornell. I find your boyish naiveté and your breathless syntax to be much more informative and endearing." Her gentle touch on my hand was electric.

By now my head was spinning wildly—from the pain of embarrassment, from the shock of experiencing such an ethereal dream of beauty in the flesh, from something pharmaceutical the waitress might have slipped into my olive juice. It was all I could do to muster a casual response: "Thank you, I think. It's a pleasure and an unforgettable occasion for me to meet you."

Lauriana turned back to Dash. Apparently, Lauriana Noire knew all about the petrified schoolchildren in the trees, the overly dramatic staging of the secondary crime scene, and the LAPD's inability thus far to identify either the bodies or the causes of death, much less the perpetrator. And as she talked about these points, I had the distinct impression that I had been in a snow globe that had been shaken up, and now all the flurried bits of luminous white began settling gently into place, as if magnetized by her words and guided by her voice; so many puzzling things began to fall into place for me.

"You say that the setting in the woods was staged by a fictitious movie company?" she asked in a velvety tone.

More interesting than her prior knowledge of the case, from my point of view, was the uncanny way in which Detective Brogan responded to her thoughts and inquiries, as though he truly admired her artistic insights and somehow valued her poetic intuition. "That's right," he said, leaning toward her conspiratorially. "The name *Art House Creations* was mentioned."

"Well then, that is your first real clue," quipped the beautiful poet laureate.

"What is?" asked Brogan, and I seconded his interrogatory brief.

Lauriana leaned her chin gracefully on her fingers and closed her eyes as she responded, "The first abstract, or metaphysical, indication of this malicious perpetrator, or perpetrators, is that they fancy themselves to be *Artistic*—and this is your first real clue."

It was about that time, nearly midnight, when Brogan's cell phone rang, and his facial expression turned from apprehension to grimness.

He ended the call and turned back to the poetess. "I'm sorry to have to drag your new admirer away so soon, Lauriana, but it sounds like someone just found the schoolteacher who belongs with that class of dangling children."

The poet laureate remained seated when Dash Brogan and I stood up to leave.

"Please keep in touch, Dr. Westerly," she said as she held out her delicate hand.

I was more than a little surprised that she already knew my last name, which had definitely *not* been mentioned in the previous conversation. But just one touch of her cameo skin—that wonder of nature in polished alabaster—and my family name, my rational mind, and my previous life was out the door and on the wind, lingering for a brief moment in the warmth of her knowing smile and then lost in the flutter of her eyelashes that reluctantly waved good-bye.

5 No Time to Be Asleep

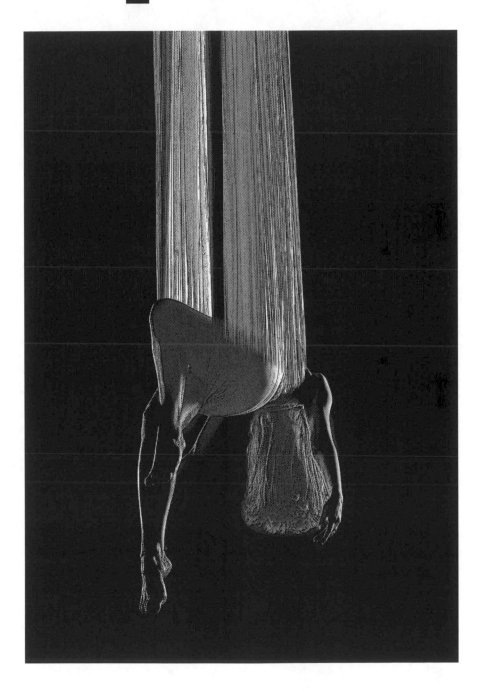

I followed Brogan out of the silken plush of the Bordello Bar and into the chill of the night. I was feeling no pain, and I could still taste the dregs of the dirty martinis. We walked in silence down the sidewalk of North Vignes Street. We passed by Brogan's mint Catalina 2+2 and past my beat-up Bimmer. Then we crossed over to the other side of the street where a dimly lit *No Parking* sign read *Nishi Hongwanji Buddhist Temple*. The borders of the gated temple grounds were tastefully landscaped with manicured hedges, miniature pagodas, and diminutive bonsai trees whose shadowy forms emerged like little apparitions from pools of abject darkness. We made our way to the corner of First Street where the narrow gardens widened and rose up upon a gently mounded berm decorated with larger iconic statues and full-size fir trees. Brogan stopped and stood perfectly still, staring meditatively into the shadowy ambiance of the Zen gardens.

Now, my understanding of this particular stream of Mahayana Buddhism is only cursory. However, I recall from my studies in the humanities that this contemplative tradition emphasizes the enlightenment of all living beings over that of personal, individual achievement. Moreover, the guiding principles of Buddhist naturalism teach that the origins of all our problems arise from rational causes rather than from vague supernatural sources. The effects of the considerable liquor intake notwithstanding, I could tell from Brogan's upright posture and his unwavering hard-boiled character that he was in total agreement with the basic tenets of this meditative sect.

I was beginning to think that Brogan had fallen asleep standing up when an unmarked police car suddenly pulled up, and I recognized the grinning face of Clive behind the wheel.

Brogan opened the passenger-side door of the jet-black Crown Victoria and slid into the front seat next to Clive. I took my place in the backseat among a slew of camera bags, trajectory rods, blood spatter kits, and crime scene tape, and we roared off into the night.

The Code 3 running lights of the otherwise unmarked Crown Victoria created a flashing, beaming, strobe-light aurora of red, white, and blue that tattooed the outside world with blazing patterns of luminous Los Angeles ink. Inside the speeding Crown Vic police interceptor, we heard only the remonstrations of the burly V8 engine, and it took me a moment or two to realize that something was clearly missing—the sirens.

"I figure we can do without the bells and whistles, considering you guys have been dipping your bills at the pink-walled watering hole."

"Fine with me, Clive," said Brogan. "I owe you one for the designated driving."

"That goes for me too, Clive," I chimed in. "Thanks for designated drivin' … an' for the photographin' … an' for the blood spatter analyzin'." I heard myself slurring my words with a mouth as dry as a dirty martini without the benefit of vermouth and olive juice. The flashing, beaming world sped by my window as in a dream. I was a cotton ball inside a jar of cotton balls.

"Sounds like the boy enjoyed himself a tad." I heard Clive speaking from a faraway place.

"Afraid so," affirmed Brogan. "Might be for the first time in his young life."

I tried to speak, but my head was suddenly so heavy it dragged me down through the camera bags and blood spatter kits to the assuring firmness of the seat cushion. I heard the words "Pasadena" and "crime scene" spoken from afar. I heard the term "Ghost College" mentioned as I drifted off to Nowheresville.

* * *

I was alone in the Crown Vic police interceptor when I awoke. I was not feeling well. Nowheresville is an okay place to visit, but I wouldn't want to live there.

I stepped out of the car and onto the spongy grass of some kind of lawn, upon which the unmarked police cruiser was parked obliquely. The street beside me was lined on both sides with a procession of stout cast-iron lampposts, each post supporting a single, dull yellow globe. The street was otherwise empty and dim. Above the antique lampposts there loomed a canopy of old magnolia trees—the kind with big, white flowers as big as pie plates—and between the old magnolia trees there were tall, overgrown palm trees whose tops all but disappeared into the dense canopy, reaching beyond into the oblivious sky. Across the street, opposite the parallel lines of streetlamps and the far rows of trees, I could see the dimly lit silhouettes of several old-money mansions constructed in what appeared to be Craftsman, Mission, and Italianesque styles. There was nothing moving; there was nothing doing but the darkness.

I returned to the Crown Vic, reached in the driver's-side door, and pulled on the headlights. The beams illuminated an ornate iron fence and a locked gate, which blocked the way to a series of sidewalks that led beyond the fence. I switched off the headlights and allowed my eyes to adjust. Then I climbed the fence and entered into a strange and elaborate series of elegant gardens and courtyards with flowing streams and water fountains that would not have seemed at all out of place in an authentic Venetian palazzo.

The electric lights that would ordinarily illuminate the steps and footpaths that undoubtedly wound their way through the palazzo were not working. The subtleties of shadow could hardly differentiate between walkway, lawn, and raised feature. I took a guess and stumbled along what I'd decided was the former, literally falling across the boundary of an Italian water garden lined with low boxwood hedges and what I painfully determined to be thorny rose bushes. The splashing sounds of what sounded like a dozen or more water jets guided me across the courtyard to the unseen edge of an elongated pool where I kneeled down and reached into the cold, dark water, splashing my face and my neck. It helped to sober me up.

I was glad of that as, just then, something strange moved in the dark recesses of the water garden. I froze. This was surely him—the perpetrator of the crime that Brogan was investigating—lurking close by, hiding in the bushes, watching my late, stumbling arrival. I was keenly aware that I had nowhere to go, no cover to hide behind, and I was quite sure that this perpetrator could make me out much better than I could him.

The figure moved slowly closer, and my heart beat against my chest. I forced my hand into my pocket, searching for anything I might use as a weapon to defend myself against this murderer who liked to render corpses faceless.

As the ghastly being made one more move toward me, I yanked my weapon—a pen—from my pocket and cried out, "Stay back."

Clearly startled, the figure (on closer inspection) headed back into the shadows, and I stood still, allowing my pounding heart to steady as the family of opossums out for a late-night stroll disappeared into the darkness.

Once calm again, I noticed what appeared to be a strobe-light flash across the way: a momentary flash that illuminated the ornate façades of a pair of ultramodern buildings standing right before me. Another strobe-light flash went off, and I could distinguish the intricate details of the stunning honeycomb façades: rows upon rows of empty six-sided cells molded in architectural concrete. I assumed these modern edifices to be classrooms and/or auditoriums of the obviously abandoned "Ghost College" I had heard Clive and Dash discussing before I passed out.

I stood there for a moment wondering if the modern architects were even vaguely aware—wondering how many people on any given college campus were even vaguely aware—of the significance of these arrays of hexagonal rings and columnar cells that enabled the dutiful honeybees to economically construct, in terms of labor and wax, the elegant combs of their beehives. These same arrays of hexagonal rings and hollow cells that enhance the structural integrity of cork, the bones of birds, and the dome of the Parthenon were utilized first and foremost in the elegant molecular structures of our genetic birthright: that is, the nucleotide bases of the primal genetic code—those heterocyclic, aromatic embodiments of purines and pyrimidines that are intricately stacked, interlocked, elongated, and preserved in the elaborate physical structures of our own DNA.

Another strobe-light flash guided me past the foreboding honeycomb structures onto a gravel path that led beyond the courtyard and the water fountains and further into the darkness. I made my way along in the pitch, following the contours of a trimmed hedge that led me around a sharp corner to a faintly lighted passageway comprised of free-standing Corinthian columns topped by stone urns with vague and weathered carvings of flames. A feeble incandescent light was coming from the recessed entrance of an ornate Italianesque villa. I could hear the sounds of voices coming from within, which might have been reassuring were it not for the bright flash of another strobe-light that shown through a span of tall, arched windows looming above the doorway, warning me that I was about to enter the scene of a crime.

When I approached the formal entrance of the Italian villa, I could see through the arched, shadowy windows that something was not right. My eyes were drawn to what would normally be a grand chandelier illuminating the entrance foyer. In the briefest flash of a strobe-light vision, I glimpsed a chilling specter—the dangling body of a woman hung motionless in repose, suspended in place of the grand chandelier.

The front door was partially open, and I quietly stepped inside. Dash nodded briefly to me and motioned high overhead. He had his game face on. Clive had taken up a position on a black-and-white marble staircase that curved around the foyer, defining the grand entrance. Clive was focusing his camera lens on the body of a naked woman hanging there, with arms and legs and long blonde hair reaching down, down, down to the cold stone floor clad in polished Arabescato marble. The lifeless body of the naked woman was supported precariously by the tensile strength of a plain white sheet. Another bright flash went off, and my mind went empty and dim.

I climbed up the staircase to get a look at the dead woman's face.

My mistake—there was no face. Clive moved the beam of a flashlight slowly over the woman's remaining visage for me to get a better look. There was the same fleshless musculature, sans facial features, that we saw previously on the eight dangling children. What's more, there were those same unnerving glasslike replicas: those same perspicuous eyes.

"Looks to me like the work of the same *artistic* perpetrator," I said with a degree of confidence that echoed perhaps too loudly in the emptiness of the villa's interior.

"D'ya think?" remarked Brogan, lighting an unfiltered cigarette and blowing the smoke upward into the air. The smoke drifted past the hanging body and into the shadows of the high ceiling above. "Anything you can tell us that we don't already know?"

"Sorry, boss, I just woke up ... I'm sorry, Clive, for not being more help."

"Forget it, Cornell," said Brogan with an upward sneer. "I sometimes wish I could sleep like a newborn babe in the middle of a crime scene investigation."

"There's not much more we can do here tonight," added Clive. "The whole place has been wiped clean as a whistle, as far as I can tell. What do you think, Dash? Should we try and work up some latent prints or turn it over to the sheriff's men?"

"Might as well let 'em in, Clive. We'll take a closer look when they bring her down. There's something I want to check for myself ... up close and personal."

Clive made a call on his cell phone and went outside to wait. I joined Dash at the bottom of the stairs, and we made our way around the spiral staircase, across the polished floors of the spacious villa, and out the back door. We traipsed in the murky dead of night onto an elevated patio that overlooked the sprawling campus of the now-official Ghost College. The lights of Old Town Pasadena sparkled in the distance between two stands of Italian cypress trees. The sounds of water falling downhill could be heard somewhere in the darkness.

"It looks like you were right when you told the coroner there would be more victims."

"Bein' right don't feed the bulldog, son. Not when you can't do a damn thing about it." Brogan leaned hard on a broad stone railing and stared out into the night. It was as though he was peering intently into some vague and distant past, or perhaps some kind of war, when evil men and evil deeds held sway, and heinous crimes were committed wholesale with impunity.

Frightened by the creeping cynicism, I tried to break the spell.

"I like to think that being right means something, Dash. At least it does to me."

"Tell that to the next dangling participle we come across."

Following Dash Brogan's line of reasoning, a slew of dead bodies filled my mind.

"I understand that we can't save the dead, Detective, and that there may be many more victims out there somewhere … dangling, as you say … and in danger." I leaned forward on the stone railing next to Brogan and peered out over the rolling hills of the Ghost College, striving to match the noblesse oblige of the discerning detective's posture, striving to catch even a glimpse of what Brogan seemed to be searching for in the far-reaching realms of his worldly experience. "But if endeavoring to accurately assess our assumptions—if striving to prove whether our working hypothesis is right or wrong—is not sufficient … I don't know what is."

"Bein' right isn't all it's cracked up to be in this dog-eat-dog world, son." Brogan turned away from his distant reveries to face me. "Being absolutely, positively correct is all well and good when it comes to answering test questions on your college exams. But when push comes to shove in the middle of the night … when there's human lives on the line and it's kill or be killed … being comfortably, agreeably correct is a piss-poor excuse for being late to the party."

"So, what's better than being accurate in Detective Dash Brogan's book?"

"Bein' *timely*, Dr. Westerly; it's better than arriving too-little-too-late with just the right answer. *Bein' timely*, young man, *bein' timely*—that's what you need to start thinking about."

"So you're saying?"

"I'm saying that it's high time to get your new crime lab in gear."

The arrival of the sheriff's men was accompanied by the boisterous arrival of the Pasadena Fire Department. The resulting assemblage of ladders that were erected in the marble foyer resembled a medieval siege upon a castle wall. It must have been the provocative allure of a stark-naked woman hanging aloft in place of the grand chandelier, for there were soon far too many men clambering up the ladders to be of any actual assistance. Eventually, the woman's body was retrieved and laid gently to rest with the sheet upon the marble floor. It's amazing how gentle men can get when they are handling a dead body. The gentleness of the manhandling was exceeded only by the level of ensuing silence brought on by the ghastly appearance of that upwardly leering face.

The onlookers backed away when Detective Dash Brogan approached the cadaver, and I followed closely in his wake. The sheet had been draped respectfully over the woman's naked torso such that the denuded face alone was visible. Dash bent down and slowly moved the sheet away, uncovering the full length of her corpse. The position of her legs remained exactly the same as they had appeared overhead, suggesting that, whoever she was, her body was fixed and plasticized just like the dangling school children. There was no doubt that this petrified body was once a beautiful woman, shapely and flawless— with the exception that the outward curvatures of her breasts appeared to be exaggerated, and the skin of her face and fingers was missing.

I simply nodded when Brogan gestured to the telltale scars on the dead woman's chest. I assumed that we would be discussing the theoretical implications of this particular feature at another place and time. I further assumed that I would soon be paying another visit to Daniel Grist at the Coroner's Office to collect the appropriate specimens for my forensic DNA analysis. I was not prepared, however, when Brogan pulled out a large folding knife from his coat pocket and extended the thick silver blade. Nor will I ever be able to forget the sound that was made when Brogan drew the razor edge of the knife blade across the lifelike luster of her unblinking eye—it was the chilling sound of hardened steel on the cusp of a large crystalline marble, like a coffin nail scoring a thin, white line on a pane of window glass.

* * *

The winding late-night drive on the Arroyo Seco Parkway back to Little Tokyo was both eerie and serene. I learned that the academic mission of the Pasadena Ghost College had been abandoned many years ago—something about corruption and betrayal of trust that bled the place dry and left the once-prosperous teaching college in the hands of some unscrupulous characters. *Far from surprising,* my mind grumbled. No one had to tell me that a board of trustees was the very last den of inequity one could actually trust.

I also learned that the Terrace Villa was one of several mansions on the abandoned college campus that were available for lease and catering for special occasions, including wedding receptions and fancy corporate meetings. Clive had gleaned from the Pasadena sheriff that the contractual arrangements for the rental of the villa had been made in cash, off the record, under the table—just as before—suggesting to me that the perpetrator, or perpetrators, in question not only fancied themselves to be *artistic,* they were equally *secretive* and *deceptive.* Since art is often considered to be revealing, I found that to be ironic.

Clive dropped us off at East First Street and bid us good night with a fading wail of his police siren. When we got to his muscle car, Dash instructed me to "Go get some more sleep." I watched him as he unlocked the handsome Pontiac coupe, climbed inside, and started the powerful engine. He reached over and rolled down the passenger-side window when he approached the place where I was standing. "But don't sleep for too long, Cornell. There's a twelve o'clock trolley you need to catch tomorrow. I've scheduled another meeting for you with the infamous Rusty Beams."

Dash could probably tell from my muted reaction that I was not looking forward to another meeting with the colorful and decrepit Señor Basilio Oxidado.

"What's wrong?" said Dash. "Does Rusty Beams make your skin crawl?"

"Nothing's wrong," I said in haste. "I was just thinking how many items of equipment and supplies I'll need to get the crime lab up and running, and I have a number of concerns."

"Don't worry, son. You just make a list of all the equipment and supplies you need to get started—I'll be there to watch your back." With that, the old-school detective gunned the engine, chirped the tires as a matter of course, and motored on down the road.

6 A Filthy, Ill-Lighted Place

The next morning, I dragged myself out of bed, donned my sweats and running shoes, and headed out the door of my monastic one-bedroom apartment in Santa Monica—jogging across the already congested Ocean Avenue out onto the lush and luxuriant footpaths of Palisades Park. The sun was just beginning to burn through the hazy layers of maritime fog that roll in from the Pacific in the evenings this time of year and wraps the entire coastline in a big, wet blanket. The scenic cliffs were breezy and dripping with that seaside ambiance of salty freshness that renews both the living and the dying. It renews the rich and the recherché who are strolling contentedly along the bluffs with their characteristic accouterments and their fashionable lap dogs. It renews the impoverished and the homeless souls, moving ever so slowly with their eclectic collections of worldly belongings. It renews a young mother and her newborn child who is staring upward and agog from the deck of a high-tech stroller that is actively charging the mother's smartphone. It renews people like me who are striving to clear their heads, attempting to outrun the last vestiges of a hangover.

I showered and shaved and dressed in a hurry, for I knew that the traffic on the Santa Monica Freeway would be moving at a crawl. I made it through downtown Los Angeles, and I parked at the same small lot atop Bunker Hill in time to prepare the list of equipment and instruments I would need to set up a forensic research laboratory. As I composed the laundry list, I knew that it might indeed be possible to set up a proper crime lab, given that the standard industrial items of DNA analysis had, in recent years, been reduced considerably in size, and that much of the muss and fuss of molecular biology was now available as convenient and disposable kits. However, given the demands for microbial sterility and quality control required for stringent DNA analysis—not to mention security—I still had severe reservations concerning the feasibility of setting up a scientifically credible research program in an old, abandoned sweatshop under the dubious patronage of someone called Rusty Beams. So I quickly made another list: a list of my concerns.

I looked around. Brogan's Pontiac Catalina was nowhere in sight.

I made my way to the Angels Flight Station. According to my watch, I still had fifteen minutes to spare. I took a careful look around the platform. I didn't notice anything out of the ordinary. The two opposing railway cars were screeching and clanking up and down the steep hill in a reciprocal manner, as before. Passengers were loading and unloading at the near and far stations with each completed cycle, as before. People were eating at tables under umbrellas, and outdoor fountains were busy splashing water on the concourse, as before. I took a seat on a concrete step near the top of the landing, and I was beginning to go over my two lists when a strange and unnerving feeling came over me—it was like I was being watched.

Suddenly, the sounds of the crowded plaza were way too loud. There were peals of resonant conversation, short bursts of braying laughter, and the distinctive hiss of fountain water that could be heard above the clambering railway cars, the incessant screeching of which assumed more and more frightening overtones. I noticed that a group of heavily tattooed individuals sporting baggy jeans and graphic T-shirts were standing close by. Three women seated at a nearby table were elegantly adorned in formal business suits, high heels, silk scarves, expensive-looking jewelry, and designer purses. Even the umbrellas that hovered over the dining tables had a previously unnoticed translucent color and a glassine texture that allowed no fluttering of the stiffened fabric. I gazed about me with renewed interest bordering on alarm. Curiously, the smell of the entire civic plaza was also sharpened, like I had just opened the door of a giant pizza oven, and all the cheesy aromas of sausages, pepperonis, onions, olives, toasted bread crusts, and the diverse spices of lunchtime in downtown Los Angeles came pouring out of its gaping maw. I caught a faint whiff of tobacco smoke and immediately turned around.

Brogan! It was Detective Dash Brogan standing right behind me—as though he had been standing there all along.

"Just how long have you been here watching me?"

"Long enough to know that you still look like a kid lost at Disneyland!" Brogan must have caught the sudden change in my attention, for he added, "But you're getting better, Doc. You did notice something, and that's better than before."

"Indeed," I said, for lack of a stronger retort.

"Do you have the list of equipment you'll need?"

"Sure do," I said, shuffling the papers in my hands. "But first I want you to hear a list of my concerns."

"Shoot," said Brogan.

"First is the need for ample electricity, in terms of the work stations and electrical outlets."

"Are you kidding?" quipped Brogan. "The place is wired heavy duty—wired for more than a dozen commercial-grade sewing machines and garment presses."

"Okay … but what about security?" I demanded. "Not only for the precision instruments I'll need, but for the various tissue samples, and the DNA samples, and the DNA analysis. You know the rules regarding evidence chain of custody and official SOPs."

I stood with my arms crossed, somewhat confident that I had a leg to stand on.

"Security is the least of your worries, young man," said Brogan, laughing. "You can rest assured that no one would get even three blocks if they took so much as a T-shirt from those premises."

"You mean to say that Rusty Beams is that dangerous?"

"It's more like he's that connected," said Brogan with a broad grin.

Connected to what? I didn't ask. What I did say was that the precision equipment I needed was not only expensive but was generally limited in availability.

"Let Rusty Beams worry about that."

"Are you sure?" I insisted.

"I'm sure," said Brogan. "Anything else?"

"I'll need basic supplies, restriction enzymes, WIFI-water, pipettes, disposable tips, reagents for gels, PCR reagents. In point of fact, there are a whole lot of fine chemicals—"

"Here, take this," interrupted Brogan, handing me an official-looking credit card. "Use this for your chemical supplies, your sterile water, and any other disposable items you need."

I was dumbfounded. I just stood there looking at the strange name on the credit card, thinking, *Who or what in the world is Esmeralda Diagnostics?* I was almost afraid to ask.

Brogan extinguished his cigarette with a turn of his shoe. "And give these to Rusty Beams—no questions asked!" Brogan handed me fresh stacks of yellow-banded one-hundred-dollar bills, more stacks than before, and I quickly stuffed the fat stacks into the bulging pockets of my sport coat as nonchalantly as I could.

"He prefers that I call him Señor Basilio Oxidado," I said. "He told me you're the only one who calls him Rusty Beams."

"No doubt," said Brogan. "Give him my regards in Spanish, if you like."

"You're not coming with me?" I said with noticeable alarm.

Brogan didn't answer; he just looked at his wrist and pointed to his watch. Then he walked over to the railing and looked out over the edge of Bunker Hill, peering well past the seething chaos of the LA streetscape in the general direction of my new crime lab.

I took this as my cue to catch the very next railway car descending from Angels Flight.

• • •

I crossed South Hill Street and worked my way through the myriad Los Angelino pedestrians with slightly more poise than I had managed previously, although I could still feel the conspicuous bulk and the attendant danger of the thick wads of hundred-dollar bills I was carrying in my coat pockets. I could feel an intensely uncomfortable sensation of cold fear and sweat rising to the surface, oozing out from beneath my hatband, dripping from my armpits, running down the nape of my neck. I nearly broke into a run as I made my way into the alleyway and clambered full speed up the metal steps of the fire escape.

This time, the steel door opened before I knocked, and there in the segue between the light of day and the darkest night appeared the disembodied face of Rusty Beams leering at me, his moldy teeth bared in a hideous facsimile of a smile. His cruel eyes squinted against the glare of the daylight as he surveyed the conspicuous bulges in my pockets, which stood out like saddlebags from the tailored cut of my sport coat. When I reached into my right pocket to withdraw one of the fat stacks—no questions asked, just as Dash had instructed— Rusty Beams suddenly opened the door wide and nodded his head, signaling me to enter into the inner sanctum of the erstwhile sweatshop.

It was a filthy, ill-lighted place of human toil and dust, with a greasy smell of something foul, as if the wretched remnants of human greed and ambition had come and spawned and died in this place, sending fatal utterances of exhaustion echoing into the rafters, leaving nasty issuances of despair seeping into the floorboards. Somehow, the slow desiccation of human labor and drudgery into the primal elements had filled the unmoving air with a fine powdery particulate that floated listlessly in the empty spaces, illuminated here and there by streams of daylight that dared to shine through the small, translucent panes of the unwashed windows.

Señor Basillio Oxidado hunched forward expectantly with his hands held together as I carefully piled the stacks of hundred-dollar bills onto his upturned palms.

"I like you much better this time," he said. *"Me gustas mucho sólo esta vez,"* he repeated with a cruel smile and a downward nod of approval.

It took me a few seconds to unfold my shopping list and to formulate my next sentence. *"Tengo una lista de cosas que necesito,"* I said, handing Rusty Beams my list of necessities.

He read the shopping list of laboratory items out loud—BioRad real-time PCR, Beckman spectrophometer, microbiology incubators, precision water baths, laboratory refrigerators, super-cold freezers, etc. I realized that Señor Basillio Oxidado was reading the list fluently, speaking English perfectly well; apparently, he was only using Spanish with me for emphasis.

"Are you familiar with this type of laboratory equipment?" I queried.

"I know a guy who knows a guy," was all he said. Then, when he came to the specific precision scales and the Mettler analytical balance, he said, "These might take some time. *Hay una gran demanda.*"

Surmising the source of the big demand for laboratory scales and analytical balances, I wondered. "How many drug dealers actually weigh out their ill-gotten wares to three decimal places?"

"You'd be surprised," said Rusty, followed by, "*Te sorprenderías, ese.*"

"How much time do you think you'll need?"

"Give me five days."

"And the rest of these items?" I asked. "You know, Señor Oxidado, some of this equipment needs to be special ordered and professionally calibrated, and then there's the matter of the requisite service contracts and warranties."

"Warranties! I don't have any warranties! I don't need any warranties! I'm not gonna give you no stinking service warranties!"

I strained at the tension that was building between me and Rusty Beams, tension that increased considerably when one of Oxidado's henchmen stepped forward from out of the shadows and glared menacingly at me.

"Now, wait a minute," I stuttered. "I—"

"What you have," Rusty broke in, his face taking on a redder shade of bronze (though his anger was apparently counteracted to some extent by the hefty weight of the fat stacks he was still holding), "is my personal guarantee that the machines I get you are *perfecto!*"

Deciding to press the issue nonetheless, I said, "And what do you expect me to do if one of these precision analytical instruments breaks down?"

"If one of these frigging machines doesn't work like it's supposed to, I'll steal you another one! … *Te voy a robar otro, lab rat!*"

"Okay, if that's the best you can do," I acquiesced, wondering which of the local universities would soon find that their molecular biology laboratories were missing these particular instruments. "Meanwhile, I need to hire some laboratory technicians who may not be as tough-skinned and amiable as I am."

"*No problema, ese.* Just give your little lab rats some of these uniforms," said Rusty, setting the fat stacks on a filthy table and handing me a black T-shirt with a big red *I "Heart" LA* silk-screened in red letters boldly across the front. "So my homeboys will know who to let in the front door." Rusty Beams reached into the large cardboard box and withdrew another handful of the black T-shirts, saying, "Here, *ese*, take as many as you need. *Tu puedes tener la caja entera,*" he added, offering me the whole box of T-shirts with a sideways scuff of his foot.

I followed Rusty Beams down a wooden staircase, which opened out into a storefront festooned with a vast array of tasteless clothing, T-shirts, sweatshirts, sweatpants, and a weird collection of counterfeit purses. Rusty signaled briefly to one of two crudely tattooed Mexican henchmen who were standing guard at the front door, using his thumb to identify me as a preferred client, or tenant, as the case may be. I nodded to the muscular henchman, admiring the LA graffiti that decorated his arms and his neck, and proceeded to walk out the front door onto the bustling sidewalk of South Broadway. I crossed the street at the corner light and looked back at the five-story building that would soon house my new crime lab.

That was when I saw the front of the building for the first time. The entire façade from the second floor on up was a windowless urban canvas bedecked with the most amazing and colossal Aztec mural. Two massive arms of gold arose from the face of a large circular mandala, arms that were reaching up to the heavens through a spectacular array of lightning bolts. The mandala itself was comprised of concentric circles of big block letters inscribing the lines of a famous poem from the Nobel Laureate Octavio Paz: *Mis pasos en esta calle resuenan en otra calle donde oigo mis pasos pasar en esta calle donde sólo es real la niebla.* Struggling to make out the painted words that were upside-down and sideways, I managed to construct a crude translation: "My steps along this street resonate in another street where I hear my footsteps crossing into the street where only the mist is real." *Crossing into a street or state of mind where only the mist is real,* I thought to myself. *If only Lauriana were here with me now, perhaps she might be able to help me grasp the hidden meaning of these strange words penned by a poet who died of cancer in 1998.*

• • •

Later in the day, I placed a Help Wanted notice at three of the local universities, specifying the basic prerequisites of molecular biology and the various laboratory techniques involved in forensic DNA analysis. The next morning, I was greeted by a long line of applicants, mostly of Asian descent, standing outside the picturesque storefront, patiently waiting beneath the most colorful mural on Broadway.

"*Nadie entra aquí sin los colores correctos,*" said the security guard, referring to the required uniform of black T-shirts with bright red *I "Heart" LA* printing on the front.

I tramped up the stairs and returned with the specified uniform and handed it to the first applicant, an austere Chinese woman with pleasing features and a disarming smile. It was a smile of supreme confidence and reserve that made me wonder how she had managed to be the very first applicant in this long line. The woman pulled the obligatory T-shirt gracefully over her street clothes and introduced herself as Dr. Liling Chen. I escorted Dr. Liling Chen up the stairs to the laboratory, as it were, and switched on the fluorescent lights—less than half of which were working. Amazingly, she did not seem the least put off by the dust and the filth; she just looked around the dusty room and calmly said, "I can see that you need some help."

I liked her immediately and decided to hire her on the spot. We talked for the better part of an hour as she recounted her scientific training and work experiences, and I assured her that I would double her current salary at the university. Then, when I asked her to go downstairs and pick out two experienced technicians to work under her in the laboratory, she simply said, "No, Dr. Westerly, you only need me," at which point I decided to triple her salary.

7 Night of the Corpora Delicti

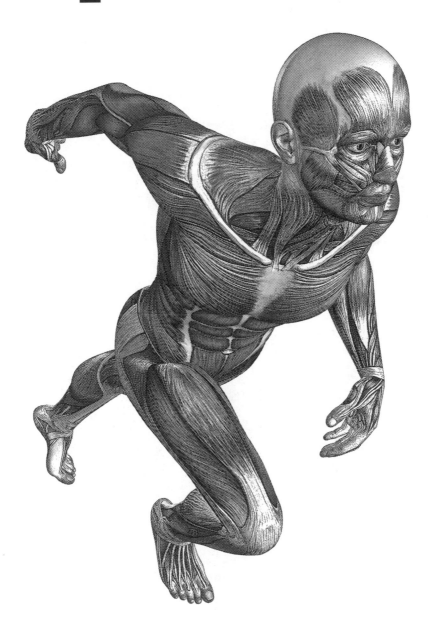

I was having dinner, munching on a barbeque-chicken pizza at CPK on Figueroa Street, when I got a call from Dash Brogan. He instructed me to meet him at the California Science Center in Exposition Park at midnight.

Foolishly, I asked, "Is the science center actually open at that time of night?"

"It's open for me and you and the night watchman. That's all you need to know."

"Okay, Dash, I'll be there. Should I bring my briefcase for collecting specimens?"

"No need," said Dash. "Just bring a good flashlight."

That night, I made my way to the sprawling museum complex, completely unaware of the scare in store for me. Little did I know that I would be frightened out of my wits by the end of this late-night investigation. Dash was waiting for me at the towering entrance of the ultramodern science center. Seated on a black-granite petal of the iconic flower-shaped DNA Bench, underneath the areal display of a thousand-plus variously sized, gold-covered hanging spheres arrayed in a circular pattern that evoked the image of a spiral galaxy and/or the interior hollows of a chromosome, the detective seemed to be meditating, perhaps on the complex connections that link the animate and inanimate worlds together. Or maybe he was contemplating the conspicuous helical design of the DNA Bench, which depicts the molecular blueprint of life. Or perhaps he wasn't pondering the formations of the universe or the origins of life but simply smoking his unfiltered cigarette. At any rate, an eerie, finely sprayed mist arose from the center of the DNA Bench and spread out like the fog of a primordial stew, melding everything together with the tobacco smoke.

"Nice night for a stakeout," I said, looking around for a clue as to what we might be doing at such a place in the middle of the night.

Dash stood up, snuffing out the remnants of his smoke, and then he handed me the Starbucks paper cup containing something other than coffee. "Here you go, Cornell. Let's try and find a match."

I pried off the plastic lid and peered into the cup. There was an eyeball, staring up at me from the dregs. Shivers ran up my spine as I recalled my college days when I used to collect dead cows' eyes for dissection from the local slaughterhouse. It was an uncanny feeling, standing there watching the wholeness of a live bovine reduced to pieces in a matter of a minute. But this was no vertebrate anatomy class; this gleaming orb looked incredibly real to me and much too human for comfort.

"Where do you reckon we'll find a match?" I asked.

"Just inside if we're lucky," said Brogan, adding with an impish grin, "Fair warning, Doc. This particular science exhibit, when viewed at night without proper lights, isn't for the faint of heart."

"I have no problem viewing dead bodies, Dash," I assured him. "It's only the manner of death of our youthful victims and their schoolteacher that concerns me now."

Brave words, I know, but these brave words soon vanished into the thinly dusted air around the bizarre spectacles illumined by my flashlight's beam. I waved my light through the cave-like den of pitch darkness behind the sign that read "The Human Body Exposed," and when my hand steadied, I saw in its beam a plasticized couple in a passionate embrace—him with his visceral organs externalized for all to see, her with her spinal cord and attached brain emerging frightfully from her splayed-open back like a dorsal fin on a dolphin. The next nightmare vision that loomed out at me was a plasticized man on a plasticized horse with all the human skin and horse hide removed, which seemed, in the gleam of my light, to be galloping toward me, appearing much larger than life. My mind began to reel when I came upon a pair of naked, skinless ice skaters who were frozen in time in an everlasting death spiral, her outstretched arms displayed in a permanent posture of mortal surrender. As I scanned the strange anatomical displays, I surmised that more than one hundred human corpses were extravagantly arrayed in various stages of dissection and dismemberment.

I turned once more and, right there in front of me, illuminated by my light's narrow beam, was a pregnant woman with her womb and fetus completely exposed. I gasped at the sight of the eviscerated baby. Next to this pair was another anatomical man whose muscles appeared to be walking away from his skeleton while he somehow managed to hold hands with the denuded skeleton of a small child walking beside him. An exploded man whose disembodied muscles and organs were strung together and supported by piano wires stood off in a corner. I moved my light again through the darkness, and goodness, a plasticized man was holding his own skin, the entirety of his epidermis draped casually over his arm as one would hold onto an unneeded overcoat. I swallowed hard. I found myself surrounded by ghoulish figures of human embodiment emerging from the stygian darkness. The midnight spectacle was so unnerving, so reminiscent of the crime scenes, that I began to feel dizzy and nauseous at the same time.

I found myself thinking of the secretive murderers we were chasing down. Perhaps they were here now, watching in the darkness. And how had these plasticized corpses—seemingly handpicked to eternally play out the scenes they were now in—truly met their demise? Notions of the murdered children ending up in a display like this and no one any the wiser and wild, fleeting preponderances of where these "victims" on display had really come from ran through my overcrowded mind. Try as I might to steady my nerves, another slow wave of fear crept over me while my flashlight searched frantically in the darkness from one nasty display to another for answers that would never be forthcoming.

Suddenly, the alarming, echoing sound of footsteps approaching set my heart to beating even more rapidly. The beam of Brogan's flashlight disappeared simultaneously with my own, and I froze, trying hard to blend in with my macabre fellows. And now it was my own corpse I pictured, doomed to become one of these plastic beings.

When at last the echoing footsteps receded, I flipped on my flashlight and flashed the beam into the glass eyes of a plasticized ballet dancer, frozen *en point*; she was staring with unflinching aloofness upon her audience of eternal night. I watched in silence as Dash approached the anatomical ballet dancer and proceeded to carve one of her glass eyes from its socket with his penknife. Completing the grisly task in a matter of seconds, Dash simply dropped the eyeball into his coat pocket as though he were pocketing a pack of gum. "Plastic people tell no tales," he said, "but these glass eyeballs might lead us to our copycat embalmer."

"So that's what we came here for," I said, deducing that the investigative nature of this little midnight excursion had everything to do with the hard evidence now in hand. "Do you think it will match the glass eyes of the petrified children and their suspended schoolteacher?"

"Too soon to tell," said Dash. "It's just the first step in establishing our corpus delicti."

We exited the "Human Body Exposed" exhibit and walked to the lot where Dash Brogan had parked his Pontiac Catalina. There was not a living soul in sight, just the drone of some anonymous cars passing nearby on the Harbor Freeway. Dash held up the glass eyeball he had just extracted from the plasticized ballet dancer and turned on the map light. I fished the dead child's eye from the coffee cup and handed it to the detective for comparison. He carefully examined the two eyeballs, turning them slowly with his fingers to match the reflections.

"The eyes don't match," said Dash, with a note of disappointment in his voice.

"Are you sure?"

"They're not even close. See here," he said, handing me the ballet dancer's eyeball. "The glass eye from this butcher's museum looks real enough at first glance, but compared to the one we took from the county morgue, it looks amateurish."

"What do you mean *we*?" I said. "You carved the eyeball out of that dead kid."

"Yeah, but you carried the coffee cup out of the morgue, didn't you? You see, Cornell, I needed to have some room for deniability when it comes to Chauncey's predictable accusations."

"It's okay by me. I'm happy to cover for you, Dash, but what do we do next?"

"We need to find the manufacturer of these realistic replicas of the human eyeball."

"And how, might I ask, are we going to do that?"

Dash pocketed the two glass eyeballs and said, "I'll make some calls and let you know. Meanwhile, it's best you go and get your new crime lab up and running as soon as possible. It looks to me like we're going to need some help from you and your DNA machines."

. . .

The next week was a whirlwind of cleaning, ordering a vast array of supplies, and equipping my new crime lab with just the right benches and tools and instruments. I could only imagine what scientific laboratories these instruments and incubators and freezers were taken from, for the telltale labels were scrapped completely off in the same manner one would obscure the identity and serial number of a stolen car. Dr. Liling Chen was a wonder of industry and efficiency, organizing all the workstations and lab benches with impressive expertise, cataloguing and stowing the various supplies that were arriving on a daily basis. Moreover, I found that Liling was pleasant to work with. She had a dignified air of authority and a serene demeanor that comes with mastery of the technical aspects of a complex field. Arrayed in her oversized I "Heart" LA T-shirt and her pressed white lab coat, Liling made herself right at home in my new laboratory, transforming the filthy, ill-lighted place into a respectable analytical lab. Replacement of more than a dozen fluorescent light bulbs overhead did wonders for the ambiance, which soon took on the inviting appearance of a modern medical research facility.

Wednesday evening, I drove to Hollywood Boulevard, where I met Detective Dash Brogan for dinner at Musso and Frank's Grill— an old-fashioned steakhouse that was once a prime destination for Hollywood's movers and shakers, including studio executives, movie stars, directors, producers, and noted screenwriters. You could well imagine F. Scott Fitzgerald, William Faulkner, Ernest Hemingway, Dashiell Hammett, Raymond Chandler, Nathaniel West, and even Charles Bukowski cozying up to the old wooden bar while the likes of Charlie Chaplin, Rudolf Valentino, and James Dean spread out in the mahogany booths eating piles of flannel cakes. You might have found Elizabeth Taylor, Rock Hudson, Humphrey Bogart, or Orson Wells seated at the linen-covered dining tables munching Welsh rarebit or filet mignon.

Dash Brogan was drinking alone at the bar when I arrived. He carried his drink to our dining table in the wood-paneled back room, and we ordered Porterhouse steaks from a vintage waiter wearing a black bowtie and a red jacket.

The old-school detective emptied his glass with a grimace and asked me how my new crime lab was coming along. I told him that we were already extracting DNA from the plasticized tissue samples and that I might possibly have something for him in the next day or so. He seemed pleased, and between thick mouthfuls of tenderloin, he informed me that Lauriana Noire would like to have dinner with me sometime soon. I literally jumped at the chance, not only because of her raving, intoxicating beauty, but because I felt she might have something important to say about the gigantic poem that was painted on the front of my makeshift crime lab building on Broadway.

Thinking now of Lauriana Noire, my thoughts returned to the poetic words on the Aztec mural. *"My steps on this street,"* presumably Broadway, *"echo in another street,"* invoking the imagination, *"where I hear my footsteps crossing over into yet another street,"* a street of unknown dimensions, *"where only the mist is real."* It was just unusual enough, just striking enough to be compelling, and in the context of the bizarre building itself, I felt compelled to figure it out. Somehow, I knew that Lauriana could help me demystify the meaning of these strange words.

* * *

Two nights later, I found myself at Musso and Frank's again. This time I was dining with the beautiful Poet Laureate of the Inner Dark who was wearing the same form-fitting evening gown that clung to her curves like angels in heaven cling to their wings. I won't recount the exact conversation because, once again, I was reduced to the dialogue of a blithering idiot by the entrancing gleam of her ethereal presence. Yet somehow I managed, between gulps of French champagne and steaming bouillabaisse Marseille, to describe the Aztec mural and the strange poem I found on the Broadway building.

I was amazed that Lauriana already knew all about the building's façade, the history of the gigantic mural, and the poem. Apparently, she had known all three artists who painted the sixty-foot-high mural on the building. She told me that the original name for Broadway Avenue, and thus the painting, was *Calle de la Eternidad* (Street of Eternity) and that the acrylic mural rendered on stark concrete was sponsored by the Social and Public Art Resource Center and the Department of Cultural Affairs. Lauriana explained to me that the two enormous golden arms lunging up to the sky not only reflected the city's high-rise ambitions, the image also offered a vision of great supplication, accompanied by two iconic figures standing beside the Aztec calendar. She said that these pre-Columbian artifacts were combined with the enigmatic poetry of Octavio Paz to explore the interrelated concepts of culture, place, and time.

When I pressed her about the cryptic meaning of the various streets, the resounding echoes, and the reality of the mist, she explained to me that the meaning of the mist and the streets was most likely intended to represent the aesthetic credo of the surrealistic poet who was attempting to recover the elusive realm of the sacred from the grips of the mundane, as sensory perception is transported into the imagination through the transformative function of poetic inspiration. Needless to say, I was inspired.

Sipping coffee from a bone china cup held gracefully in her

delicate hands, Lauriana told me that she liked me from the start and that she desired to get to know me better. She put down the coffee cup and smiled at me and stroked my hand in a most seductive manner. Her touch was as electric as it was before; it was the kind of touch that goes right to the very center of a man; it was a touch I could feel all the way to my hip pocket.

We drove in my beat-up Bimmer to her luxury apartment on Wilshire Boulevard, and then, like a dream come true, I was invited into her sumptuous bedroom where I was thereupon seduced and ushered to a heightened precipice of poetic ecstasy.

"Here is our moment of love's first embrace," she said tenderly, "when we fly toward our secret place in the sky …"

The warm softness of her whispering lips soon blossomed into a deep, passionate kiss that aroused and alarmed all my senses.

"We prompt our lingering strands of silken veils to fall away, away …"

She spoke softly, confidently as we began to undress—she and then, more urgently, me.

"Letting go of all that binds us and keeps us apart …"

Her warm, velvety hands guided my impassioned actions unto her heavenly body.

"Ahhhh, my young lover …" She sighed. "Let us to soar aloft together and dance in the air without shoes …"

Mis Pasos Resuenan en Otra Calle

I awoke the next morning feeling the lingering sweetness of countless shared pleasures, thinking what a wonderful privilege it was to be alive—to breathe, to enjoy, to make love to a beautiful woman all night long. Like a stained-glass window that was set above and apart from the mainstream crowd, Lauriana sparkled and shined when the spotlights were on her, but then, when the spotlights were turned off, and the shadowy darkness of the nighttime set in, an even deeper beauty began to emanate from the countenance of the woman with the blossom of an enchanting light from within. I was still partly dreaming, basking in the glow of the poet laureate's sumptuous stained-glass beauty, when I realized that I was actually facing the glow of the morning sunrise. I opened my eyes and found that I was alone in her bed.

There was no trace of Lauriana to be found, only the lingering jasmine-sandalwood smell of Samsara and two empty wine glasses to remind me of the night we spent dancing in the air without shoes. I dressed and walked out of the Wilshire Margot, a stylish five-story collection of luxury apartments fashionably located between Westwood Village and Beverly Hills. I worked my way west on Wilshire Boulevard to the Armand Hammer Museum, where I turned north on Glendon Avenue and stopped in at Espresso Profeta to get some of the best coffee and cranberry bread in the vicinity of UCLA. Located in one of the oldest brick buildings in Westwood, the Seattle-style espresso bar was manned by committed baristas who drew thick espresso shots using dark, chocolaty dolce beans from Seattle's famed Espresso Vivace. Sitting there on the patio, sipping a steaming cappuccino, I was feeling a bit curious as to Lauriana's whereabouts, but I was feeling no pain in any other aspect of our romantic relationship.

I retrieved my beat-up Bimmer from the underground parking garage and headed off to the Angels Flight Station and my crime lab in downtown LA. I knew that it was up to me as a forensic scientist to make something happen—that much I knew for sure. What I didn't know was which types of the various probes and screens for DNA polymorphisms—discrete genetic variations that tend to differ in unrelated individuals—might yield a definitive clue. When in doubt, it is best not to guess at such things but to explore as many aspects of genetic typing, sequencing, and profiling as possible, given the constraints of time and energy.

On Saturday, I worked the whole day with Dr. Liling Chen, showing her the various protocols I routinely used for DNA extraction, amplification, and hybridization, only to find that her practiced techniques were at least as good as, if not better than, the standard forensic SOPs. By the end of the day, we had extracted and amplified sufficient DNA from all eight of the dangling children and were getting the results of our first restriction digests. I should mention that only one-tenth of 1 percent of our DNA—about three million bases in all—differs from one person to another, and we forensic scientists can use these variable regions to generate a unique DNA profile of a given individual.

Upon mapping the variable lengths of the enzymatically digested restriction fragments with gel electrophoresis, one can begin the hybridization process using specific probes that bind to complementary DNA sequences present in each sample. Following Y-chromosome analysis (for boys) and analysis of simple restriction fragment length polymorphism (RFLP), one can then probe more specifically for short tandem repeats (STR) in the genomic DNA samples using the standard FBI-approved set of thirteen specific STR regions, enabling the resulting data to be input directly into CODIS (Combined DNA Index System), a software program that operates across local, state, and national databases, containing DNA profiles obtained from convicted offenders, unsolved crime scenes, and assorted missing persons. Given the odds that two individuals would have the same 13-loci DNA profile is about one in a million, I knew that we were searching for a needle in a haystack—yet we were not searching blindly. Surely ol' Desiderius Erasmus knew what he was talking about when he espoused in Latin, *"In regione caecorum rex es luscus."* In the land of the blind, a one-eyed man—make that an observant forensic scientist—can indeed rise to the top and become king of the hill.

The next two days were much of the same, with the exception that we added mitochondrial DNA (mtDNA) analysis to the mix. Since the tiny mitochondria of each new embryo come exclusively from the mother's egg cell, this can be extremely important in matching a potential maternal relative in the case of a troublesome missing person's investigation. Mitochondrial DNA analysis recently helped scientists to crack one of the great mysteries of European history, as such tests were used to conclusively prove that the lost son of the executed French King Louis XVI and Marie-Antoinette had died in prison— using mtDNA extracted from the heart of the slain child's remains for comparison with the mtDNA extracted from a lock of his mother, Marie-Antoinette's, hair. A similar analysis was used to identify the parentage of several of the "Disappeared Children of Argentina" who were consigned to orphanages or illegally adopted after their parents were killed by Argentina's military dictatorship in the 1970s and early 1980s. From Holocaust victims of WWII to the murdered war victims in Bosnia, Rwanda, and Ethiopia, mtDNA analysis is now commonly used by forensic investigators to reunite missing persons with their families, to match the remains of the "politically disappeared" with their surviving relatives, and to amass genetic evidence for trials involving international war crimes and other crimes against humanity.

I was seated at my new desk, pouring over the films and autoradiographs, trying to make sense of the curious patterns of blobs and blots I was seeing, striving to match assiduous observation with experience, straining to find something that might stand out as unusual, when Dash Brogan called.

"Well, college boy," he said, announcing his impatience with my extended time-on-task, "what do you have for us to go on?"

"I can't say for sure ... at least not yet ... but I suspect that there is something very wrong with this collection of samples."

"You mean you can't get the DNA you need from the plastic bits and pieces?"

"No, Dash, the extractions were fine, the PCR went well, and the quality of the resulting DNA is excellent. What I don't understand ... rather, what I can say at this point is that these maps do not look like a normal random distribution of genetic profiles. There is an unusual amount of restriction fragment length variability and redundancy that is indicative of gene amplification. And there are at least two or three apparent chromosomal translocations that are certainly not normal, as far as I can tell."

"Tell it to me in English, Doc. You're not talking to a chemist, a judge, or a jury."

"I wish I could say more at this time, but I want to be right about my suspicions—"

"And your suspicions are?"

"My suspicions are just that—it's speculative at best, Dash," I said with a degree of discomfort. "We'll know more in a day or so, after I prepare some specific probes for some of the common oncogene sequences. It's only a guess, mind you, but the implications are sufficient for me to be cautious, even cryptic, at this point in time."

"Can you tell me anything else?" pressed Brogan.

"Not right now," I answered reluctantly, "but soon."

"Well then, make your probes as quick as a bunny, and let me know what pops out of the rabbit hole as soon as you can."

I sensed that I was on to something—I could feel it in my bones—but I needed more proof.

It was late in the afternoon when I sent Dr. Liling Chen home for the day, wrapped up the developed films in a brown paper bag, and left the crime lab, removing my heart-emblazoned T-shirt as I exited by the storefront door. I crossed the street at the end of the block and looked back at the soaring Aztec mural, the top of which was bathed in the spectral glaze of the setting sun. I repeated the words of the Octavio Paz poem to myself, first in Spanish and then in English, as I walked the walk from Third Street to the LA Law Library on West First Street where I stopped in to photocopy a complete set of the films and autorads. By the time I finished at the library copy center, the curvilinear panels of the Walt Disney Concert Hall were beginning to glow pink and gold and purple in the sunset. The luminous colors reflected by the stainless-steel surfaces of the concert hall appeared surrealistic to me, like those passages of the poem, like those footsteps in the mind.

But nobody ever listens to the sounds of their own footsteps here in downtown Los Angeles, not on a night like this. On a night like this, the marine layer was already coming in heavy, dropping a cold, gray curtain over the setting sun, making the cool sea breeze misty enough to be almost fog-like. On a night like this, the brilliance that was the LA skyline by night was reduced to a few sleepy yellow lights somewhere off in the distance. If there was life behind the windows of the public buildings that surrounded me this evening, I did not notice it. I was alone with my thoughts, wondering if there were any others like me who were listening to the sounds of their own footsteps, wondering if there were any others who could even imagine the echoes of footsteps resounding in yet another street, yet another *calle*.

I followed the hard concrete footpaths of the darkening city, thinking about the poem and its possible relation to our crime scene investigation, thinking about the dangling children and their presumptive schoolteacher, listening for the sounds of a footfall in other conceivable dimensions, as a steady stream of cars hissed by and an occasional bus filled with Los Angelinos roared out loud in low guttural notes. Somehow I knew I needed to cross over something, but when and where to cross over that mysterious something? And, perhaps more importantly, how?

• • •

By the end of the first week, I finally had the definitive results I needed. It was nearing the middle of the night. Nevertheless, it was time to set up a meeting with Detective Dash Brogan.

Not wanting to waste a single day, Dash told me to meet him right away at a restaurant called the Pacific Dining Car, which was about the best one could do when such late hours of the evening tend to turn into the wee hours of the morning. Operating in a replica of a railway dining car since 1921, the Pacific Dining Car was a favorite late-night haunt for assorted Los Angeles night owls, movie stars, and film crews who did nighttime shots, doctors and nurses working the late shifts at the Good Samaritan Hospital, stockbrokers who liked to arrive early for the opening of the New York Stock Exchange, and public servants, like us, who whether by choice or dire necessity ended up working around the clock.

The ambiance of the place was nostalgic elegance a la early 1950s, a postwar mise-en-scène with vintage low-key lighting, green-velvet armchairs, linen tablecloths, and curved mahogany ceilings. Dash was already munching his steak-and-egg breakfast by the time I arrived. I ordered eggs Benedict, black coffee, and orange juice from the late-night menu that was brought to me on a slate by a bleary-eyed waiter in a black vest and tie. Dash looked up from his plate and stared at me expectantly, signaling for me to spill the beans, so to speak.

"Some of our dangling children don't appear to be murder victims, Dash," I said, playing nervously with my silverware. "There is clear evidence of cancer markers in some of the DNA samples. I need to check the bodies again to be sure, but it looks to me that some of these children may be cancer victims."

"Cancer victims!" shouted Dash, a little too loud for a crowded steakhouse, even one that catered to night creatures and was open for business twenty-four hours a day, 365 days a year. "What the hell are we dealing with, Doc? Is it murder investigation, or is it something else entirely?"

"It might be something else, Dash," I said, leaning in to quiet and slow the conversation. "Again, I need to check the bodies physically and to get some DNA samples from actual tumors to be sure, but it is looking more and more like the staged scenes we encountered were intended to show us something other than murder."

"Okay, Cornell. That's definitely more than we had to go on

with our old-school police forensics, given the fact that our belated autopsies have been placed on hold by the county coroner. I'd like to say good work or well done, son, but I have an uneasy feeling that you and I are very far from being finished with the severe nastiness of this case."

"I agree with you, Dash. I would be a lot happier with a formal time and cause of death determined with some certainty by a competent medical examiner. But I'm beginning to think that we're being led down the garden path by an artistic perpetrator who's trying to tell us something. The logical next question being, *What in the world is this perp trying to say?*"

The waiter brought my coffee, orange juice, and eggs Benedict, and I hurried to catch up with Dash.

"Slow down, Cornell," said Brogan sympathetically. "Enjoy your food. You look like you haven't eaten for days, or even slept for that matter."

"I do tend to get engrossed in my work, particularly when the findings are still a mystery."

"Engrossed, you say?" prompted Brogan, purposefully narrowing his focus.

"More like fascinated," I said, avoiding his penetrating gaze. "That is to say, fascinated by a mystery that creates a sense of wonder rapt in awe, yet the wonder and the awe are always tempered by the scientific comprehensibility of man and nature, which ultimately leads an inquiring mind from utter darkness to the brink of a greater understanding."

"Sounds to me like you are engrossed all right … engrossed in the seams and silk stockings of a lovely poet laureate we both know."

"You can't expect me to talk about that, Dash. You know as well as I do that a gentleman never tells."

"You don't have to tell me anything, Cornell. Lauriana already told me all about your little sleepover with the Poet Laureate of the Inner Dark."

My surprised expression must have betrayed my discomfort, which bordered on chagrin.

"Don't worry yourself into a tizzy, Cornell. Lauriana always tells me everything I need to know—we always communicate on a need-to-know basis. Besides, I think she might have done you some good: you're beginning to sound a tad poetic yourself when you go on about utter darkness leading to a greater understanding."

"Whatever happened to privacy? Whatever happened to discretion?" I lamented.

"Come now, Cornell. Between an LA detective and a Poet Laureate of the Inner Dark, do you really think that carnal knowledge is off limits as a topic of adult discussion? I've known Lauriana longer than you realize, and there is nothing that we don't know about each other."

"And I'm supposed to be comfortable with this?" I asked incredulously.

"You're not supposed to be comfortable, young man. You are supposed to be brilliant, and you know it. That's why she likes you, and that's why I chose you for this job."

"I don't know what to say ..." I relented, slowly munching on the remainder of my eggs Benedict while the waiter refilled our coffees.

"Just finish your breakfast while I make a phone call," said Dash. "I'm going to get our friend Daniel Grist out of bed to open up the catacombs for us before Chauncey gets wind of what we're up to."

. . .

Dr. Daniel Grist, forensic pathologist and medical examiner, was waiting for us at the front door of the coroner's office. It was the first time I saw him without his surgical mask. It was the first time I saw him smile. His pockmarked face was as impressive as a bucket of mud.

"Any progress with the official death certificates, Danny?" queried Dash.

"You mean: did the congregation of experts from out of town come up with one iota's worth of useful evidence?"

"That's exactly what I mean, Danny boy," said Dash. "Guess

not, huh? Lucky for you that Dr. Westerly is hot on the heels of the perpetrator of this case," he added as he lighted an unfiltered cigarette and headed toward the elevator.

"You do know that there is no smoking in public offices?" remarked Daniel Grist. He nodded to me in deference, and then he looked me over from topknot to toe tag before following Dash Brogan to the elevator.

"I won't tell anyone if you don't," said Dash. "Besides, the smell of burning tobacco leaves is a lot more pleasant than the stink of the chemicals you use in your line of work."

The steel doors closed harshly, and we headed down to the labyrinth of dank corridors and foul vestibules that defined the LA County Morgue. The cold autopsy room was the same morbid necropolis as it was before, with one exception: in addition to the eight rolling gurneys, there was another gurney with a body bag on it. I could see that the bag was filled with something larger than the others, and I assumed that the additional body bag might contain the lifeless plasticized corpse of the suspended schoolteacher we found at the Pasadena Ghost College.

"Tell Danny what you found, Cornell, and what you came here to do," said Dash. "Tell him what grisly business you need to take a look at and what kinds of tissue samples you'll need." Dash extinguished the remains of his cigarette in the hollow of a stainless-steel sink. "And while you're at it, you might want to take some samples from the petrified schoolteacher over there."

Danny's eyes lit up as I explained the implications of my preliminary findings, and I think that he was smiling, although though it was pretty hard to tell with his surgical mask back in place. When I told him what we needed to do to confirm my suspicions, Daniel grist seemed reluctant at first, reminding us of the coroner's strict orders.

"You have no idea how hard it was for me to cover for you the last time you were here," exclaimed Danny. "I had to invoke the Code of Hammurabi—an eye for an eye—to fill in the hole." Danny zipped open one of the body bags and pointed accusingly at the obvious ocular replacement. "The medical-grade eyes that are available to me aren't nearly as realistic as these marvelous jewel-like babies," he added. "Lucky for me, the coroner and his so-called experts weren't very observant."

"The Code of Hammurabi, huh?" quipped Dash. "I've heard tell a lot of codes of conduct in my day, but I never heard the words of an old Mesopotamian king spoken anywhere near the Department of Justice."

"Justice would be well served if you did," remarked Daniel Grist. "You see, the Code of Hammurabi is all about justice and law and order in an otherwise wicked world."

"Do tell, Danny boy. What did good ol' Hammurabi have to say about justice in this city of fallen angels?"

"Plenty," said Danny, who proceeded to count with his fingers. "First, the enlightened king had plenty to say about the need to bring the rule of righteousness to the land. He intended to destroy the wicked and the evildoers so the strong should not do harm to the weak. He intended to chastise the unruly land of Babylon and to further the well-being of all mankind."

"I didn't know you were such a scholar, Danny boy," said Dash as he clapped the medical examiner on the back and lit another unfiltered. "Does the Code of Hammurabi have anything to say about cancer doctors and their terminal patients?"

"You bet, Detective," said Danny brightly. "In addition to the rules of ownership, civil rights, debts, marriage, divorce, and incest, the Code of Hammurabi specify the amounts of payment for doctors and surgeons, the latter of whom suffered severe punishments for their fatal errors."

"Severe punishments, you say," said Dash, expelling a great plume of tobacco smoke.

"Yes, I'd say severe, particularly by today's standards. You see, the Code of Hammurabi decrees the following judgment: *if a physician makes a large incision with an operating knife, and inadvertently kills the patient, his hands shall be cut off!*"

"Sounds fair to me," said Dash.

Knowing all too well the current state of defensive medicine, where doctors generally escape accountability and responsibility under the guise of malpractice insurance, I nodded and affirmed that I was inclined to agree with the former Mesopotamian king.

"Speaking of dramatic incisions, Danny boy," said Dash. "I'm gonna have to ask you to look the other way while Dr. Westerly performs some major surgery on these here corpses."

"Major surgery!" said Danny, hunching over his lifeless brood like a lion over a kill.

"Minimally invasive," I said, correcting the exaggeration. "I only need to sample the lungs and the livers, where cancers tend to spread. The rest of the story we can get with simple x-rays."

"And what justification am I to use this time, Detective, when the coroner takes me to task?" Danny protested weakly, knowing full well the dire necessity of the tissue samples.

"It's called *probable cause*, Danny boy. Besides, you're likely to be a hero around here when Dr. Westerly confirms the probable cause of death. But I highly recommend you get a move on before any more experts from out of town come out of the woodwork and invade your princely domain."

9 They'll Never Get to Hollywood

The next day, I got a call from Dr. Daniel Grist with the results of the x-rays. We had reexamined the scarred legs and arms of two of the dangling children, which looked like they had undergone and recovered from limb-salvage surgery some time before their actual deaths. He told me that, indeed, there were titanium rods inserted in the place of the tibia of one child, and the femur of another should have been. So far, so good. He was moving on to the histology slides to probe for the presence of cancer markers. The rest of the story would have to come from my newly established crime lab, where I was busy with Dr. Liling Chen, analyzing the lumps and nodules of tumor biopsies I had pulled out of the livers and lungs of the deceased.

Then I got an urgent call from Detective Dash Brogan. "Meet me at the La Brea Tar Pits," he demanded, "and make it fast!" I was almost afraid to ask; I could tell from the insistent tone of his voice that I would be walking smack-dab into the nitty-gritty of another disturbing crime scene.

I parked my car in the lot at Hancock Park and walked past the Page Museum to the banks of the bubbling tar pits where a crowd of onlookers was already gathered. The late winter's day was overcast and cold. I was alarmed to see a number of photographers and reporters assembled in the crowd just beyond the police barricades. Dash Brogan was deep in conversation with Clive, who was busy focusing his camera on something that was floating in the oily asphaltum. It was bodies: lots of bodies, female bodies, beautiful bodies that appeared to be swimming. Only none of them were swimming; they were only floating half-submerged in the dire ooze, rocking in the wake of the foul-smelling gas bubbles that were rising up from the depths of the antediluvian quagmire.

There among the entombed fossils of mastodons, giant sloths, camels, and saber-toothed cats that once roamed the Los Angeles Basin in ancient times were the bodies of at least a half dozen bathing beauties, which is not at all unusual in this town that attracts the most beautiful women in the world to its swimming pools, movie studios, and casting couches. Lured to the trappings of Hollywood, California, they come in search of money, power, and fame, only to find that the glamour and the glitz of Tinseltown is only another façade manufactured by specialists practiced in the art of deception. As many who have come to these Pacific shores in search of stardom, as many have had to settle for considerably lesser roles in the entertainment business and/or the vainglorious sex trade, which tragically lures the beautiful and the unfortunate. In many ways, Hollywood, California, is much like the La Brea Tar Pits: this sepulcher by the sea is a death trap that devours the innocent and the predators alike, leaving only the embalmed, exanimate husks of what was once the nobility, dignity, and grace of the virtuous. Approaching the banks of the largest of the tar pits, where Dash and Clive were standing, I knew one thing for sure—these lifeless bathing beauties would never get to Hollywood.

"Hell of a thing to be photographing," I said to Clive. "Hell of a thing on such a gray day."

"Hell of a thing on any given day," responded Clive. "Dash here tells me that you may be on to something with your DNA analysis."

"I don't know what to make of it in relation to our prospective corpus delicti, but I suspect that the perpetrators of the previous crime scenes we discovered are not the actual commissioners of the crimes."

"Okay, smart guy," chimed Dash. "What do you make of these young lovelies? These tar babes appear to be young and healthy enough to be fashion models. Are you going to tell me that these women died of cancer too?"

"To be certain of that, I would need to take a careful look at the torsos without their bathing suits on. Then I would need to take some deep tissue samples to be sure."

"Well, you're not going to get a chance to do that here," said Brogan. "Not until we get these girls bagged and tagged and carted off to the county morgue. I'm not about to have my young protégé photographed peeping under ladies' bikinis by the local paparazzi."

"Protégé," I said with an irrepressible smile. "I like the sound of that, Dash."

"Well then, do like I do—wipe that shit-eating grin off your face and help Clive finish up with the walk-through and the official photographs." Pacing the shoreline of the tar pits right in front of me, Dash added, "This place gives me the creeps!"

The La Brea crime scene, with its bubbling pools of tar and its reedy, palm-lined banks, resembled an establishing scene from an old science-fiction movie. Searching the foul-smelling scene in an ever-widening semicircle, from the banks of the tar pits to the yellow tapes and police barricades, it was clear to me that there was no way to preserve and protect the entire perimeter of the crime scene. The first responders had apparently notified the local paparazzi and the press at the same time they had called in their reports of the floating bodies. With so many people wandering through the area before it was secured, any physical evidence on the banks was rendered useless, as was the perpetrator's entrance and exit. It was all we could do to exclude the unauthorized personnel from further encroachment and to photograph the setting and the positions of the floating bodies before they were fished out of the oily waters by the LAPD. In an effort to document the mounting spectacle of the overcrowded crime scene, Clive took an array of long-range and midrange shots for perspective, followed by some close-up photography of what amounted to seven lovely ladies, each of which were just as petrified and just as plasticized as the previous victims we had encountered. The only obvious difference between these victims and the others was that several of these oil-encrusted bodies still had undefiled faces on them.

* * *

Back at the morgue, I was able to examine the breasts, as well as the livers and lungs of the victims, and to gather the tissue samples that would hopefully provide the confirmation I needed. At first glance, the tumors I found on these floating women were quite different from those of the dangling children. Whereas the telltale tumors of the children were found deep inside the body cavities, it was immediately evident that these bathing beauties were victimized by the invasive fingers of breast cancer, which had resulted in the radical excision of the normal breast tissues in one or both breasts, and the replacement of the resulting voids with various prosthetic implants. Moreover, a thorough examination of the voluptuous schoolteacher revealed the same cosmetic surgery. Although her natural breast tissue appeared to be normal, her outstanding mounds of feminine distinction had been substantially augmented by a plastic surgeon sometime prior to her demise. Nevertheless, I obtained more tissue samples from the liver and the lungs and the swollen lymph nodes of the suspended schoolteacher, as well as the seven tar-spangled women, and I headed off to the crime lab to probe for a broad spectrum of molecular tumor markers, including a series of genetic markers for bone, brain, and breast cancers.

Later that evening, Dash called to see how I was doing and to tell me that the public spectacle exhibited at the La Brea Tar Pits—including graphic photographs of the floating bodies—had landed on the front page of the *Los Angeles Times*. He told me that thousands of irate Los Angelinos were already gathering for a candlelight vigil on the sidewalks of Wilshire Boulevard. Dash suggested that I make an immediate appearance at the place where a life-size statue of a female mastodon appeared to be trapped in the Lake Pit, bellowing out a fatal warning to her helpless family standing on the banks. I asked him if it was really necessary for me to accompany him at this time, given that the official walk-through was completed hours ago and the bulk of the physical evidence was already removed from the staged crime scene.

The silence on the other end of the phone call suggested that I might have been somewhat less than responsive to the detective's explicit instructions. I started to explain that I was currently knee-deep myself, mired in the extraction and DNA analysis of the new tissue samples we had just gathered, when Dash interrupted me. What he said came as a complete surprise.

"I didn't say for you to meet *me* at the candlelight vigil, college boy. Clive and I are already out of the picture. I was just thinking that you might want to check out this scene of public outrage for yourself, being that the lovely and affectionate poet laureate is present in the madding crowd."

• • •

I parked my car in a lot on Wilshire Boulevard, crossed the street at the Los Angeles County Museum of Art, and made my way to the adjoining section of the tar pits that Dash had described. An eerie scene greeted me. From a distance, the gathering crowd of candle-wielding hoi polloi lined up along the fences looked like a massive candelabrum made of dark, shadowy figurines whose faces alone were bathed in the jaundiced glow of the votive candles and chemical glow sticks. I saw this glowing inner mass through an even larger crowd that surrounded it and was spilling out from the sidewalks into the street, blocking traffic in the first two lanes.

As I drew closer to the human constituents of the living candelabrum, I could begin to make out the details of the individual faces, each appearing for a brief moment in chiaroscuro, like the subjects of an old Rembrandt painting.

I searched the agitated crowd for the angelic face of Lauriana Noire. What had previously seemed a candelabra was now a moving, writhing sea of tormented, mourning sardines. I pushed forward awkwardly against the grain of the enveloping multitude, taking in the sounds of the angry mob's anguish. My breath came short, and my heart rate sped as an uncomfortable element of danger took hold of me. The increasingly rabid mourners squeezed ever tighter between the moving automobile traffic and the iron fences that separated the sidewalks from the bubbling tar pits. Bumping shoulders with strangers as if I were the silver ball in a pinball machine, I struggled to keep my balance as I made my way to the fences bordering the simmering Lake Pit. I could make out the life-size statues of several terror-stricken mastodons that stood out like pale specters from the engulfing darkness of the tar pits. I was holding on to the rods of the iron fence for support, staring at the half-submerged hulk of the terror-stricken mastodon, when Lauriana found me.

"Can you hear it, Cornell? Can you hear the mother's desperate cries? Can you imagine the look of fear in her eye? Can you see that she is not only sounding the alarm for her husband and her child? Can you see that she is pleading for us all to become more aware of the ever-present dangers, sending out a warning of grave portent for all the modern world to see?"

I seized Lauriana and held her in my arms while the mob and the pits and the benighted metropolis swirled around us. I blew out the votive candle she was still holding oh-so-gracefully in her delicate hands, and then I kissed her lips like there would be no tomorrow. Lauriana dropped the votive candle, the glass of which shattered on the sidewalk, and she returned my kiss with such passion that my mind began to reel. She kissed my lips and my throat as she unbuttoned my shirt, and then she reached further down with her soft, cool hands as she spoke to me in an evocative tone.

"I want you to take me and love me, Cornell. I want you to take me and love me again."

"You mean right here, right now?" I said in surprise.

"No, silly man," she whispered with the softness of a kiss. "I want you to walk me home."

10 More Than Lamps Symmetrically Arranged

The walk down Wilshire Boulevard to Lauriana's apartment that evening was an exercise in consummate bliss. Arm in arm, we left the bubbling caldron of the La Brea Tar Pits and the raucous candlelight vigil behind us, drawing closer and closer to the soft firmament of satin sheets and pillows of illusion that move a man from one dream of beauty to another. We passed by the concrete frontage of the art museum and were approaching the site of the "Urban Light" exhibit when the night sky opened up, and it started to rain.

The rain fell heavily, fitfully in large, silvery drops that were briefly illuminated by the light of hundreds of antique streetlamps—202, to be exact—arrayed by size and by style in rows that formed the orderly grid pattern of the "Urban Light" exhibit. Designed by the artist to appear at night like *a building with a roof of light*," the raised platform of the outdoor exhibit offered little protection from the elements, and so we ran through the columns of Victorian streetlamps to the cover of an open-air pavilion located just behind the exhibit.

Lauriana drew me close and tenderly kissed my lips. The heady smell of her perfume was intoxicating. Then she turned me around to face the luminosity of the Urban Lights as she stood behind me with her arms clasped around my waist. I melted into the grasp of her embrace.

"Tell me what you see, Cornell," she said, with her voice raised above the clamor of the rainstorm.

"I see symmetrical rows of vintage streetlamps arranged like pieces on a chessboard."

"Oh, my poor, dear Cornell. Life is more than a series of streetlamps symmetrically arranged; life is a luminous halo, a semitransparent envelope surrounding us from the beginning of consciousness to the end."

Suddenly, I was at a loss for words.

"Can you see the luminous halo, darling? Can you feel a radiant envelope surrounding you yet?"

"No, I can't," I said in confusion. "I see rows and rows of lamps with glass globes glowing in the dark. That's all I see ... What were you saying about the beginning of consciousness?"

"I said life is more than a series of streetlamps symmetrically arranged; life is a luminous halo, a semitransparent envelope surrounding us from the beginning of consciousness to the end."

"That's beautiful," I said, nearly shouting above the din of the downpour. "Did you just make that up off the top of your head?"

"No, silly man, I'm quoting Virginia Woolf for your benefit ... and the benefit of your unsolved murder case, of course," she added.

"My murder case?" I said incredulously. "What do these cast-iron lampposts have to do with the case of the dangling schoolchildren? Or the suspended schoolteacher or the tar-soaked bathing beauties that we just fished out of the bog?"

"Everything," she said with her arms still clasped firmly around my waist. "Everything or nothing at all, depending on your ability to interpret the whole of your present surroundings."

"I don't understand," I said, feebly attempting to turn around and face her directly.

"You will," said the poet laureate, turning me back around to view the Urban Light exhibit with her hands placed firmly on my hips. "Now close your eyes and clear your mind ..."

As she spoke these curious instructions in my ear, Lauriana deftly unbuckled my belt and slid her hands to the place where my pants had been. There in the relative darkness of the outdoor pavilion, with the rain pouring down in sheets all around us, and the wind blowing steadily in vigorous gusts, her velvet hands moved fervently, rhythmically upon me as I closed my eyes, inhaled her perfume, and awaited her next instructions.

"Think not of materialistic things, my young lover," she said. "Think not of your conventional interpretations … I want you to open your eyes and look again, more deeply this time, at the whole of the present art form."

I stood there trembling but unmoving as she changed her position from the dorsal to the ventral side of me, kneeled down, and continued her vociferous encouragements with increasing vigor and pace. I obediently opened my eyes.

"Life is more than rows and rows of individual lampposts symmetrically arranged, my darling," she said, looking up at me from a kneeling position. "A lamppost is just another lamppost, no matter how straight and tall it is. What I want you to see—what I want you to feel—is the luminous halo of love and light that surrounds you now … the halo that envelops you and stimulates your consciousness to yearn and grow."

It was more than my consciousness that was yearning and growing, but I stood up to the task and allowed the Poet Laureate of the Inner Dark to take control of my sensory impressions.

"Look at the Urban Lights again, Cornell, not with materialistic eyes that look upon the unimportant things of life and make the trivial and the transitory appear to be true and enduring. Look within and feel the spontaneous flow of your own spirit awakening. Feel the stream of your consciousness straining for release. And as you do, your life and your mind, it seems, is expanding to even greater proportions … As you search for the meaning of the messages in the medium, you will see that this is far, far, far from an ordinary day or night."

I was straining to appreciate the provocative perspective she was lavishly flourishing upon me, almost as much as I was straining to contain myself within myself.

"The mind of a man," she asserted, "receives myriad sensual impressions every living minute: some trivial, some fantastic, some evanescent and fading into imperceptibility, while others are substantial enough to be engraved upon the soul with the sharpness of steely teeth."

My mind reeled with the rapture of extreme delight as I strived to embrace the profundity.

All the while, Lauriana continued to coax me to new heights of poetic understanding. "From all sides they come, an incessant shower of sensory impressions that merge and shape themselves into meanings like atoms that assemble into crystalline forms. And yet a man is encouraged to delight in the wholeness of his surroundings ... the aspirations of his intellect ... the splendor of his body ... the meanings of his memorandums ... until every feeling, every thought, every quality of brain and spirit is enlivened. Is he not magnified by the experience and compelled to look more deeply beyond the staging of these public spectacles ... compelled to look beyond the evidence of appearances—to see the mystery, the unsolved case, the dark tragedy now at hand—to look beyond mere manifestations that are common to the art and to see the luminous halo of love and light that surrounds him now? Is he not flooded with a great surge of infinite possibilities that come alive and extend the meaning of his own fictions into the realm of the sublime?"

It was then and there, in the opulent grasp of the poet laureate of the inner dark, that I let go of my inhibitions and I felt and I saw the luminous halo of the Urban Lights for the first time.

· · ·

Graced by another heavenly night in the arms of an angel, I was anxious to extend my newfound psychological perspectives further into the enthralling folds of this criminal case.

I worked day and night to complete the genetic profiles: amplifying specific sequences in each DNA sample with PCR Polymerase Chain Reaction (PCR), separating the DNA sequences with gel electrophoresis, probing the various restriction fragments with fluorescent probes, mapping the results with autoradiography, looking for telltale patterns in the scientific ink blots. Daniel Grist was also working feverishly in the histology laboratories of the coroner's office. He was working overtime, overseeing the paraffin embedding and chemical staining of each tissue sample from the excised tumors, trying to determine the cellular origin and derivation of the cancerous tissues in a systematic process of differential diagnosis. Meanwhile, Dash and Clive were busy working to match the close-up photography of the three bathing beauties that still had skin on their faces with the national and international databases of missing persons. Unfortunately for us, there were no exact matches to be found. Apparently, these plasticized stiffs were not missing persons. But what else could they be?

So far, we had not been able to positively identify even one of the victims. There were no useful fingerprints obtained from any of the plasticized bodies, and there was no evidence of drowning, strangulation, stabbing, gunshot wounds, or blunt-force trauma. We were not even able to determine the exact times of death, due in part to the vagaries of decomposition introduced by the artful taxidermy. All we could determine at this point was that some of these victims had probably died of metastatic cancer, which would normally be classified as natural causes. Only there was nothing natural about the way that these terminal cancers were being promoted, nothing natural about the way they were theatrically presented to the public at large.

Three days and as many front-page headlines from the *Los Angeles Times* and public demonstrations for the LAPD to contend with, I was summoned by Detective Dash Brogan to a formal meeting at the coroner's office. By the time I arrived on the scene, the press and the paparazzi were camped outside the building in full force. Dash Brogan met me in the visitor parking lot and escorted me through the throngs of reporters and camerapersons who were clamoring for any and all official announcements about the case. The waves of paparazzi parted like the Red Sea when Brogan held up his hand, and we were soon heading up the winding staircase of the red-brick hospital building to a conference room on the second floor.

Midway up the staircase, Dash Brogan stopped and lit an unfiltered. I could tell by the hurried manner in which he lit the cigarette and immediately drew the smoke into his lungs that this was going to be a difficult meeting.

"I want you to let me do the talking today, Cornell," said Brogan with an anxious air of grave portent. "I'll ask you directly if I want you to reveal anything you found in your lab at this time." He snuffed out the half-smoked butt with a turn of his shoe, looked me directly in the eyes, and said, "Got it?"

"I got it, boss," I said, nodding.

"Good," said Brogan. "Trust me, Cornell, you don't want to start off on the wrong foot with Chauncey and Philiac."

"Philiac?" I queried. "What kind of a name is Philiac?"

"His name is Philip Dickinson," said Brogan. "He got the nickname from the simple fact that his nose starts bleeding before you even hit him."

"You mean he has a congenital form of pseudo-hemophilia, like Von Willebrand disease?"

"I mean he picks it," said Brogan starting up the stairs. "You'll see."

I followed Dash Brogan into the coroner's office, where Chauncey was seated in a high-back swivel chair behind an oversized mahogany desk. Dr. Daniel Grist and a fellow whom I assumed to be Philip Dickinson were seated in two lesser chairs positioned directly in front of the coroner's desk. Dash strode into the center of the room, and two of the three men rose from their seats. The coroner, who did not rise to greet us, introduced the new man as Dr. Philip Dickinson MD, PhD, and informed us that he would be acting as the assistant chief coroner for this high-profile case. I noticed Dr. Daniel Grist wince in a transient expression of pain when the coroner explained that the new man was going to be personally supervising all the autopsies from here on out. A slight pout, a lopsided tightening of the upper lip, and a look of what can only be described as contempt spread over Danny's pockmarked face in a blush that lasted but for a moment and then disappeared into the familiar bucket of mud. I shook hands briefly with the newly designated assistant chief coroner, and then I took a seat in a black-leather davenport off to one side of the room, where I was able to eyeball the new man obliquely when he and Danny regained their seats.

Whether standing or sitting, the man exhibited the sinuous posture of a slug. He had a rather smallish head with pale yellow hair the color of dried cornstalks and a sickly yellowish complexion that is rarely found among the living. His anemic, jaundiced appearance made me wonder whether his red blood cells, as well as his platelets, were functioning normally. It made me wonder if he had even half of the five liters of blood that are normally contained within the body of a healthy seventy-killogram male.

"Come on, Chauncey," growled Dash, leaning his full weight on the coroner's desk. "You know as well as I do that Philiac may have the right letters after his name, but he does not have the kind of experience needed for this particular job." Brogan stood up and turned to face the man in question. "Philiac here never treated a single patient, and he never contributed anything worthwhile to either science or humanity. You know I'd rather work with Danny here."

"That's the problem, Detective Brogan," said Chauncey, pushing back on his swivel chair to create distance between him and Dash. "You get to choose your forensic scientists, and I get to choose my assistant chief coroner. That's the way it works around here!" Chauncey inched his chair back to a position behind the executive desk and continued. "Besides, Dr. Dickinson was chief resident at Stanford and he has excellent recommendations from UCSF."

"I don't care if he was the chief ball washer at Pebble Beach!" boomed Dash. "I don't want some incompetent asshole with no pertinent experience whatsoever mucking up the progress we already made on this case."

"Progress?" echoed Chauncey, shifting forward in his chair.

"That's right … progress!" affirmed Brogan, taking a seat on the coroner's desk. "While you and your gaggle of so-called experts were busy doing *nothing*, Danny and I have made real progress on this case. We work well together, Chauncey, and I want it to stay that way—that is, unless you would like to get another intimidating phone call from the mayor."

"How do you know that the mayor called me, Brogan?"

"I have my ways, Chauncey. I certainly have my ways. So unless you want to put the man in the moon in charge of this case, I guess we're done here." Brogan stood up and headed for the door.

Chauncey rose to his feet. "Not so fast, Brogan. I want you to tell me what you know."

Detective Brogan turned back around.

"I told you there would be more victims, didn't I?"

"Well, yes. You were right about that," admitted Chauncey.

"And I told you I needed to remove something round and shiny from the bodies?"

"Well, yes. But you did so against my direct orders. And that is precisely why I am replacing Danny with Philiac here," he said, glancing over at the pale anemic slug of a man. "I mean, Dr. Dickinson," he added, too late to do anything but compound the faux pas.

The nervous look on Dr. Dickinson's face made me think that he was struggling hard to keep from inserting his index finger into his nose. A faint rim of dried blood on his left nostril attested to the frequency of this behavior, as well as the appropriateness of his unusual nickname.

"The fact that Danny had the good sense to trust me to solve this case moves him to the top of my bookshelf," said Brogan with a wink to Daniel Grist. "Without a thorough examination of those glass eyes that were used in the fancy taxidermy, we'd still have nothing to go on. And you and your resident ball washer here would have zilch."

"So, out with it, Brogan!" demanded the coroner, whose face was growing redder by the minute. "Just what were you able to discern from your investigation of those artificial eyes?"

"No dice, Chauncey. You can't have it both ways. You're either with me or against me."

"If you want me to keep Danny on this case, you're going to have to give me something solid to tell the mayor."

"I can only tell you what I found out from my personal contacts in Hollywood."

"Hollywood?" exclaimed the red-faced coroner. "What does the murder of sixteen innocent people have to do with Hollywood?"

"More than you and your best boy here would ever suspect, Chauncey," quipped Brogan, adjusting the flexible brim of his fedora downward. "You see, Hollywood is the only place in the whole world where extreme realism is considered de rigueur. And I understand that there is only one eyeball factory in the whole wide world that can manufacture such a fine product." With that, Dash Brogan headed for the exit, nodding for me to follow him out the door.

11 A Thousand Unblinking Eyes

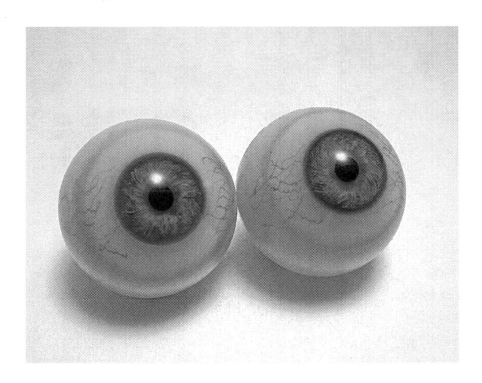

ash Brogan and I were soon heading south in his Pontiac Catalina, motoring down the 405 on our way to Newport Beach. The old-school detective informed me we were heading to a factory called High-Tech Oculars, where we were scheduled to meet with the new CEO. The old CEO had apparently gone missing a few months ago, leaving no trace of his whereabouts.

It turned out that High-Tech Oculars was uniquely qualified as a place of interest in this bewildering case. Known throughout the entertainment business for superior quality workmanship, the specialty company made artificial eyes of all kinds: doll eyes, mannequin eyes, cat eyes, horse eyes, dinosaur eyes, creature eyes, whale eyes, dolphin eyes, puppet eyes, alien eyes, and animatronic eyes that moved and blinked for special effects, as well as realistic human eyes of a quality that far surpassed standard medical-grade prosthetics.

Dash Brogan parked the vintage muscle car on a pine tree–lined street in front of a concrete tilt-up bedecked with a gallery of blue-mirrored windows that reflected the palm trees and the long-stemmed bird-of-paradise bushes in the landscaping. The place was as secure as an ATM machine, with surveillance cameras that moved along with us as we approached the building. Dash pushed a button on the intercom box, and a disembodied voice emerged from the speaker.

"We're from the LAPD," grumbled Brogan. "We're here to see the chief cook and bottle washer of this establishment."

A buzzer sounded, and we entered the lobby of the eyeball factory. We were greeted by a pretty, young, sandy-haired girl wearing high heels, a black, leg-revealing slit-skirt, and a red sweater that was at least two sizes too tight. The girl ushered us into a spacious conference room with a large table shaped like a surfboard, and then she turned around and left the room. I noticed the gallery of framed pictures on the wall: pairs of glass eyeballs staring out at the observer, cool and expressionless. The surfboard table was flanked by two rows of ergonomic designer chairs, which were much more comfortable than they looked.

A man entered the room and introduced himself as "Troy, a businessman with a vision." He was a tall, pigeon-chested man in his early forties. The smell of cheap cologne entered the room with him. You could tell that Troy was the head honcho of this eyeball factory from the exorbitant deepness of his suntan, which must have required considerable time at the beach and the golf course to acquire.

Dash Brogan reached into his coat pocket and withdrew an eyeball; it was the one from the Body Exposed exhibit at the science center. He looked it over and then rolled it across the table to the new CEO. The resulting sneer of disgust—signified by a slight wrinkling of the nose and a momentary curl of the lips—told me that the quality of the workmanship was not up to Troy's high standards.

"I'm sorry, Detective, but this is definitely not one of ours," he said, rolling the eyeball back across the conference table."

"Are you sure?" urged Brogan. "This is a serial murder investigation we're talking about."

"I'm positive," said the suntanned CEO as he rose to his feet. "Now if you'll excuse me, I have some urgent paperwork I have to see to."

"Not so fast, sonny boy," said Dash as he reached into his coat pocket and produced another eyeball. It was the perspicuous eye he had extracted from the dangling child. "How about this one?" he added.

Even before Dash Brogan rolled the second eyeball across the table, the CEO's expression changed dramatically, and he swallowed hard in the process. The executive officer looked the eyeball over carefully, and then he affirmed the obvious. "Yes, this is definitely one of ours."

"How can you be so sure?" prompted Brogan.

The suntanned CEO sat back down, and he turned the gleaming eyeball in his hand, rolling it deftly with the tips of his fingers. "In order to create such stunning reproductions of human eyes that are considered film-worthy by today's standards, we go to great lengths to make our glass eyes sparkle with dynamic realism." Rotating the eyeball with a clear expression of pride, he continued: "Each artificial eyeball is made by hand with a patented process that combines resin glass, polymers, and acrylics to achieve an incredible realism needed for wax figures and authentic-looking human reproductions. See here," said the CEO like a proud father, pointing to the bloodshot vessels in the milky sclera. "It's simply amazing the way that our artisans at High-Tech Oculars imbed this fine meshwork of blood vessels and capillaries into the multilayered sclera of each individual eyeball, creating an added realism that is shockingly lifelike—don't you agree?" he prompted, pointing the perspicuous eyeball directly at me.

I couldn't resist the temptation to nod my head in affirmation.

"What else can you tell us about this bloodshot eyeball of yours?" pressed Brogan.

The CEO rolled the eyeball back across the table as he explained the nuances of the craft. "This particular eyeball incorporates some of our newest proprietary technologies. You see the blood vessels embedded in the multitone sclera?" he said, waiting for Dash Brogan to eyeball the orb. "This distinctive feature accommodates a wide variety of skin colors, and the slight dilation of the pupil serves to create a dynamic realism that is unmatched in the industry."

"So you can tell us exactly who you made this fancy eyeball for?"

"Well, not exactly," said the CEO, somewhat nervously. "I know for certain that it's one of ours, but with these new features ... it had to be a special order."

"Great," said Brogan. "Now show us the invoices for all the special orders you have for eyeballs with these features."

"That's going to be a problem, Detective," said Troy sheepishly. "You see, I've just been promoted to this position. And the original CEO, who was also the founder of the company—by the way—recently disappeared, leaving us with a whole lot of eyeballs, but no head to speak of."

"This is no time to get cute with me, sonny boy," growled Brogan. "What does the disappearance of the company's founder have to do with the list of special orders?"

"It appears that all the invoices and the paperwork for the previous orders disappeared with him."

"That's rather convenient for you and your tax attorneys, buster, but you can't expect me to believe that you know nothing about these special orders for eyeballs." Brogan rose and pushed his designer chair back so hard it slammed into the wall.

The suntanned CEO swallowed hard and said, "I'd really like to help you, Detective, but these orders were not processed on my watch."

"You can't stonewall me, Troy," said Brogan. "One more wise crack out of you, and I'll haul you in for obstruction!"

The chastised CEO immediately changed his cocky tone to that of sincere sheepishness. "Seriously, Detective, I was never involved in either sales or production. I was only involved in quality control," he cleared his throat, "supervising the pairing of mannequin eyes, mostly."

"Well then, dammit," barked Brogan, "take me to someone who knows something useful about the production of these dilated eyeballs!"

"I'm afraid I can't do that, Detective," said the replacement CEO. "Like all high-tech industries, this is a very competitive business. Many of our customers in the motion-picture industry demand strict confidentiality and discretion—"

Before the reluctant CEO could complete the sentence, Brogan rounded the table and dragged the frightened man up by the collar of his sport coat. It looked like Brogan was about to handcuff the trembling executive officer—either that, or beat him to a pulp.

"Okay, okay, you convinced me," said the ruffled CEO. "Let me make a call first … to see which one of our experienced artisans might be free to speak with you."

"No deal, dumbass. It's either my way or the hard-core highway!" barked Brogan. "Now take me to the eyeball artist who fabricated this thing!" he said, pocketing the eyeball and pushing the bedraggled CEO out the door.

We entered into the inner sanctum of the eyeball factory, a large industrial hangar with high ceilings and industrial venting overhead. It immediately appeared to me that this was more like an organic chemistry laboratory setting than the robotic assembly line I had imagined. There were rows and rows of individual workbenches supporting arrays of rubber molds, weighing scales, mixing devices, and plastic measuring beakers. Several of the workbenches were staffed by eyeball artisans wielding paint brushes and airbrushes. Others were populated by electric-drill rigs upon which individual eyeballs were mounted, and ocular artisans were busy wet sanding and polishing the finished products. I recognized a symphony of distinctive aromas in the air: the sweet smell of acetone and nail polish mingled with the more noxious odors of casting resins and polymers curing, producing a heady bouquet of acrylics, urethanes, polyester resins, phenols, and spray paint that permeated the eyeball factory.

Troy, the suntanned CEO, led us past a series of folding tables whereupon we were greeted by at least a thousand unblinking eyes staring blindly up at the outside world from the recessed chambers of what looked like cardboard egg cartons. The reluctant CEO led us to a workbench where a man in a white lab coat and a respirator was busy wielding a forceps in one hand—skillfully applying fine red yarns onto the sides of a single mounted eyeball—followed by a gentle wave of a tiny air gun, which he held in the other hand and sprayed a fine mist of what looked like clear polymer that melted the red yarn into the sclera of an eye. "I'm certain that this is the eyeball artist you're looking for … I mean, the one you were asking to speak with."

Removing his respirator and gloves, the eyeball artisan, an elderly man in his sixties, slowly rose from his bench and faced the replacement CEO. "I would prefer that you refer to me properly, sir, as an ocularist," said the man with an air of pride, if not authority.

"Very well," said the CEO. "This is the ocularist you want to speak with."

"I'm Detective Dash Brogan from the LAPD, and this is my apprentice, Dr. Cornell Westerly. I need you to answer one question for me, old-timer." Brogan reached into his coat pocket and produced the eyeball in question. "Did you make this here bloodshot and dilated eyeball yourself, or did someone else help you with it?"

"There is no one who could make such a fine specimen but me," said the prideful ocularist with an attitude that bordered on arrogance. "I would never let anyone even polish my artwork."

"Can you tell me *who* you made this particular eyeball for, old-timer?" pressed Brogan.

"I never met the customer in person," explained the elderly ocularist. "I do remember that this specimen was part of a large order of various eye colors and sizes."

"How large?" demanded Brogan.

"As I recall, it was an order for ninety of the finest artificial eyes I could create—forty-five matching pairs, that is." The elderly ocularist sat back on his stool and looked off into the distance. "I remember now … it took me several months of solid work to complete the order."

"Is there *anything* that you can tell me about the customer you made these eyeballs for?"

"Yes, yes, I remember clearly now. The order, as I recall, was from a newly established motion-picture company called Art House Creations. Being a true artist myself, I can appreciate the aesthetic connotations of the name."

• • •

The sun was dropping low in the western sky when we pulled up to the Pelican Grill, a trendy seaside restaurant that overlooked the ocean along the Newport Coast. Dash Brogan had a few words with the maître d' about impromptu reservations and his preferred seating, and we were summarily escorted to the terrace, an elegant alfresco setting on a grand deck lined by Greek columns and enclosed by a low wall of clear glass that attenuated the evening sea breezes. Dash ordered the wild salmon special, and I ordered crab cakes and pasta primavera. We ate our meals in silence, sipping espresso coffee and imported sparkling water, gazing at the Pacific Ocean as it slowly, inexorably consumed the last remains of the setting sun.

Watching Dash Brogan meticulously pick out the stray pin bones of the baked fish that lay before him, I envisioned the two of us on an old-time hayride, each of us striving to capture that one needle in the haystack that could tie everything together, that one piece of vital information that might serve as the crucial clue that would prevent Art House Creations from utilizing the remainder of its eyeball order.

"So tell me, Cornell," said Brogan. "Are you having any luck with your DNA analysis?"

"It's not a matter of luck, Detective," I assured him. "It's more about persistence, fidelity to basic methodologies, adherence to scientific principles, and the personal dedication needed to keep an open mind to emerging patterns and interpretations, based on the accumulation of raw data gleaned from painstaking observations."

"If you're trying to tell me that the devil is in the details, I'm not buying it."

"I'm trying to tell you that the *majesty* is in the details, Detective," I declared, sipping the last vestiges of a double espresso. "The majesty of the biological kingdom is ever present in the genetic code of each and every life form, from the lowest of the microbes and viruses to the very top of the food chain. The majesty is hidden in the molecular-genetic details, Detective."

"Well then, smart guy, tell me something about your emerging patterns and interpretations. We need something solid to go on—and quick!"

"I can tell you at this point that the majority of our victims appear to have malignant tumors that had spread throughout their bodies while they were alive. Plus they have quite a variety of chromosomal abnormalities and classic tumor markers in and around the cancerous tissues." I shook my head sideways and said, "What I still can't figure out is why there are so many different types of cancers represented in this set of victims. We have sarcomas and bone cancers in the dangling children, we have a yet unidentified cancer in the suspended schoolteacher, and we have breast cancer and lung cancer in the oil-soaked bathing beauties."

"Are you trying to tell me that *none* of these petrified corpses are bona fide murder victims?"

I looked around to make sure that no one was listening to our graphic after-dinner conversation, and then I answered Brogan's question in a decidedly hushed voice. "I'm telling you that I found evidence of a potentially fatal disease in every single stiff."

"You know what this means?" said Brogan.

"No, I have no idea what it means, Dash." And I didn't. "Tell me what it means to you."

"It means that the perpetrator of these public spectacles is not a cold-blooded murderer in the first place or the second place. It means that he or she is some kind of showman who is trying to prove something to someone or to tell us something important in a brutally theatrical manner."

"May I ask why you didn't want me to tell the coroner about my preliminary findings?"

"I'm protecting you from yourself, college boy," said Brogan. "The last thing we need right now is to have Chauncey and his bevy of bottom-feeders challenging your findings for the wrong reasons. With all the press and the hoopla surrounding each public exhibition, the powers that be are out for blood—human blood." Brogan waxed surprisingly philosophical in his reasoning. "While you're up there in your lab pointing fingers away from the obvious, the rest of the law enforcement in this City of Angels is looking for someone to blame," he stared pointedly at me, "looking for someone to arrest ... looking for someone to shoot, hang, or beat to death!"

"So what do you want me to do, Detective?"

"I want you to get together with Danny and his histologist to compare notes and confirm your findings. I understand that Danny was able to independently categorize some of the tumor types you mentioned. I want you to make darn sure that your DNA data can be verified by Danny and his histologist, using his own slides. Can you do that for me?"

"I think so, Dash," I said, recalling a recently developed method. "Danny and I can use fluorescence in situ hybridization (FISH) and a newer, more sensitive method of in situ RT-PCR to confirm my results, using Danny's histological slides as the source material."

"Good," said Brogan, picking his teeth with a salmon bone. "Let me know what you find."

We motored back to LA while a giant bruise in the western sky slowly faded from bright crimson and purple to somber shades of gray. I was wondering what kind of message it was that was hidden in the midst of these public spectacles, what kind of motivation could be behind these brazen theatrical acts, what kind of abnormal psychology could propel this artful yet secretive perpetrator to conceive such an elaborate plan, let alone to repeat such an atrocious endeavor.

"What do you know about the psychology of motivation, Dash?"

"You mean, why did Sigmund Freud smoke twenty cigars a day?"

"No, Dash, I mean abnormal psychology ... as it relates to criminal profiling."

"I know that fear, greed, pride, and lust cover the bases. Why? What are you thinking?"

"I'm trying to figure out what kind of abnormal psychology might be behind the orchestration of these shocking public exhibits."

"You mean like paranoid or schizophrenic assholes who shoot first and ask questions later? I doubt if our body-snatching perpetrator fits that profile," said Dash. "Our artful dodger may be sneaky and eccentric, but he doesn't fit the description of someone with trust issues."

"I was thinking more about Cluster B personality disorders ... you know, antisocial, narcissistic, and histrionic disorders. Each of these syndromes is associated with deceitful activities, an inflated sense of self-importance, and excessive attention-seeking behaviors."

"You mean our perpetrator is deceptive, defiant, and dramatic, don't you?"

"Well, yes," I said, mulling over the amazing clarity of Brogan's thought process.

"So much for abnormal psychology, smart guy. We already know, in fact we already agreed, that our mysterious perpetrator is nothing if not theatrical."

By the time we made it back to my car at the coroner's office, the time was half past dark.

12 Clutching a Handful of Smoke

ack at my off-Broadway crime lab, Dr. Liling Chen and I worked feverishly to prepare new sets of PCR-primers and to assemble the collection of restriction enzymes and probes needed for the in situ hybridization procedures. In addition, we assembled the reagents needed for me to confirm the results with reverse transcriptase—polymerase chain reaction (RT-PCR) in my lab, using total RNA extracted from duplicate serial slides. Once I had all the reagents needed for DNA amplification, probe hybridization, and signal detection in hand, I headed to the county morgue where Dr. Daniel Grist—at Dash Brogan's insistence—and his molecular histologist were burning the midnight oil.

Fortunately, the molecular biology methods—which are far superior to standard immunohistochemistry using specific antibodies—were familiar to Dr. Grist and his lab technician, which made for quick work in setting up the comparative analyses. The combination of conventional histology and immunohistochemistry with Danny's in situ hybridization and in situ RT-PCR assessments would provide powerful insights into the identification, cellular derivation, and staging of the biopsied tumors, as well as additional insights into the presence of characteristic tumor markers and chromosomal abnormalities that are associated with, if not causal to, the clinical development of the various malignancies. It would take a full forty-eight hours for Danny and his molecular histologist to process and probe the complete set of slides. I used this time to validate Danny's assays with additional controls and high-stringency RT-PCR performed in my own lab.

Two days later, I contacted Daniel Grist, and we set up a private morbidity and mortality (M&M) conference. For those who are not familiar with such propitious traditions held by medical services at academic centers, M&M conferences are forthright discussions of issues, complications, and errors—that is, peer reviews of autopsy outcomes and mistakes that occurred during the care of patients, already dead or dying. The enlightened thinking behind the M&M conference was originated in the early 1900s by Dr. Ernest Codman, MD, FACS, at Massachusetts General Hospital in Boston. Unfortunately for Dr. Codman—who lost his staff privileges at the hospital after suggesting the evaluation of surgeon competence— such refined ideas aimed at improving clinical practices were adopted rather slowly, and it was not until 1983 that the Accreditation Council for Graduate Medical Education began requiring that accredited residency programs conduct a periodic review of all complications and deaths. Indeed, in both forensic science and medical practice, the *end result* matters.

Danny and I met in his office at noon, a time when the coroner would be out for a three-martini lunch. Danny had taken it upon himself to x-ray the suspended schoolteacher, which led him to believe that she died of some form of brain cancer. I was glad that he, and not I, had the displeasure of opening the woman's skull to obtain the confirmatory biopsies. We went over his molecular biology results, and not surprisingly, Danny came up with the same genetic markers in the biopsied tissue samples as I had found previously. Moreover, the control amplifications and the total RNA samples processed by RT-PCR in my lab provided additional confirmation of the results: each of these plasticized corpses was riddled with the molecular signposts of cancer, and each of the different cancers exhibited its own distinguishable molecular pathogenesis. Like fingerprints left behind on a hunting knife, or footprints in the snow, the pathogenesis of every cancer leaves behind a progression of molecular breadcrumbs in the wake of its flagrant course.

While we couldn't be sure that the cause of death in each case was the metastatic cancer or something else, we finally had something new to go on, something solid, that indicated that the coroner and his cohorts were all barking up the wrong murder tree. But before we patted each other on the back in celebration, I realized that we were no closer to collaring the perpetrator of these outlandish theatrical displays than we were before. I was beginning to think that each and every day we tarried in darkness was a day that someone somewhere was bound to lose.

"How do we go about convincing our bosses that the probable causes of death might indeed be cancer in all of these alleged murder cases, Danny?" I wondered out loud. "It doesn't bring us even one step closer to uncovering the identity of these victims or our serial taxidermist." I shook my head in dismay, lamenting the lack of a singular causal element. "I sure wish we could do more to tie these disparate cancer cases together. Do you have any ideas about that?"

"Well, there is one thing that you overlooked in your search for genetic mutations, chromosomal abnormalities, and oncogenes," said Dr. Daniel Grist, with more than a glimmer of professional pride. He slowly unwound the sealing string on a large manila envelope and slid the opened folder over to me.

"What's this?" I asked, leafing through a familiar set of fluorescent micrographs, examining the remarkable consistency of a bright signal in all sixteen plates. "Is this a positive control you put in? If it is, it's a good one."

"I wish it was," said Danny.

"What is it then?" I demanded, turning over each of the photos one-by-one to see what information might be encrypted on the reverse side.

Daniel grist looked extremely worried when he blurted, "There is one tumor-associated DNA marker that is common to all sixteen of these cancer victims."

"What tumor marker would that be, Danny?" I said, taken aback. "And how did I miss it?"

"I found …" Danny started, gulping back the glaring fear that spread across his face, the expression of a man who's just stepped on a landmine. Then he continued, more resolutely, "I found evidence of SV40 sequences in each and every one of the tumors we excised in our exploratory autopsies."

My mind swooned as I heard the words, and my face must have reddened—not so much from the embarrassment of having missed the screening and detection of a highly oncogenic virus, but from the ramifications of Danny's findings, which forced us into the crux of a colossal scientific controversy—a controversy that went to the very heart of modern medicine.

"How could I have missed this?" I asked with an equal measure of curiosity and dismay. I was so busy looking for intrinsic chromosomal features, classic mutations, and oncogenes that it didn't even occur to me to test for an infectious agent. In my experience, SV40 is never screened for in the course of genetic profiling. We routinely probe for all the classic cancer markers known to man, but we never screen for a monkey DNA virus in our human tissue samples. "I don't get it, Danny. How did I miss something as obvious as this?"

"Well, first of all, you're not a pathologist, Dr. Westerly," said Danny with an irrepressible smile that came and went in an instant. "It's my business to diagnose the causes of disease, as well as the fatal consequences. Second of all, the general public is not supposed to know!"

"Really?" I said with alarm. "So you think that the SV40 might be a contributing cause in each and every one of these categorically different cancers?"

Danny looked around him, as though he was afraid to speak out loud. He swallowed hard, his face darkened, and a grim specter of fear intensified in his expression. "I'm almost afraid to say it," he whispered sheepishly, "but I'm fairly certain that the answer to that question is yes."

We sat in silence, contemplating the interpretations ... contemplating the repercussions ... contemplating the angst and the consternation that would surely result from Danny's findings.

We vowed not to say anything to anyone until I could verify the SV40 results with high-stringency RT-PCR in my own lab, and until I could do some additional research of the available medical literature.

What I would find was not what I had expected, for as cynical as I had become from my own harsh and horrid experiences within the academic community, the shroud of darkness and deception I would uncover in my research and interviews over the next few days would spread out over the medical establishment like a thick velvet pall spreading over a coffin.

It didn't take long to corroborate Danny's results, for I worked through the night and early-morning hours to complete the battery of assays. Then I spent the better part of the afternoon in the UCLA medical library gathering detailed information and review articles on SV40: what it represented, where it came from, how in the world so many human beings became exposed to this cancer-causing monkey virus. I spent hours on the Internet tracking down leads, following the key opinion leaders and their peer-reviewed publications, and discerning the official postures and conclusions of the federal regulatory authorities—which changed quite dramatically and inexplicably over the years. What I found was chilling. What I found revealed to me, in no uncertain terms, why Danny looked so scared.

It was time for us to bring Detective Dash Brogan into the mix. It was time for Danny and me to spill the beans.

• • •

Dash Brogan paced the floor anxiously as I outlined our findings and recounted the broad spectrum of cancers and the wide variety of tumor markers we found. I told him that we were able to confirm that each of the plasticized victims was indeed suffering from metastatic cancer, which might certainly have been the actual cause of the deaths. In each case, we were able to determine the histological type of the cancer involved, both from the immunohistochemistry and the molecular biology. In addition to bone and soft tissue sarcomas, there was breast cancer and brain cancer and lung cancer represented in the collection.

Brogan nodded in appreciation when I credited Danny for

discovering a figurative smoking gun that was common to each and every one of our petrified victims.

"Now that's interesting, boys," said Brogan as he continued pacing the floor. "I like smoking guns. The only problem is that I have no experience in determining the actual trajectory of this monkey virus of yours. The gun might be smoking, as you boys say, but I still don't understand a damn thing about the motivation behind the murders! Is it Mother Nature we're looking at here? Or is it human nature at work? Tell me more about this monkey virus."

I explained what I had found in my literature searches, and Danny filled in the blanks. It turned out that SV40 was inadvertently introduced into the human population on a grand scale in the 1950s. It first appeared as a contaminant in the polio vaccines, which were produced using the kidneys of Rhesus monkeys. Unfortunately, SV40 was only one of more than forty simian viruses that were found to be contaminating the early polio vaccines that were distributed worldwide, but simian virus no. 40 turned out to be the worst of the bunch. Simian virus no. 40, or SV40, was determined by scientific investigations to cause cancers early on in the federal vaccination program. However, it was much, much later that the medical community began to listen to the scientific community and to even acknowledge, let alone accept, the idea that such a renowned polio vaccine could ever do more harm than good. By the time the truth was revealed, it was too late: millions of human beings were summarily exposed to and were now carrying a live virus that was known to be a potent carcinogen—that is, a bona fide cancer-causing agent.

"How the hell did this happen, Danny?" demanded Brogan. "And how did you know to look for this lethal SV40 bullet in our collection of Barbie and Ken dolls?"

"I knew to look for SV40 because I was trained in a research laboratory of a distinguished professor of microbiology, who happened to study the virus. From my postdoctoral work with Dr. Marcel Mandel, I knew to look for SV40 in our petrified corpses because it is the most underappreciated villain in the entire field of cancer research."

"By underappreciated villain, you mean cover-up don't you?" boomed Brogan.

"I would be afraid to use that term, Detective," Danny said matter-of-factly, attempting to avoid Brogan's gaze. "I would be very afraid," he said more softly, as if to emphasize his point.

"Afraid of what, Danny boy?" prompted Brogan, anticipating the answer. "Whatever happened to this distinguished microbiology professor of yours?"

"After years of ad hominem attacks against his medical research, including the loss of tenure, termination of his federal funding, and aggressive suppression of his scientific papers, he went into hiding. Nowadays, Professor Mandel consults independently for the Biotech Industry up in San Francisco, changing his address often and operating under an assumed name."

"Well then, I want you boys to get on the next plane to Frisco to do some actual detective work for me."

"Exactly what do you mean by detective work, Dash?" I asked in earnest.

"I want you to find out something from this professor that we don't already know!" barked Brogan. Then he grabbed his hat and headed for the door. As he was leaving, he turned back to us and said, "Meanwhile, we should all put on our thinking caps and try and figure out why the hell some overambitious exhibitionist is trying to showcase the sad story in this day and age!"

• • •

The Price of Veracity—I made out the sailboat's name, suppressing a chuckle as Danny and I neared the two-masted schooner moored discretely at a floating dock at Oyster Point Marina. The royal-blue paint, though not old, blended into the gray mist that hung over the docks as if it was a part of the sea. Professor Marcel Mandel, a.k.a. Dr. Jonathon Doe, appeared on the weather-pocked, cream-colored dock of his new home and offered his raised hand in greeting. Danny and I had flown from LAX to San Francisco that morning, where we took a cab north to the marina on the western shoreline of San Francisco Bay. The sixty-foot schooner barely shifted in its moorings when we stepped on board.

"Ahoy there, Daniel," shouted the gray-haired professor of microbiology. "Long time, no see," he said, shaking Danny's hand with vigor. The professor, who must have been in his late sixties, wore a full beard, a Patagonia jacket, faded blue jeans, and Sperry topsiders, which gave him a distinctly nautical appearance. He looked me over and offered his hand, which was thickly calloused from working the ropes.

"I'm Cornell Westerly from the LAPD forensic team, Dr. Mandel," I said, by way of introduction. When attempting to gain undisclosed information from an academic source, it is always best to be forthright in your affiliations. Realizing that it's also best to be clear about your mission and intentions, I added, "Danny and I have come to ask for your help in solving a very troublesome and potentially explosive case of serial exhibitionism in the City of Los Angeles."

"I did hear something about some plastic corpses turning up in unexpected places," said the wizened, gray-haired professor, shaking his head. "Danny already gave me a head's up as to the SV40 connection." The aging professor opened up the cabin door, and then he looked around the docks suspiciously before he headed inside the cabin, inviting us to join him. "Come on in, boys. I've got some gourmet sandwiches and soft drinks set out for us in the galley, where we can keep the content of our conversation out of earshot of the electronic seagulls."

Danny thanked the professor with a nod, and we both stepped inside behind him.

Once inside the sailboat's cabin, Professor Mandel began to speak freely. "If you want to know the real story about the SV40 debacle, you've come to the right place. But I have to tell you that you're asking me to open up a can of worms, young man ... a very real and very nasty can of worms. I also have to tell you that everything I say to you must be kept confidential, strictly off the record. I truly want to assist you with your investigation, but I've spent too much time hiding from the hangman to want to go down that road again anytime soon."

"Fair enough, Professor," I assured him. "We simply want to get at the truth of the matter and its possible relation to some rather disturbing exhibitions involving postmortem theatrics."

The seaside luncheon was filled with tasty morsels awash with spine-tingling intrigue. We munched on ham-and-cheese and chicken-salad sandwiches catered from the Oyster Point Yacht Club while Professor Mandel laid out before us one of the biggest blunders in medical history.

Professor Mandel explained to us the social context of the cover-up—that is, the cover-up of the polio vaccine contamination by live SV40 virus particles and its possible health effects, linking both the oral and the injectable polio vaccines to rampant SV40 infections and cancer. While the extreme dangers to the unwitting public were reported early on by members of the scientific community, the federal regulators turned a blind eye to any and all warning signs. Hell-bent on keeping the dangers and the liabilities of the vaccination program under wraps, federal health officials were determined not to alarm, or even inform, the general public about the health dangers resulting from SV40 contamination. Since the public health program was mandated and enforced by the federal government, in concert with no less than five pharmaceutical companies, it was considered to be more important to prevent alarm and/or litigation than it was to prevent iatrogenic (doctor-caused) disease. Dr. Mandel explained to us the concerted falsification of research due to legal and financial conflicts of interest. Apparently, the federal government used superficial surveys and bogus epidemiology studies to refute the early cancer warnings, citing no differences in the cancer incidence of US citizens having received noncontaminated vaccine versus contaminated vaccine lots—only to find that nearly all of the polio vaccine lots were, in fact, contaminated with live SV40 virus, thus undermining the entire basis of the contrived epidemiologic comparisons. For many types of tumors, including brain cancers, bone cancers, lung cancers, leukemias, and lymphomas, the incidences increased dramatically over the twenty-year period spanning the 1950s and 1960s, as SV40 infections spread throughout the human population and more than one hundred million healthy individuals were exposed.

Of course, eradication of polio is a marvelous thing in and of itself. The error was not in the medical intentions. It was in the ensuing deification of the biotechnology and its proponents to a point that left little room for constructive criticism, most notably, constructive criticism of the vaccine production methods that used monkey kidneys—the body's sewage plant that filters blood into urine, making it one of the dirtiest of all organs, microbiologically speaking—for a cheap and easy expansion of the stocks of polio virus to produce the vaccines. While the live, attenuated polio vaccines were teeming with live SV40 virus, even the injectable vaccines, in which the polio virus was sufficiently inactivated by formalin treatment, the SV40 virus was still functionally alive and kicking. Once the extent of the SV40 contamination was exposed, the next stage of the cover-up extended to the dissemination of erroneous dogma: the belief that the SV40 virus in the tainted vaccines was harmless.

Even more damming was the concerted efforts of federal spokespersons to minimize and discredit the reported health effects of SV40 infections in humans. There was no vaccine recall, no changes in the manufacturing process that continued to use SV40-infected monkey kidneys—which could have prevented the contamination in the first place—and there were no changes in the official position that SV40 was anything other than a harmless wee beastie. Each and every scientist who dared to speak out, including Dr. Mandel, was either censured or punished for rocking the medical boat, so to speak, and yet each and every scientific study linking SV40 to cancer was ultimately validated by the preponderance of the clinical data that was coming in from around the world.

Today, there is no doubt that SV40 is a potent human carcinogen, as well as a potent co-carcinogen—that is, a tumor promoter that transforms normal cells and cooperates with other carcinogens, like asbestos, in the formation and development of cancers, such as mesothelioma.

Today there is no doubt that the policies used to justify the continued exposure of human beings to live SV40 virus were biased and severely flawed; no doubt that SV40 infections are found in association with a large number of human tumors; no doubt that the global infections of this cancer-causing virus, which were initiated by the contaminated polio vaccines, are still continuing to this day, perpetuated by both vertical (mother-to-child) and horizontal (person-to-person) transmission. It turns out that SV40 is far more dangerous than anyone had ever expected. Even more insidious is the tendency for SV40 to cause human cancers with a long latency, meaning that SV40-containing cancers tend to show up many years after the initial exposure to the oncogenic virus takes hold.

"How could something like this happen, Professor Mandel?" I asked excitedly. "How could it have gone on so long without anyone in authority taking this deadly monkey virus seriously?"

"If you want to know the real story that links bad drugs to bad science to bad medical practice," said the old professor, "you should look in the direction of the fame and the fortune. In other words, you should follow the money flow!" He leaned back in his seat and polished off a Diet Coke. "This unholy alliance between government officials and the pharmaceutical industry continues to be reinforced to this day by the sheer number of federal regulatory officials who take a cushy job in a grateful pharmaceutical company as soon as they have completed the minimal requirements for their government pensions."

"How many federal authorities are to blame for this fiasco?" I inquired, with a mouthful of chicken-salad sandwich.

"Let me see. The National Institutes of Health and its sister institutes, the Center for Disease Control and the National Cancer Institute, were all directly involved in proliferating misinformation, as was the American Medical Association, whose card-carrying pediatricians would otherwise have been more than a little concerned about *doing harm* to their patients—Hippocratically speaking. Even the FDA, it seems, was far more interested in maintaining public confidence in US licensed vaccines than it was in protecting the health and welfare of US citizens. That is, of course, not to mention the total failure of the free press, which conspicuously and negligently ignored the hot topic. This is *not* to say that the polio vaccine was a bad idea in the first place—it was effective in eliminating the threat of polio in much of the world. It is simply to say that the persistent exposure of unwitting patients to SV40 infection for years and years and years is now as lamentable as it was then preventable. If the federal regulators of the pharmaceutical industry had simply heeded the scientific studies and early warnings, the polio vaccine could have easily been produced more cleanly, without extraneous viral contamination."

Professor Mandel paced the floorboards of the galley as he continued to explain. "The lobbyists from the cartels of pharmaceutical manufacturers have been unduly influencing public policy from the days of Franklin Delano Roosevelt to the present administration—influencing public policy, that is, for the benefit of the pharmaceutical industry. When you realize the full extent of the cover-up, you will realize how hard it would be to remedy. After years of muddying the waters to the extent that no definitive conclusions could ever be made, the gaggles of guilty parties in official government robes were hard pressed to accept the ultimate scientific realities: that hundreds of millions of healthy individuals were unnecessarily exposed to live SV40 virus; that SV40 kills people by a well-known mechanism of action; and that SV40 is still killing people to this day."

Danny popped the tab on a Diet Coke as he waxed philosophical. "If I understand you correctly, Professor, you're saying if the regulatory authorities admitted to being blind to the dangers, they would be innocent, but since they claimed that they could see no evil, their guilt remains."

"Yes, Danny, that's it exactly! But I do believe I have heard that analogy before," laughed the old professor. "Let me put it another way: in a land where profits are king, nearly everyone who is anyone is officially blinded."

At this point, I felt fairly well versed in the controversy. I knew that hundreds of millions of people around the world have been exposed to a damn dangerous vaccine cocktail, manufactured by cheap and dirty methods using SV40-infected monkeys, and that the regulators allowed the distribution of the SV40-contaminated vaccines to continue for decades until the causal links to cancer eventually became overwhelming. I knew now that this was a health disaster of enormous proportion, and that the cause-and-effect relationships pointed to an iatrogenic plague that was almost too monstrous to contemplate, let alone admit. Still, I remembered what Detective Dash Brogan had ordered us to attain from the savvy and conscientious professor of microbiology, and I endeavored to push our conversation in that direction.

"Thank you for your time and the generosity of your tutorial, Professor Mandel. I agree that there has been a catastrophic failure of regulatory oversight across the board. But everything you have told Danny and me so far is readily available in the scientific literature, such that anyone with access to either a medical library or a laptop computer could eventually have come to the same conclusions. I have been asked by my mentor at the LAPD to ask you for something that we don't already know." I looked around through the cabin windows to be sure that no one else was nearby. "What we desperately need," I said imploringly, "is a break in this case of serial exhibitionism involving SV40-ridden corpses. And we need something other than ancient history to solve this case!" I exclaimed. "We need something that is happening *today*—something that might be upsetting enough to encourage the outrageous theatrics of a demented serial taxidermist who is currently running amuck in the City of Los Angeles!"

Professor Marcel Mandel nodded in silent sympathy and appeared to be thinking. Then he stood up and looked out the windows and portholes of the sailboat's cabin for quite a while. He turned on a small black-and-white television screen, which must have been connected to a video camera up on the deck, for it slowly scanned the surrounding area of the docks, providing a rotating view of the walkways. Satisfied that no one suspicious or officious was listening, the professor reached into a cabinet and pulled out a bottle of Jamaican rum and three glasses. Placing the three crystal glasses on the table, he said, "If you're asking me to move from ancient history to current events to help you in your ongoing criminal investigation, I'm going to need something stronger than Diet Coke to wet my whistle."

"Can you think of anything else that is not commonly known, Professor Mandel?" I asked, gingerly slurping a healthy bolus of my rum and Coke. "Something that's even more disturbing? Something that might be still happening today ... something that might, if truth be known, be upsetting enough to encourage such outlandish serial theatrics?"

The distinguished professor emptied his glass and refilled it with straight Jamaican rum. Out of courtesy and decorum, I promptly emptied my glass as well, and the professor promptly refilled it. I could feel a wave of alcohol warmth extending from my spine to my limbs.

"There is one thing that's exceedingly upsetting, which is not widely known, though I'm surprised that you didn't think of it, Danny," chided his old mentor. "As I recall, when you were in my lab, you used the SV40 large-T antigen to immortalize quite a few human cell lines."

"That's right, Professor," said Danny, "I did work with the SV40 large-T antigen, and I have my suspicions about what you're thinking, but I much prefer to hear it from you."

"Very well. If I had to speculate as to the most upsetting thing about SV40 imaginable ... something that is current and clearly discernable, and yet beyond the scope of most academic scholarship, it would have to be the molecular mechanisms of action of SV40 and its cause-and-effect relationships to the most aggressive and intractable cancers ..."

"Yes, yes, Professor," I said, perched on the edge of my seat. "Please explain."

"The precise mechanism of action—that is, the biochemical manner by which SV40 not only immortalizes but transforms human cells—involves the production of a series of proteins that disable the natural controls of cell lifespan, genetic fidelity, and cell proliferation. Once these tumor-suppressor proteins, including p53 and p107-Rb, are knocked out by SV40 in infected cells, the transformed cells are a thousand times more likely to progress to tumor genesis and to malignancy." The distinguished professor took another gulp of straight rum before he continued. "Now, here comes the punch line," he said dryly. "Given the fact that both radiation and chemotherapy rely on tumor-suppressor proteins like p53 and Rb to initiate apoptosis, or programmed cell death, the inactivation of these tumor suppressor proteins by SV40 makes the cancer cells impervious to conventional cancer treatments."

"Are you saying, what I think you're saying, Professor?" I uttered with my head in my hands. I glanced over at Danny, who was sipping on his drink, visibly trembling with fear.

"What I am saying is that the presence of SV40, which inactivates p53, et cetera, allows the cancer cells to survive conventional cancer therapies. Indeed, these SV40-transformed cells, in turn, tend to become even more malignant due to the increased incidence of ungoverned genetic mutations caused by the DNA-damaging treatments. In the presence of SV40, the mutations, which would normally be recognized by the cellular machinery and would normally result in apoptosis and cell death, are allowed to persist, thus making the cancers more aggressive in many cases, in addition to making them unresponsive to standard cytotoxic therapies."

"So you're telling us that the presence of SV40 in a tumor, which is a considerable incidence in many types of human cancers, not only participates in the development of the cancer, its presence dramatically impacts the efficacy, or rather the ineffectuality, of the most common forms of cancer therapy?"

"It's sad but true, laddie. And what's even worse—and possibly upsetting to someone—is the current lack of any kind of screening or profiling of human cancers for SV40 in an effort to construct more rational therapies. At present, there are no prospective tests or clinical trials in which SV40 status is used in clinical decision making."

"It's like they don't even want to know," affirmed Daniel Grist.

"Well, that's outrageous!" I shouted, nearly spilling my glass. "Who is responsible for this unconscionable state of affairs? Isn't there someone, anyone, who can be held accountable?"

The distinguished professor reached across the dining table and placed his hand on my shoulder as he said softly, in a hushed tone, "Trying to hold someone accountable for wrongdoing in the modern medical community is like clutching a handful of smoke."

13 My Lady in the Lake

When I got back to LA, Dash Brogan was waiting for me in his vintage Pontiac Catalina, parked just outside my apartment. I climbed inside the Catalina 2+2 where Brogan filled me in. He told me that his men had been busy comparing Clive's photos of the three bathing beauties—the ones that still had faces—with the Federal Database of Missing Persons and the FBI Database of Faces and Biometric Data compiled from public surveillance cameras. When nothing turned up in these files, which were scanned with sophisticated facial-recognition programs, Dash and his men endeavored to scan the National Databases of the Newly Deceased, including the Unidentified Persons Database, containing information provided by coroners and medical examiners. They also scanned the Unclaimed Persons Database, which contains information about diseased persons who have been identified by name, but for whom no next of kin or family member has been identified or located to claim the body for burial or other disposition. There were no hits, thus no useful leads to be found in the official files.

I told Dash that we had indeed found something interesting from our conversation with Professor Mandel, a.k.a. Dr. John Doe— something that we didn't already know.

Brogan nodded understandingly and said, "Lets take a walk."

We crossed over Ocean Avenue to Palisades Park, where we found an empty bench overlooking the Santa Monica Pier, with its Victorian carousel, its solar-powered Ferris wheel, and its arcade pavilions, framed by the vanishing edge of the oceanic horizon. The afternoon sky was clear and bright with a slight onshore breeze.

Dash Brogan looked out upon the amusement park, without any amusement—he had his game face on.

"So what did you and Danny find out that we didn't already know?" he asked.

I filled Dash in on what the distinguished professor had confirmed and revealed. I summed up our initial investigative scholarship concerning the contaminated polio vaccines and the failure of the US regulatory authorities to respond appropriately to the inherent dangers to the human population. I told him that the distinguished professor essentially confirmed that the official cover-up was broad and relentless, implicating nearly everyone in the upper echelons of both federal regulatory agencies and major pharmaceutical concerns.

Brogan shook his head in disgust as he pulled out a package of cigarettes from his coat pocket and planted an unfiltered in his mouth. The following plume of aromatic tobacco smoke rose and disappeared in the loft of the gentle sea breeze. A phalanx of seagulls dressed in black and white winged silently up from the sandy beaches and disappeared into the foreground. The sun itself hung silently in the sky, as if waiting for something specific to herald its inexorable downfall, something tragic, something unearthly to signal its downward descent.

Dash Brogan looked over at me inquisitively. "Spit it out, Doc," was all he said.

That was when I told Brogan about a true crime against humanity: a crime that was not something out of the distant past, a crime that affected millions of innocent people, a crime that persists to this very day. "The failure to screen for SV40 sequences in contemporary cancer patients is not simply a matter of oversight, it seems, but a policy that is steeped in secrecy and official misinformation."

"Since when is *not* doing something a crime against humanity?" exclaimed Brogan. "It seems like a crime of gross administrative negligence as opposed to malicious intent."

"I'm afraid it goes much further than that, Dash," I continued. "You see, the presence of SV40 renders the tumors refractory to standard treatments—that is, radiation and chemotherapy. The very presence of this virus essentially inactivates the tumor-killing pathways, making the cancers more aggressive and rendering the conventional cytotoxic treatments completely ineffective. In this day and age, the failure to determine a patient's SV40 status prior to administrating standard cancer therapy goes well beyond simple negligence, in my opinion. It might even be considered medical malpractice, if the whole truth be known."

"You're telling me that modern-day oncologists treat a large number of cancer patients with radiation and chemotherapy, knowing full well that the darn apothecary is ineffectual?"

"That appears to be the case, Detective."

"That's like giving a person a death sentence before they've had a proper trial." Brogan crushed out his cigarette and spat a glob of his viscous discontent into the sandy ground. "This *is* new! This is important—good work, Cornell. This hidden travesty of medical ineptitude might actually be the provocative missing link—something that's worth crying out loud about!"

"So you really think this might be a drama that's worth the time and effort to showcase theatrically?" I inquired. "For the world to see the aftermath up close and personal?"

"Could be, son," said Brogan, shaking his head in disgust. "It sure makes *me* mad as hell." Brogan looked out along the vanishing edge of the Pacific Ocean as he ground his right fist into the palm of his left hand. "What's this modern world coming to, Cornell? In my day, it was much easier to tell the good guys from the bad guys. In my day, the *touch of evil* and the *imp of the perverse* were clear and easy to read. These days, you can't trust anyone … not the butchers … not the bankers … not the feds … not even the doctors, whose hands are far from clean."

"I couldn't agree with you more, Dash," and I meant it. "In fact, there are numerous scientific surveys in which the vast majority of practicing physicians admit that they would refuse chemotherapy for themselves—when they were asked to imagine that they had cancer—based on their clinical understanding of the ineffectiveness of chemotherapy and its unacceptably high degree of toxicity. The finding that SV40 infections are capable of rendering standard chemotherapy even less effective than usual certainly compounds the offence, as far as I'm concerned."

"It's a damned dirty business, if you ask me," said Brogan defiantly. "If I had my way, I would personally spill the beans and ask all the cancer patients to preserve their last urine samples, so they could piss on the graves of each and every cancer doctor that betrayed their trust!"

Taken aback, I said, "You don't really mean that, do you, Dash? What if the public took you seriously? What if thousands and thousands of cancer patients were outraged enough to do exactly what you say? What if it spiraled out of control and everyone cast a critical eye upon the practice of medicine and actually pissed on the graves of all the responsible parties?"

"And you think that would be a bad thing?" remarked Brogan.

"I guess not," I acquiesced in my confusion. Not wanting to extend the discussion of medical ethics beyond the immediate cases at hand, I focused on the amusement park before us, taking the colors in before expressing my newly gathered thoughts. "Everybody already knows that the whole multi-billion-dollar business of chemotherapy began with experiments with deadly chemical warfare and mustard gas. Everybody already knows that the term *effective*—which should logically mean cure—has been displaced with the guise of temporary tumor shrinkage. Everybody already knows that standard chemotherapies tragically suppress the patient's own immune system, which might otherwise assist in the surveillance and eradication of tumors. What they don't already know is that the contents of the polio vaccines they gave their children have unleashed a contagious plague of SV40 upon the land that dooms these dark-age treatments to even greater failure. It's hard for me to imagine what would happen if the public learns the truth about the origins and the present-day implications of this cancer-causing virus."

"Exactly," said Brogan as he impatiently ground his fist into his palm. "I'm beginning to get a clearer picture of what our theatrical perpetrator is attempting to showcase here in this blighted City of

Angels. The only question in my mind is what he or she is going to show us next ... and what the hell we are going to do to finally solve this case."

I squinted into the glare of the afternoon sun and realized that I had nary a clue.

Walking back to his car, Dash Brogan told me that we should hold off on reporting our findings to the coroner, who was bound to be skeptical, and the mayor, who was already dealing with a number of mass demonstrations, complete with car burnings, that were breaking out across the Los Angeles Basin. It seemed that nearly everyone in the Greater Los Angeles Area was mad at someone, but no one knew exactly whom it was they were actually mad at—so, the natural thing to do was to riot.

Dash Brogan advised me to steer clear of the massive gridlock that was forming around the MacArthur Park and Hancock Park areas, where spontaneous rallies of outraged citizens were currently assembling. He must have realized that I would be attempting to hook up with Lauriana ASAP after checking in with Dr. Liling Chen at the crime lab. Brogan knew that the hordes of protestors at both MacArthur Park and the La Brea Tar Pits would be directly in my path if I headed west along Wilshire Boulevard, which runs from Downtown Los Angeles through Beverly Hills and Westwood Village on its way to the beach and the deep blue sea. Taking the savvy detective's advice, I managed to skirt MacArthur Park and the La Brea Tar Pits entirely—the main staging areas for the burgeoning mass hysteria—by driving on the freeways from the 101-South to the 10-West to the 405-North—a round-about route, but an expedient way to approach Lauriana's apartment on Wilshire without getting caught up in the demonstrations.

• • •

I parked in the visitor's parking lot of the Wilshire Margot and nodded confidently to the man at the front desk, indicating to his satisfaction that I knew the person in the apartment where I was headed. I didn't announce myself, for I wanted to surprise Lauriana and to take her out for a romantic dinner. Moreover, I was anxious to share our latest findings and suspicions with the lovely poet laureate and to gain her insightful poetic impressions on this unsolved case.

Brimming with heartfelt anticipation, I took the elevator up to Lauriana's apartment on the fifth floor, and I was about to press the buzzer when I noticed that her apartment door was cracked partially open. I slowly pushed the door open further and entered into the foyer of the living room, where I was confronted by a shocking scene of sartorial disarray. Her black evening gown was rumpled in a heap on the floor, along with her high-heel shoes and her black brassiere. There were several more items of discarded clothing arrayed in a haphazard line of sorts that led from the living room to the hallway of the master bedroom.

I froze in my tracks when I noticed that there was not only women's clothing heaped on the floor: there was a pair of man's shoes and pants by the sofa and a dress shirt and tie draped across the back of an elegant upholstered chair. Soft strains of classical music from the Romantic era were playing espressivo on the stereo, which seemed strangely incongruent with the chaotic scene of disarray. If I had to guess, I would guess it was one of Beethoven's ten violin sonatas, but I didn't want to guess at anything. I wanted to be certain, I wanted to investigate the actual facts of the matter, I wanted to detect the exact nature of the intrusion that started my heart pounding so wildly, my blood surging so alarmingly in my chest, up my neck, to the throbbing center of my brain.

I reached down into the rear pocket of the men's trousers, and I found a black-leather wallet filled with large bills and business cards, which did nothing but intensify my panicked curiosity. The name "Barrett Berghoffer" on the driver's license was accompanied by the appellation "Vice President of International Sales, Imperious Pharmaceutical Consortium, Basel, Switzerland" on the nested set of business cards. I literally froze in my tracks again when I heard the dreaded sounds of a woman's moans emerging from the open door of Lauriana's bedroom. Inching closer, I could make out another tortuous sound: the sound of a man striving and grunting in the climactic throes of ecstasy. It was an ecstasy that should have been mine to strive for, mine to enjoy, mine to revel in and remember forever with fondness and satisfaction.

I dropped the wallet, covered my ears with my hands, and hurried out of the apartment with the violent, convulsive movements of a wounded animal. By the time I made it back to the silent safety of my car, my heart was raging with the angry pulsations of unrestrained protest, and my mind was seething with the frightening forces of righteous indignation. It was all I could do to breathe.

• • •

Nobody ever gets over something like this completely, not when one is forced, against their will, to walk blindfolded off the plank of true love into a veritable sea of disillusionment and despair. I could feel the flood of a cold, cruel immersion into darkness—the darkness of a realization that I was loathe to accept—the darkness that begins as a lump in the throat, a sense of wrong, a homesickness, a lovesickness. The mentality of despair is not a turning loose of negative emotion, but an escape from emotion, an escape from that elusive dream of beauty that makes life worth living. It is an empty place where all human happiness is but an echo, and all hope of salvation is about as useful as asking a shadow to dance.

As natural as it was for me to wallow in the dregs of my despair, I was not allowed to extend this period of mourning beyond the end of the week. By not allowed, I mean I got an urgent call from Detective Dash Brogan that slapped me back to my senses. He told me to meet him by the banks of the Silver Lake Reservoir, where the sheriff's men were busy dragging the lake. Apparently, someone had reported seeing two men throwing a body into the water. By the time I made the drive from Santa Monica through East Hollywood to Silver Lake, the sheriff's men had already fished a woman's body out of the lake.

Silver Lake Reservoir is a concrete-lined expanse of water that is several times longer than it is wide, stretching out across a depression between two sloping hillsides populated by an eclectic assortment of Bohemian wood-sided bungalows and historic modernist gems. The sky was cold and overcast without sun, the way it is on winter days when a low-pressure system moves in from the coast. The surface of the lake was a dull gray continuum, interrupted by an occasional line of whitecaps that arose haphazardly as if in protest to the jagged gusts of a biting, sharp wind. I parked at the designated dog park and walked over to the grassy shore by the recreation center where Dash was standing with his arms akimbo. Clive was already taking photographs of the crime scene. I stepped over the plastic yellow tape that demarcated the grassy area. I nodded silently to Dash and to Clive as I donned a pair of medical gloves and bent down to look over the naked body of the diseased, which was still entangled in the netting.

Peering into the lifeless half-closed eyes of the woman in the net, I immediately grew sick and dizzy. My first impulse was to shrink away from the danger of such a grim reality, but, unaccountably, I remained steadfast, resolved to faithfully examine the sodden features of the dead body. The sickness and the dizziness increased alarmingly into a fearful sensation—a sensation that chilled me to the very core of my being with the terrible fierceness of the worst imaginable horror. The dead woman's body caught up in the net was unmistakably the lifeless corpus of Lauriana Noire, my beautiful Poet Laureate of the Inner Dark.

I looked up and over to Dash Brogan, who must have surmised the dire context of my burning anguish, for he immediately took off his hat and walked up to the place where I was kneeling, trembling in the entanglement of netting. He bent down and lifted me up firmly by my left arm. "Go home, Cornell," he said. "You can't be involved in this case."

14 Looking Deeply into Indifference

own, down, down, into the darkness of the grave they go, the beautiful, the tender, the wise, the lovely, the kind … I can't for the life of me remember what the sainted poet said next in her famous dirge without music, but I think she said something about lovers and thinkers who have gone to feed the roses, even though the lights in their eyes were supposed to be more precious than all the roses in the world. All I could remember on that dreary, despondent morning—the morning we laid Lauriana to rest in the grassy fields of Forest Lawn—was the sainted poet's final refrain: *I know, but I do not approve … and I am not resigned.*

Standing there in the Forest Lawn Memorial Park outside the town of Glendale, I felt like I was depressingly alone in the gathering congregation of mourners: alone with my thoughts and mixed emotions, alone with my cherished memories of her, alone with a staining tincture of regret that dripped and seeped and spread throughout the barren hollows of my mind. I didn't pay any attention to the reverential words that were spoken over her grave or the personal testimonies of Lauriana's many admirers. I hardly noticed the funeral procession, the heaps of floral wreathes and garlands at the graveside, the rows of sunken headstones in the nearby fields, the pastoral sylvan surroundings of the memorial park. I was lost and alone in a world of my own making, struggling amid the clamorous onslaughts of my seething heartache, straining against the punishing manacles of Lauriana's willful betrayal of my love while striving to comprehend the dreadful finality of her death.

A gust of cold wind swept across the rolling green hills of Forest

Lawn Cemetery and tarried nervously around the gaping hollow of the open grave, agitating the towering evergreen trees that sighed and swayed in unison, sending an alarming chill through my body—a chill that began at the top of my neck and descended rapidly down my spine into the very marrow of my bones. Curiously, I felt like I was being watched. I was standing at a comfortable distance from the now-silent gathering of mourners, shivering with an unwholesome intermixture of fear, alienation, and remorse. I looked over the somber, downturned faces of the congregation for the source of my immediate anxiety. It was then that I first saw her: a delicate yet statuesque goddess of a woman who was standing slightly apart from the others; she was staring directly at me, staring intently into the innermost depth of my being.

She was dressed entirely in black: black-leather gloves; a small, black purse that hung gracefully from her left wrist; a black woven scarf draped over a black silk blouse that draped low at the neckline; a short, black half jacket with velveteen lapels and a form-fitting cut that was perfectly tailored to hug the alluring feminine contours of her thin waist and her womanly hips. She was wearing a tight, black skirt that was slit high on one side, extending just below her waistcoat to a hem below the knee. The slit skirt revealed a glimpse of the exquisite shapeliness of her legs, which were wrapped in black silk stockings that originated from a place I could only imagine and descended to the point where the stockings disappeared into the hollow recesses of her black high-heeled shoes. I raised my gaze to the top of her head—which was only partly covered by the adornment of a stylish black hat crowned with a small tuft of black feathers—and then down to the level of her eyes, which were still staring at me intently.

She was exceedingly blonde—the kind of ice-cold platinum blonde that many men would willingly die for. She had the mesmerizing appearance of a Hollywood star. In fact, her mesmerizing appearance reminded me of Jean Harlow, the glamorous Hollywood star from times gone by. Although I couldn't place this mysterious woman in black definitively in the rarified au courant registry of the contemporary Hollywood pantheon, I couldn't dismiss the uncanny impression that I had seen her face somewhere before.

Suddenly, Detective Dash Brogan appeared out of nowhere like an animated apparition standing on top of the cloth-covered mound of burial dirt. Without saying a word, the grim-faced detective gingerly surmounted the dirt pile and stepped right up to the verge of the grave.

He pulled a small paper scroll from the inside pocket of his coat jacket, carefully unfurled the parchment, and paused for a moment with his head bowed down and his hat in his hand before he glanced up decidedly and addressed the startled congregation. "On this, the most sorrowful of days, I would like to read from a work in progress—something that Lauriana was working on when she died. Those who knew her well know that Lauriana was passionate in her abiding love of poetry, her high-spirited lust for life, and her relentless quest for truth. Those who knew her well know that the demands of such poetic truth are severe. Whatever else Lauriana was working on, whatever she was investigating the day she was murdered by cowardly hands ... these, I believe, are the last words she left us." A hushed wave of confusion infused with an air of anticipation spread over the graveyard as Dash Brogan cleared his throat and began to read aloud the following poem in a rough, nicotine-soaked voice:

"The Corruption in the Vial"—by Lauriana Noire

There is enough treachery, collusion, deception, and contempt in the average pharmaceutical company to supply any given army on any given day ... and the best purveyors of poison are those who attempt to deny it ... and the worst at treating disease are those who stubbornly ignore it ... and the best at practicing deception are those who end up promoting it. Those who preach medical science, know no science ... those who train physicians leave connivance in their wake ... those who preach regulation officially bury their mistakes.

Beware the doctors. Beware their teachers. Beware the knowers who should have known better. Beware continuing medical education, for it rewards ignorance. Beware those who detest medical alternatives and are too proud of it. Beware those who are quick to prescribe, for they are actually point-of-sale. Beware those who are quick to condemn, for they only condemn themselves. Beware of those who seek political approval, for they are already bought and paid for. But most of all, beware the mediocre men of medicine and pharmacy; beware the mediocre women. Beware their counsel, for their counsel seeks conformity. Beware their motives, for their motives perceive your physical illness as a profitable, renewable resource.

But there is genius in their methods, in their contempt for your humanity. There is enough genius in their contempt to kill you, enough to kill anybody!

Not wanting progress, not understanding progress, they will attempt to destroy all competition. Not being able to innovate themselves, they will denounce all challenging medical innovation. They will consider their outright failure as innovators only as a failure in their marketable share. Not being able to trust in science, they will proclaim all opposing data is flawed and incomplete. Not being able to effectively treat disease, they will bottle their animosity in tainted vials of detestable and ineffectual apothecary.

And then their contempt for you, the helpless patient, will be perfect: like a shining lozenge, like a sharpened syringe, like a vial of hemlock or arsenic or chemotherapy, like a bolus of plutonium infused without your informed consent. In the end, their contempt for your humanity, your vulnerability, your gullibility, shall remain their highest art.

I nearly keeled over when Dash Brogan finished reading this frightful condemnation, this final castigating pronouncement from the Poet Laureate of the Inner Dark. I was overcome by a new and disturbing perplexity of emotions. Indeed, this new realization was stunning—this acute awareness that Lauriana Noire, my erstwhile lover, might have been helplessly compelled by the very nature of her dark passions, her lusts, her quests that might otherwise be misconstrued as wanton promiscuity. The thought that Lauriana Noire was actively investigating something dark and dangerous and relevant to the case at hand left me bobbing in the wake of mortal confusion. If it weren't for the steadying hand of Detective Dash Brogan, who promptly appeared at my side, I would certainly have succumbed to the gravity of the situation as I stumbled in vain by her graveside.

Dash Brogan walked me to my car without saying a word. He rolled the parchment scroll tightly with both hands, and then he handed it to me. "Here ... keep it," he asserted. "I think you should know, Cornell, that poetry like this is often nearer to the truth than history." And then he turned and walked away.

● ● ●

It wasn't until a swarm of human arms and legs began floating up on the beaches that the coroner and the mayor began to take Dash Brogan, Danny, and me seriously.

The next month, the weather turned almost balmy with a blush and glimmer of the coming spring. Early flowering trees that lined the roadsides began to blossom with pastel shades of color. In the night, however, it was the cherry tops of the police cruisers, ambulances, and fire trucks that painted the spaces between earth and sky. The warmer weather brought more people out into the streets and more chaos throughout the metropolitan area. Bonfires, car fires, and building fires were set by enraged rioters from the posh districts of West Hollywood to Culver City and South Central Los Angeles. It seemed that the winter of nearly everyone's discontent was spontaneously bursting into flames—not from racial tensions or from economic inequities, but from the deleterious manifestations of a collective form of social exasperation that was fed up with deceitful governing authorities who deemed it either proper or practical to keep the general population completely in the dark. The more the official authorities stonewalled the forensic details of this high-profile case, the more outraged the populace became. Ironically, while the general public was actively protesting having been kept in the dark about the material facts of the serial murder investigations, little did they know that these staged scenes would ultimately reveal a much more extensive, damaging, and truly horrifying case of their being kept totally and reprehensibly in pitch blackness.

Eventually, the army national guard and a division of marines from Camp Pendleton were called in to support the LAPD in their efforts to control the frenzied mobs, the fires, and the looting. A dusk-to-dawn curfew was finally imposed city-wide to help abate the destructive civil disturbances, which tended to increase dramatically each evening under the covering shroud of night.

Detective Dash Brogan was fitfully immersed in his own ongoing war with the coroner, who—just as Dash had expected—refused to discuss publically or even consider the medical and scientific implications of our findings. Thus, the lack of an evil perpetrator displayed in the public pillory or even a communicable motive for the frightful human taxidermy did little to satisfy the fear of the outraged citizenry.

The floating limbs first appeared at El Matador Beach in Malibu. By midmorning, there were reports of truncated human appendages found bobbing and rolling en masse in the shoals of Venice Beach, Newport Beach, and Laguna Beach, with several clusters of amputated limbs reaching as far south as Dana Point.

Driving south down Ocean Avenue on my way to meet Dash Brogan at Venice Beach, I heard wild speculations on the radio ranging from a massive flotilla of great white sharks, to an unfathomable tsunami that might have mysteriously inundated the Channel Islands, to an invasion of extraterrestrial aliens that were targeting and mutilating surfers and fishermen. By the time I met up with

Dash Brogan on the palm-lined promenade that ran parallel to the beach, there were already scads of news reporters and TV network vans with their high-definition video camera equipment lined up along the shoreline. I pushed my way through the milling crowd to join the uniformed officers of the LAPD's Pacific Division, who were accompanied by several recognizable members of Detective Dash Brogan's independent investigative team.

"From the looks of it, men, these body snatchers are more deliberate than they are finicky," barked Brogan. "See what you can do to cordon off that perimeter—from that lifeguard stand over there to the breakwater," he said, gesturing to the attentive group of uniformed officers who immediately departed with a number of orange cones and several rolls of crime scene tape. "And don't touch a damn thing until we get a better handle on this situation," added Brogan.

Then Brogan turned with instructions for Clive and me. "Try and get some photos of the crime scene before the tide comes back in, Clive … and take Cornell with you to help figure out what's going on over there," he added, pointing to what looked from a distance like a school of large fish trapped in the shallows.

"Will do, boss," said Clive to Dash Brogan, who stood immobile, looking out to sea.

I looked over to Clive, and I shrugged with the arm that was holding my briefcase.

"Better bring that briefcase with you, son," said Clive. "You might want to get some tissue samples while the getting's good."

Clive took photographs of the curious objects that were trapped in the shallows. I immediately noticed that these objects were not fish but the legs and arms of human beings that were actually tethered together, one after the other, with what looked like a yellow fishing line. Upon Clive's instructions, I pulled the entire string of human appendages out of the shallow water and up onto a dry section of sand while Clive took pictures of the process. "They're all plastic, Clive!" I shouted over the sound of the ocean waves smashing on the breakwater.

As might have been expected, there were no fingerprints to be obtained, since the epidermis and musculature of each fingertip had been surgically dissected down to the bone. I labeled each detached limb with an identification number, as required, before I took a tissue sample, and I proceeded to catalogue the entire set of thirteen limbs within an hour. Standing back and surveying this ghoulish catch, I was struck by an eerie observation. "Something wrong here, Clive!" I shouted. "It doesn't look like there are any actual pairs of arms or legs that physically match up!"

"What?" Clive shouted back. And as he walked up to the sand-encrusted lineup of amputations to snap a series of close-up photographs, I explained that, based on size, shape, and skin color, along with the spread of the distal phalanges, otherwise known as fingers and toes, no obvious matches were to be found.

"I'd say that's a mighty strange baker's dozen, if you ask me," Clive commented contemplatively. He paused for a few more close-up shots. "What do you make of these purple patches on this one?" He pointed out a number of raised bluish-red lesions on the plasticized skin of one arm. "And this one?" he asked, motioning to the same marks on a second, otherwise disparate right arm. "Looks pretty similar to those purple patches I see on that hairy leg over there," he added, zooming in and snapping another close-up photograph.

I kneeled down in the sand to take a closer look at the wounded yet perfectly preserved skin that covered the two arms. "Clearly, these are erythematous violaceous cutaneous lesions, which must have been present for some time before death and embalming. I can't tell for sure what they are without working up a surgical biopsy," I said, opening my briefcase for additional specimen vials. "Maybe Daniel Grist can help us out with that."

"I like a man who knows what he knows for certain and what he don't," said Clive with a smile, "a man who isn't afraid to admit it when he doesn't have a clue." Clive bent down and grabbed a length of the bright yellow line that was hanging free from the last limb in the lineup. He examined it closely for a good long moment, and then, with the toe of his shoe, he lifted one of the arms and rolled it over in the sand. He examined the string that was underneath the tethered wrist, protected from the sun. Even from a distance, I could see that the segment of line on the tethered wrist appeared much less yellow and much less bright. Clive drew a folding knife from his trench coat pocket, opened it up with a flick of his wrist, and severed a short piece of the line.

Expecting Clive to give me that same blank admission that I had just given him, I inquired into the nature of the mysterious cordage. "What do you make of this magical golden thread?"

"Nothing magic about it, son," said Clive. "This here golden thread is a length of Berkley Trilene Transoptic Clear-to-Gold Fishing Line, the ultimate line-watcher's line. It's the first and so far only nylon monofilament fishing line that physically changes color so that the fishermen can see it clearly, but the fish don't." Clive handed me the severed sample of golden thread and continued with his astute explanation. "You see, this here fishing line is activated by UV light—much like luminol—but in this case, the color of the line changes from nearly invisible to bright gold in direct sun light." Clive must have surmised my amazement with such detailed esoteric knowledge, for he explained, "I guess you didn't know that my hobby is sport fishing … when I'm not out with Dash Brogan chasing down the bad guys." The crime scene darkened considerably when the brightness of the afternoon sun all but disappeared behind a dense bank of clouds. "Like, I said, nothing magic about it, son."

A man from the sheriff's department arrived with a body bag, and we placed all of the disembodied limbs into the one bag. After we zipped up the overstuffed body bag, I added the snippet of the protean thread to my grisly collection of tissue samples.

The sun was falling fast from its heavenly perch, behind the veil of a purple cloud that stretched across the western sky like a giant unhealed wound. I caught a whiff of that familiar tobacco smoke and turned around to confirm its source. There was Detective Dash Brogan standing silently in the sand, smoking, looking out over the restless waters and the wounded sky as if engrossed in a penetrating contemplation of recent events … looking out over the restless waters and the wounded sky as though he was looking deeply into the vague indifference of our modern times.

15 With a Finger to Your Lips

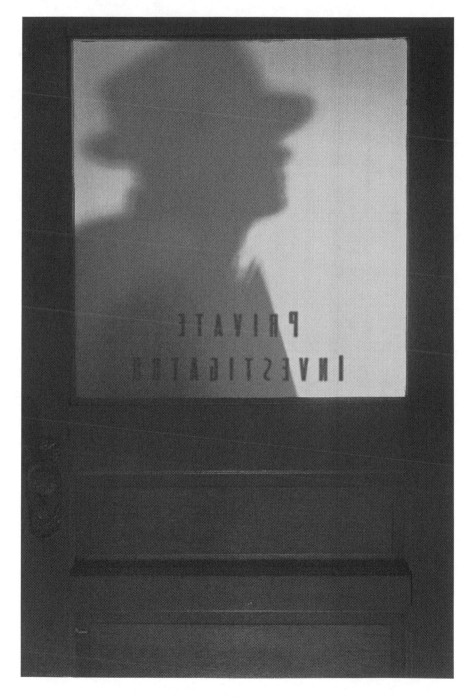

I t took the better part of the week for us to gather up all the arms and legs that were strung so neatly together on the pristine beaches of Southern California, given that each of the various coastal municipalities had their own police departments and their own commencement of spontaneous social disturbances to contend with. It took Danny and me another two days to catalogue this gruesome harvest by the sea and to match up all the individual appendages into pairs—a feat that was only possible when the entire collection of plasticized limbs was arrayed in succession, according to size, in the labyrinth of the Los Angeles County Morgue.

There were exactly one hundred human appendages—fifty pairs from twenty-five different individuals—which struck Danny and me as suspiciously informative, in a morbid sort of way. We determined that each individual set of amputated limbs was purposefully strung out at a different location, yet taken together, the pairing and quadrupling of the disparate body parts could be examined collectively in the methodical, albeit partial, reassembly of exactly twenty-five cut-up victims. The confusing precision of this random distribution, as well as the overall exactitude of the final tally, led Danny and me to the unavoidable conclusion that our theatrical perpetrator had something very different and very diabolical in mind this time. But the exact nature of whom or what he or she was attempting to *show us* this time remained a mystery.

I informed Dash Brogan of our preliminary findings over the phone, and he was none too pleased. He told me to hurry up with the genetic analysis of the tissue samples, "… to help us get a handle on this case, before the whole blasted metropolis is carried off to hell in a handbasket!"

Daniel Grist and I decided to split up our efforts. Dr. Liling Chen and I would run the entire set of tissue samples against the known chromosomal abnormalities, oncogenes, and viral sequences we had found previously while Danny and his assistants would concentrate on the raised cutaneous lesions that appeared on some, but not all, of the plastic appendages. It was clear to me that Dr. Daniel Grist, being a medical pathologist at heart, had some intriguing ideas he wanted to explore. Whatever he thought these lesions might be, he sure wasn't telling.

In the meantime, with Dr. Liling Chen working diligently on the molecular-genetic analyses, I met up with Dash Brogan at Carney's Express Limited Restaurant on Sunset Boulevard in West Hollywood. Much like the Pacific Dining Car, only cheaper, more casual, and more limited in its menu, Carney's was an iconic greasy-spoon diner set in an old-fashioned Union Pacific railway car painted bright yellow. Whether Dash Brogan, as a man on the move, naturally gravitated to the historic nostalgia of vintage dining cars, I couldn't rightly discern; I only knew that his favored cuisine was strictly Americana. We ordered the unabashed specialties of the house: chili burgers, fries, and chocolate shakes.

"I've been thinking that the freakish distribution of body parts we're dealing with can't be random," said Brogan with a mouthful of chili burger. "What do you and Danny make of it?"

"We both agree that the assortment of plasticized limbs is not likely to be a random distribution, but a purposeful, statistical *clue* of some sort."

"Tell me more," said Brogan, reaching for his chocolate milkshake. "It's been a while since I boned up on my crime scene statistics."

"We're assuming that all twenty-five of the dismembered victims we reassembled must have something molecular and/or genetic in common. We don't know what that missing link is quite yet, but I'm certain that we'll be able to sort it out pretty quick."

"That's good. Anything else?"

"Yes and no, Dash. You see, Danny seems to think that the subset of exactly five victims exhibiting external lesions out of the twenty-five dismembered bodies must mean something, since these cutaneous lesions originated well before the time of death. Danny is working hard and fast on his own personal hunch—I mean hypothesis—but he's understandably hesitant to speculate on the underlying pathology until he can be sure."

"And what do you think about Danny's hunch?

"It's hard to say at this point in the analysis ... but statistically speaking, I'd say that five out of twenty-five is exactly 20 percent. It's a nice round number, Dash. But other than that, I have no idea." I felt a wave of futility descend upon me like a dark cloud.

Watching me swirl a clutch of french fries aimlessly in the smeared ketchup on my plate, Dash Brogan attempted to probe into the recesses of my disconsolate state of mind. "Why the long face, Cornell?"

I looked away, attempting to hide my burgeoning despondency, along with my grief.

"I know you must be missing her terribly ... maybe even more than I do," said Brogan sympathetically. Dash flashed a finger-on-hand writing sign to the waiter, signaling him to bring the check. "You know that I can't have you working directly on the case of the lady in the lake—as much as I know you want to."

"And why the hell not?" I asked in a tone that surprised even me. "You and I both know that her murder is related to all these unsolved cases ... somehow ... in some insidious way!"

"Now let's not go and lose our objectivity over it, son," chided Brogan. "You're too close to this case to be of much use to anyone. And besides, you have plenty of work to do as it is."

We sat in silence for several long minutes. I figured he was giving me time to wallow in my emotions and the last pathetic smears of ketchup remaining on my plate. I knew that Brogan was right about my being too close to the case, but the violent death of Lauriana Noire had left more than a gaping hole in the dank cemetery ground; it left a gaping hole in the innermost chambers of my broken heart, a hole that wasn't filled with a coffin and with dark earth.

Dash Brogan sipped the last dribbles of chocolate shake loudly through his straw in a feeble attempt at humor. When I looked up in surprise, he said, "I think I've got a perfect solution for you, son. There *is* one way you can investigate Lauriana's murder without encountering official conflicts of interest. It's a nifty way that you can participate in this onerous murder investigation and advance your career at the same time."

"Really, Dash?" I could feel my sad face brighten with the dawn of anticipation.

"Let's take a walk, son. I think it's high time you graduated from Dash Brogan's Benevolent Institute of Crime Scene Investigations."

• • •

We headed west along the sidewalk of the congested Sunset Boulevard. I found myself gawking at the myriad giant billboards that emerged on metal stanchions from every possible angle, springing up from the tops of low-rise motels, looming skyward along the broadsides of every office building over ten stories tall. I couldn't help but think that all the skill, the industry, the artistry, the imagination, and the spiritual aspiration that once flourished in the time of the Renaissance had somehow been transmorgrified in our contemporary times into the blatant audacity and ingenuity of commercial advertising in this desperate age of mass entertainment and consumerism on demand. At least that's how it might appear to any normal person walking or cruising these days along the vainglorious Sunset Strip.

We crossed Kings Road, which branches to the north into a residential district, and continued on Sunset Boulevard, past the ramshackle House of Blues and the Comedy Store with its subdued signage, up to the front of a handsome Italian villa that seemed completely out of place on this stilted boulevard of conspicuous consumerism. The five-story building was laid out as two massive symmetrical wings, with antique stonework, tall, arched windows, and elegant, green awnings. The architectural wings were separated by an expansive entryway—an entryway that was set well back and was accessed by climbing one of two lateral stone staircases flanked by classical balustrades rising together from street level to an open terrace. The dual staircases embraced a gurgling marble fountain, rising upon a meticulously landscaped escarpment that displayed the street number, 8439, and the lofty title of this historic landmark building, namely Piazza del Sol, embedded in the greenery.

Dash motioned for me to follow him up the right staircase. He stopped for a smoke at the top of the landing, which opened up onto the broad terrace that led visitors across a marble patio to the magnificent archway of the grand entrance.

Thinking it was a good time for me to ask what we were doing here at this impressive Italianesque villa, I offered up a casual observation. "Looks like a luxury apartment complex if you ask me. But it's hard for me to guess what we're doing here, Dash, and it's even harder for me to imagine what a fancy place like this has to do with my budding forensic career."

"It used to be luxury apartments. At one time, this was a fairly prestigious address for a number of the elites of Hollywood's entertainment industry."

"Used to be?" I inquired.

"Used to be," Dash explained. "This whole place was masterfully renovated a few years back into a one-of-a-kind office building. If you play your cards right, it could turn out to be the prestigious address of a brand-new private eye in this town."

Dash placed the butt of his cigarette into the firmament of a giant urn, swiped a key card past a card reader, and we entered the antique building under the gilded ironwork that graced the curvature of the arched entranceway. Inside the villa, there were more marble fountains, more giant urns sprouting palms and ferns, a golden chandelier that hung from an arched dome, and white-marble floors that spanned the entire entrance lobby and ran past two pairs of large wooden doors that opened up into the respective wings of the splendid Piazza del Sol.

I followed Dash Brogan up four flights of stairs, down a corridor to the end of the hallway, where we stopped, and he handed me two items: a modern card key and an antique metal key. I noticed we were standing in front of a wooden interior door with a large pane of frosted glass. Across the glass, the words "Private Investigator" were professionally stenciled. With more than a little anticipation, I inserted the key into the antique lock, just below the doorknob, turned the key in the lock, and slowly opened the door.

I explored the interior of the office in silence. There was a simple reception area, two windowed offices with high ceilings, a storage closet, and a private restroom. The windows of both offices faced west, offering views of the Hollywood Hills to the north and the Sunset Strip to the south. The reception area and the first office were clean and empty of furniture; the second office had a single wooden desk and swivel chair in the center of the room. Upon the desk was a laptop computer with its screen upward-facing but dark. I pressed the on-button, and the screen immediately brightened with a homepage that displayed the title of an Online Private Investigator Training School and an American eagle emblem with an official-looking gold shield surrounded by a circle of green laurels. I studied the homepage for a few seconds, noting the assurances: "Study at Home; No Classroom Needed; Become a Private Investigator in 3 to 4 Months." I turned to Dash, who had just opened a window, letting fresh air in. For an expectant moment or two, I must have appeared like the West Coast poster boy for puzzlement.

"I bet you could complete that online course in half the time … if you really put your mind to it!" declared Dash. I could tell that he was struggling to hold back a smile, like a proud father.

"What's all this about, Dash? Whose office is this? What are you trying to tell me?"

Without answering any of my urgent questions directly, Dash Brogan simply said, "The office belonged to a private investigator we sometimes used in ticklish situations—that is, until he was retired."

"Did this private detective retire voluntarily?" I asked with obvious apprehension.

"They never do," he said frankly. "Speaking of that, you'll need to get some training in the skillful operation of handguns. That'll be a minimum of eight hours of formal training on basic safety, laws, and ethics, and at least six hours practicing at the LAPD shooting range."

"For what purpose, Dash?" I demanded. "What do I need a handgun for, anyway?"

"It comes with the territory, son. And you better get used to it."

"Okay, if you say so, but please tell me exactly why we're here in this office, and what, precisely, do you want me to do here in the first place?"

"I want you to learn, college boy," Dash reminded me, "and fast … as if someone's life might actually depend on it."

I sat down in the swivel chair and couldn't resist the temptation to spin it around like a schoolboy. "What do I need to learn, Professor Brogan?"

"I want you to learn how to tiptoe through the tulips like a professional, with your finger to your lips."

"Seriously, Dash, where do I begin?"

Detective Dash Brogan sat on the far corner of the desk and sternly continued with my instructions. "Let's see. You've got a pretty good bead on the intents and purposes of basic crime scene procedures, thanks to the advanced training you recently received at my benevolent institute. But you'll need to learn a lot more about personal background investigations, document retrieval, legal investigations, and interrogation methods. You'll need some formal instruction in the areas of business crime, industrial espionage, arson investigations, computer-tracing skills, bounty hunting, kidnapping investigations, arrest tactics, and the fine art of surveillance. Can you do all that in a hurry, son?"

"I think so," I said too cautiously. "That's not right. I know I can!"

"That's good. Then you can start right away, as long as you can keep up with Danny in the continuing operation of your newly established crime lab."

"You know I'll try and do whatever you ask, but first, I have one more question I simply have to ask you."

"Spit it out, son," Dash said bluntly.

"Who's going to pay the rent for all this and for the operation of the crime lab if I'm not working for you or the LAPD directly?"

Dash Brogan lit an unfiltered cigarette. "That's what's we call a client, son. You're about to meet a paying customer with more than a little spending money ... a paying customer who can teach you more about the ways of this world than I can ... a paying customer with more than casual interest in the murder of Lauriana Noire." He flicked a segment of ash onto the top surface of the desk and watched it crawl across the polished hardwood in the breeze of the opened window. "As I recall, you may have already met her—that day at Lauriana's funeral."

I thought about that dreadful day, and then I blurted, "You mean that blonde bombshell that was dressed head-to-toe in black? She's the client you have in mind?"

"That would be the one, Cornell. But the funeral wasn't the right time or place for me to introduce the pretty lady in black to you. Besides, we can't have a classy lady like that meeting with our brand-new private investigator in the attic of Rusty Beams."

• • •

Time passed by in a blur of studious activity. Long days stretched out into long weeks; long weeks lengthened into months. Spring came and went as I worked day and night to complete the Online Private Detective Training Course in record time. As soon as my diploma arrived in the mail, I called Dash Brogan with the good news. He told me that he already knew that I was a wiz at formal coursework, but that I didn't do well enough to write home about at the LAPD shooting range—having barely passed the test for my marksmanship merit badge by the skin of my teeth.

The bad news was that none of the twenty-five victims that washed up on the beaches carried classic chromosomal rearrangements or tumor markers associated with cancer. The screen for SV40 was equivocal, at best, having picked up signals in only two of the victims, albeit at the lower limits of detection. Things were not looking good for us to crack this case anytime soon. The only consolation was a conspicuous lull in the public exhibitions; there were no new crime scene extravaganzas to be investigated, compliments of the serial taxidermist.

Then one day, I got a phone call from Dr. Daniel Grist who told me to meet him after work hours at the entrance of the Los Angeles Zoo. When I reminded Danny that the zoo puts the animals in for the night around four and that the gates close to the public at 5:00 p.m. sharp, he told me he already knew that. He said, "I need to talk with you urgently … at a public place that no one else would suspect … at a public place where no one else can hear."

It was fast approaching the high tide of rush hour when I left my laboratory via Angeles Flight—making sure that I wasn't being followed—and I joined the mass migration heading east out of the city. I rounded the great mound of Dodger Stadium where I turned off onto the Golden State Freeway, otherwise known as I-5, and headed north for about five and a half miles to the exit at Zoo Drive. By the time I got to the zoo, the parking lot was nearly empty, making it easy for me to park just outside the main entrance. I was standing in a planting of tall palm trees at the gated entrance plaza, watching the shadows on the concrete lengthen with each passing minute, wondering what Danny could possibly have on his mind that could be so urgent and so secretive.

After about fifteen minutes of watching shadows grow longer, Danny drove up in his gray Volvo station wagon. He waved frantically for me to come and hop into his car. I climbed inside and waited for Danny to start the conversation. He told me we needed to get to a more private place, and looking around suspiciously, he drove off in a hurry.

Danny drove south on Zoo Drive to the point where it becomes Crystal Springs Drive and veers off into the green fields of the Harding and Wilson Municipal Golf Courses. We turned west onto

Griffith Park Drive, and within a few hundred feet, we turned into the parking lot of what looked like an old, overgrown picnic area.

"This is the site of the original Los Angeles Zoo," said Danny as we walked along a crumbling footpath into the strangest ruins I had ever seen. Although it was quite difficult to make out many details of the abandoned zoo in the fading twilight, I could see a series of old, dilapidated enclosures, dark stone caves, and rusty cages that once housed a menagerie of exotic animals. It gave me a creepy thrill to imagine the appearance of wild animals emerging from the mouths of those old cages and caves that were embedded in the hillside, eerily overgrown by olive trees and dense bushes with the passage of time. We came to a small enclave of wooden picnic benches standing in front of a massive stone wall of dark and gloomy animal caves. Danny stood with his hands in his pockets while I took a seat on the top of a dusty picnic bench.

"What's up, Doc?" I said to break the ice.

Danny kicked the sandy loam with the toe of his foot. Then he looked around to make sure that no one else was listening. "I figured out what the raised cutaneous lesions are made of," he said, "and that led me to investigate something that's even more terrifying."

"Well, what are they?" I demanded.

"Kaposi's sarcoma," said Danny with obvious pride. "They are histologically and cytologically Kaposi's sarcoma."

"Isn't that type of malignancy commonly associated with AIDS?" I surmised.

"Exactly!" said Danny, looking nervously over his shoulder. "And that's how I managed to connect the dots to the other disembodied victims. They're all HIV (acquired immunodeficiency virus) positive!"

"Even the ones with no visible lesions?"

"They're all HIV positive!"

"Great Scott! You hit the jackpot this time, Danny!" I shouted.

"Keep your voice down, you idiot," scolded Danny. "This is even more dangerous than the previous connection we made to the tainted polio vaccines."

"Okay, okay," I said in a hushed whisper. "I'll run the samples in my crime lab with real-time PCR to confirm your findings. But what do you make of these Kaposi's sarcomas in relation to our previous cancer victims? And what, if anything, do you make of the curious percentage of overt Kaposi's sarcoma in this subset of disembodied unfortunates?"

"That's where things get curiouser and curiouser," said Danny. "You see, Kaposi's sarcoma was relatively rare until modern times. It's known to be caused by a sexually transmitted herpes virus: human herpesvirus 8, or HHV-8, to be precise. While HHV-8 infections are prevalent in a number of high-risk populations, the incidence of Kaposi's sarcoma is still very low. However, in the context of an HIV-positive immune-compromised AIDS patient, it appears that the two viruses interact cooperatively to bring about the neoplastic transformation.

"That's interesting," I said, with my mind racing to catch up with the forensic implications of Danny's diagnosis. "And the exact percentage of Kaposi's sarcomas seen in a given population of HIV/AIDS patients is ...?"

"Approximately 20 percent."

"Are you sure about that, Danny?"

"I'm afraid so," he said, visibly trembling as he spoke. "I am very much afraid so."

"Goodness, this means that our plastic fantastic embalmer has shifted gears entirely! This means that he, or she, is clearly trying to show us something very different this time!"

"Shhhh," warned Danny, shifting forward on his feet. "This is more dangerous ... this is more explosive than any revelation we ever made before." Danny kicked the ground nervously as he lamented, "If you think the coroner was upset about our previous SV40-polio vaccine tie-in, just imagine how he's going to react this time."

"You know what this means?" I said.

Danny nodded.

"This means that we go directly to Dash Brogan and no one else."

On the way back to the car, I asked Danny if he knew anything about the cause of death of Lauriana Noire.

"I'm not supposed to discuss that case with you," said Danny, "for one or two good reasons."

"What good reasons might that be, Danny?"

"First of all, I'm not allowed to discuss active investigations with a private operator—congratulations, by the way."

"Thanks. And the other reason is …?"

"The other reason is that you were personally involved with the lady, and Dash tells me that you were in too deep for your own good. In fact, we shouldn't even be talking about this."

"Ah, come on, Danny. Be a sport. You can at least tell me the official cause of death."

"Are you sure you want to know?" he asked, stopping dead in his tracks as he spoke.

"I'm sure. I'm terribly, painfully, agonizingly sure. Come on, man, spit it out!"

Danny inhaled deeply and uttered, "Shit," under his breath. "If you must know, that lovely lady in the lake was strangled to death with a Sprague Rappaport stethoscope. She was strangled with the tubing sometime before she was tossed into the lake."

"She was strangled with a stethoscope?" I gasped. "How can you be so certain?"

"In addition to the two parallel abrasions on her neck and the subconjunctival hemorrhage in both eyes, we found one of the ear pieces of the murder weapon—it was caught up in her brassiere."

16 Chilling Moments of Uncertainty

Detective Dash Brogan was seriously impressed by our latest revelations describing the natural history of the disembodied limbs. However, Dash agreed with Danny that we would be summarily chastised by the county coroner for grasping at straws, or worse—for attempting to make a veritable castle out of a few fragmentary traces in the sand. Apparently the pressure coming from the top for us to identify the perpetrator of the staged crime scenes was intense, regardless of the actual causes of all these deaths, which were still officially undetermined. Once again, we were tied up and gagged for the time being—that is, restricted from reporting any of our recent scientific and forensic findings to anyone but Detective Dash Brogan.

In this self-imposed hiatus, Danny and I endeavored to investigate the etiology of HIV and HHV8 infections, looking for lapses in medical judgment that might be associated with the spread of HIV/AIDS and/or possible federal and/or pharmaceutical exploits that might tend to disturb the sensibilities of our elusive but artful serial exhibitionist. I used my newfound training in business crime, document retrieval, and computer-tracing skills to begin to make a number of incriminating connections while Danny continued to connect the dots on his end.

It didn't take too long for us to drill down to the bloody marrow of another medical controversy, another official cover-up, and another pharmaceutical outrage. Still, something vital and important was missing from the big picture, for it would take us quite a while to string *The Case of the Dangling Children and the Suspended Schoolteacher and the Bathing Tar Babes* together with all these dislocated arms and legs that were so ruthlessly, so deliberately, so publically displayed on the sandy beaches of Southern California.

The following week, Dash Brogan sent me on an errand that would change everything. It would be my first official outing as a bona fide private investigator, and I was anxious to make a success of it. Dash said it was about time for me to meet the mysterious lady in black. I still had no idea who she was or what my first case was all about; he just told me to act professional when I met with this mysterious femme fatale at my new office in the Piazza del Sol.

I was staring out the window of my fourth-floor office when I heard the outer door open and close, followed by the distinctive sound of high heels traipsing upon the wooden floors of my reception room. As stunning as the view of the Hollywood Hills from my office was, in the glaring light of day, it paled in comparison to the mystifying vision of loveliness that strolled into my office that day and stood before me with a provocative glamour that arrested my attention and a penetrating look that plunged my mind into an abyss.

I spun my chair around and stood up to see the alluring lady more clearly. She was dressed fashionably in black again; this time, it was a tasteful cocktail dress with lace sleeves, a form-fitting bodice, and a hemline that was located well above the knees. I recognized the seductive scent she was wearing—it was La Petite Robe Noire. The lady was clutching a small black purse, and I noticed that she was wearing a string of black pearls that matched the bracelet on her right wrist and the chandelier earring that dangled from the exposed right ear where her blonde hair was pulled back and around to the other side. Before I could offer the alluring lady a chair—the only piece of furniture that I had added to my office at the time—she combed her fingers lightly through her long, champagne locks and sat herself down as gracefully as a falling black feather.

"My name is Isadora Vanderbilt," she said unpretentiously, with a voice as soft as the velvet petals of a blue dahlia. "I have come to enlist the services of Dr. Cornell Westerly to investigate, perchance to avenge, the murder of my sister."

"I'm Cornell Westerly," I said guardedly, attempting to avoid another soul-piercing gaze.

"Obviously, Dr. Westerly, but I am also here to help you."

"Help me?" I said.

"Yes, Dr. Westerly. To help you in a truly personal way with this *intimate* private investigation," she said softly.

Our eyes met, and I immediately felt a chilling moment of uncertainty. As I struggled to adjust my demeanor to the arresting quality of her appearance, the appealing fragrance of her perfume, and the invasive quality of her gaze, Isadora Vanderbilt clicked opened her purse and pulled out a black-leather checkbook. She tore out a check—which was already filled out, signed, and dated—and handed it over to me. "Here is a retainer," she said casually, "for your professional services and your expenses."

I nearly gasped when I saw the amount—it was six figures: a single one, followed by five zeros with one well-placed comma but no decimal point. Somehow, I managed to stifle my surprise as I adjusted my eyes to withstand the intensity of the woman's soul-piercing surveillance.

"This is a very generous amount for a retainer, Miss Vanderbilt, but I am not at all certain how I can help you solve this horrid crime … as much as I am inclined to … as much as I would love to. But first, for the sake of clarity, may I assume that your sister is Lauriana Noire?"

"You may," she said bluntly. "And also, for the sake of clarity, I am retaining you to investigate, perchance to *avenge*, the murder of my sister."

Taken aback by the disturbing aspect of vengeance, I attempted to parry the thrust of such punitive intentions. "I am quite happy to investigate the violent death of Lauriana Noire as a private investigator and interested party. In fact, I am delighted to be involved. But I am certainly not the one you would want to depend on when you entertain the dubious business of revenge."

"*Au contraire, mon jeune homme insensé,*" she spoke in a scolding tone, "I am assured by the most reliable of sources that you are the one and only man for the job."

"Okay, Miss Vanderbilt, I won't argue the point. But I am rather curious. How, exactly, do you think or expect that *you* could help *me* with this particular investigation?"

"I can help you to realize your full potential as a private eye," she said, with consummate nonchalance. "I have come forward, not only to sponsor your private detection, but to inspire you to even greater levels of understanding."

"It sounds a bit mystical to me, Miss Vanderbilt."

"Mysticism," she said, rolling her eyes and shaking her head, combing her long blonde hair with her fingers, "is too commonly associated with occult practices and all sorts of irrational world views. I prefer to use nonderogatory terms, such as inspiration and vision, to describe those ultimate questions pertaining to the true nature of reality."

"That still sounds like mysticism, if you ask me."

"But I'm not asking you, Dr. Westerly. I am attempting to make a passionate assertion that there is a hidden unity that underlies the drama of our existence, a unity that underlies the diversity of observations that you have so cleverly revealed by your forensic investigations."

"If you're trying to tell me that Lauriana's murder is somehow related to the plasticized exhibitions of human taxidermy that are occurring all over this sprawling metropolis, I am more than intrigued; I am genuinely interested. But I have to tell you that I am a man of science, first and foremost, and I am not easily taken to frivolous notions of unproven cause and effect. I'm not at all sure that our points of view are compatible."

"*Au contraire, mon jeune homme consciencieux*, I am certain that we will get along beautifully, perhaps even affectionately, as we explore this unsolved mystery together." Isadora Vanderbilt crossed her lovely legs and adjusted the hem of her skirt accordingly.

I shifted uncomfortably in my chair. Sure I was intrigued by this beautiful woman who looked like a movie star, dressed like a fashion model, and smelled like the House of Guerlain. Thinking of Lauriana, I attempted to stifle my attraction to this client—her sister, of all people—even as my desire was aroused by the woman's attractive appearance, her provocative boldness, and her tantalizing scent, even as my resolve was stiffened perceptibly by the mere thought of such intimacy.

"I generally work alone, Miss Vanderbilt. Rather, I generally work with other detectives."

"That's not what my sister told me," she said, moving the tip of her tongue ever so slowly across the sexy, crimson fullness of her lower lip.

She had me there. I was still brokenhearted and bewildered by the death of Lauriana Noire, a woman who had been my lover, my poetical confidant, and much more than a friend. But, I have to admit, if such truth can be told, I was already falling in lust with her seductive sister.

"Okay, Miss Vanderbilt, you have me right where you want me. But I have to ask, before this partnership goes any further: how can you help me find the actual clues ... the solid facts of the matter that will help me to solve even one of these disparate cases?"

She looked deeply into my eyes again, this time with an assuring feminine smile. "*Oh mon beau, mon jeune homme chéri*, you already have the finest of clues in your possession."

That was when Miss Isadora Vanderbilt uncrossed her shapely legs, arose from her chair, and traipsed right out of my office. I listened to the delightful sound of her high heels clattering, receding across the hardwood floors of the outer office. A door opened and closed, leaving me alone with another chilling moment of uncertainty, leaving me alone with the struggle to apprehend the hidden meaning behind the lady's final enigmatic pronouncement.

I looked around; the room was bare, with the exception of the old oak desk, two chairs, and one clueless gumshoe. Not knowing what else to do, I opened the top drawer of the desk and peered into its hollows. There was a single solitary business card that I had unconsciously placed into the drawer some time ago. It was the business card I took from the wallet of that grunting bastard that was having his way with my beloved Lauriana. In all the confusion and despair, between Lauriana's violent death and the recent swarm of shoreline dismemberments, it had completely slipped my mind.

• • •

I worked like a madman—wielding my library card, the Internet protocols of the World Wide Web, and my newly developed computer-hacking skills, which came in handy for tracing and retrieval of classified documents. The first thing I found was that the grunting bastard, Mr. Barrett Berghoffer, Vice President of International Sales, Imperious Pharmaceutical Consortium, Basel, Switzerland, was traveling under an assumed identity. In point of fact, there no longer was an Imperious Pharmaceutical Consortium in Basel, Switzerland, or anywhere else. I found that the entire defunct corporation had morphed and disappeared, only to resurface again under the cloaks of a wide variety of corporate conglomerates in a gigantic shell game that was attempting to flee with misdirection from the mounting liabilities that stemmed from the selling of tainted blood products.

In the 1980s, when the FDA banned the company from using certain blood products that were found to contain live HIV, these guys did the unthinkable. They sold the tainted blood products to foreign countries with no warning that they contained anything harmful. Rather than discard the pooled and contaminated blood products, which were used in the treatment of hemophilia, the misbegotten bastards of Big Pharma had decided to ensure their profits at the expense of product safety, at the expense of human decency, as they shipped off the tainted batches to doctors and nurses of lesser-developed countries. Even after a certified heat-treatment protocol was established and a sterile purification of the blood factors was developed, the distribution of the HIV-tainted products continued to flood the unsuspecting markets.

I had a field day in tracing down the dozens of class-action lawsuits that attempted to pin the tail on the corporate donkeys—to the tune of many hundreds of millions of dollars—before the cascade of corporate mergers and acquisitions and divestures could successfully hide the "pea" of culpability under the "shells" of nouveau corporate indemnities. I also found that the US FDA had, astoundingly, failed to ensure the quality control, i.e., the destruction, of these tainted blood products, well after the assays for HIV were routinely available, and well after the time when purified, virus-free batches of the blood products were available. Worse yet, I found that the investigative journalists and major newspapers at the time were conspicuously silent on the matter. It's bad enough to have the debilitating illness of hemophilia to contend with, but it's manifestly worsened when one has to contend with the additional ravages of HIV/AIDS.

So that's what Lauriana was up to! She was nailing a pharmaceutical philistine, so to speak. No wonder Lauriana's last poem was so uncharacteristically caustic, so righteously indignant. She had found out, in her own way, what I had just found out in mine … that the petrochemical-pharmaceutical conglomerates that emerged in the detritus of WWII were pulling all the strings, and that the prescribing physicians and the federal regulators and the sponsored scientists and the corporate lobbyists were nothing but puppets in the lucrative process of perpetually treating, rather than actually curing, a host of human diseases. Although I will never fully understand how Lauriana Noire could have betrayed my undying love, and broken my heart in the process, I like to imagine that she was delving into the murk with a purpose sublime, delving into the murk in her own avant-garde manner, delving into the murk as the gorgeous and licentious Poet Laureate of the Inner Dark. Still, as much as I would like to forgive her and move on, my battered heart is a far cry from forgiveness.

* * *

The next evening, I was cordially invited to meet with Lauriana's glamorous sister, Isadora Vanderbilt, for dinner at the notorious Chateau Marmont. The place is a veritable old-world castle modeled after the royal Chateau Ambroise located on the banks of the River Loire in France. The towering chateau with its turrets-and-balconies architecture is perched high on a hill in Hollywood, overlooking the Sunset Strip. I handed my car keys to a uniformed valet, and he deftly secreted my beat-up Bimmer away from the entrance of the ersatz French chateau.

I made my way across the landscaped driveway on a pavement of cobblestones and strode into the grand chateau through a high-arched Gothic colonnade with vaulted sea-green ceilings and antique chandeliers. I could feel the ghosts of Old Hollywood emerging from the lofty recesses of the stone archways, dancing and romancing behind each Doric column. Clark Gable and Jean Harlow trysted at the Chateau Marmont in the thirties, as did Nicholas Ray in the fifties—he trysted with Natalie Wood, Shelly Winters, Jane Mansfield, Marilyn Monroe, and Judy Holliday, to mention but a few. I hear tell that a great many of the modern-day celebrities have discretely followed suit. Apparently, the Chateau Marmont is an excellent place for trysting, a contention I would soon confirm for myself.

I found Isadora Vanderbilt in the adjacent courtyard restaurant, standing beside a dining table. She was wearing a black, sleeveless, strapless corset, sheer black stockings, and what I assumed was a wraparound skirt. The laces of her corset were tied loosely at the top, which served to reveal a flawless bosom. She was wearing diamonds—lots of diamonds—in a geometrically pleasing configuration that descended from a glittering band at the base of the neck in the geometrical form of an arrow, an arrow that all but pointed to the delicate cleft that lay between her uplifted breasts. Isadora Vanderbilt brushed back her long, blonde hair and smiled the kind of smile that stays with a man long after the pleasantries of introduction are consummated.

"Why are you standing, Miss Vanderbilt? You could have started without me."

"What fun would that be, Dr. Westerly?" she said as she brushed my cheek with a delicate *faire la bise*. "Dining is one of the many things I prefer *not* to do alone."

"Aren't you a bit cold, Miss Vanderbilt?" I said, offering my jacket.

"Now that the sun is down for the count, I can feel the chill of the marine layer creeping in from the coast."

"Don't you like my new outfit, Dr. Westerly? I bought it just for you." Her eyes glittered brightly as she spoke. In the muted lamplight of the courtyard, I could say with some certainty that the sparkling lights in those come-hither eyes far outshined the brilliant lavalliere of diamonds.

I politely pulled back a chair from the dining table, and as Isadora Vanderbilt was gracefully settling down in the chair, I signaled for the waiter to light the gas patio heater. A few clicks of the igniter button, and our dining area was ensconced in the luxury of mild radiant heat. In addition to the welcome sensation of warmth that was added to the setting, the golden flames of the patio heater brought an aura of candle fire to the romantic lights that danced and dazzled in the enchantment of her eyes.

We dined like a king and a queen holding court, removed from the fast-paced world that raced and rallied on the Sunset Strip beyond the outside walls. Cloistered in the old-world ambience of Chateau Marmont's garden restaurant, I dined on king salmon that was decorated with an assertive saffron aioli while Isadora Vanderbilt nibbled on thyme-roasted chicken with celery root–parsnip puree. In the course of our dinner, we agreed to communicate with each other on a first-name basis, which instantly brought us closer together.

"Okay, Isadora, I'm happy with the informality. But I'm interested to know something more about your immediate family. May I ask if Lauriana is, or rather was, your younger or your older sister?"

"Does it really matter?" she replied.

"No, I guess not. I was just curious. Like Lauriana, you appear to have an ageless, timeless quality about you."

"I'll take that as a compliment, *mon homme avec du charme*. Now tell me something, Cornell. What have you uncovered by following that paper clue you have in your possession?"

In the consummate privacy of this well-heeled chateau, I told Isadora what I had found out about Lauriana's twisted mister. She listened intently and without so much as a tear while she meticulously picked through a crumbly cake that was topped with pistachio gelato.

"The time is fast upon us when you, and only you, will have to put all these pieces together," she said as she polished off the last vestiges of her vintage French Chablis.

"And exactly how do you expect me to do that, my glamorous and presumptuous partner?"

"With my help, Cornell, I sincerely believe you can do anything and everything you want. With my help, you can reach beyond your intellectual limitations. With my help, you can seek and soar and ultimately find an unseen world that is above and beyond your world."

"Seriously, Isadora, as inspiring as you are … as encouraging as you intend to be, I am not at all certain that I have it in me to do anything of the sort."

"*Au contraire, mon amant réticent*," she said with a laugh. "All I have to do is fill you with sufficient desire and direction … knowing full well that the entire universe lies within you."

I finished off my crème brulee in silence, gingerly sipping a steaming double espresso. I needed a moment to compose myself, in the chill of yet another moment of uncertainty. I felt like I was being torn between the carnal, the mystical, and the professional as the guiding light of my life. And then the waiter came by with the check, the tally of which reminded me to be sure to add a healthy aspect of financial considerations to the confusion of the mix.

It nearly emptied my wallet to cover the dinner and the tip. When the waitress left, I asked the lovely Isadora if she would like me to walk with her to her car.

"There's no need for that," she said. "You can walk me to my cottage, which is just beyond the swimming pool."

"You mean you're staying here as a guest of the hotel?"

"But of course, Cornell. I always stay at the Chateau Marmont whenever I come to Los Angeles. The ambiance here is a lot like my home in Paris: this is my home away from home."

At this point in the dinner date, I was torn between my physical attraction to Lauriana's sister—compounded by my still-painful feelings of betrayal—and the psychological prohibitions of a professional private eye who strives to conduct himself with at least a modicum of integrity. This was a sudden clash of principles, to be sure, and I knew that some vital yet unexpressed part of me was being put to the test. Would I, could I, remain true to my fond memories of Lauriana Noire, who had raised my budding forensic investigations to the highest aspirations of poetic justice? And if not, would I, could I, form a novel partnership with her beautiful, mystical sister, a partnership that would not only inform the living of the dark tragedy at hand, but would, in the fullness of time, honor those who were dead as well as those who were not yet born? Suddenly my high ideal of spotless loyalty was overshadowed by the pull of another spellbinding moment: I found myself walking hand-in-hand with Isadora on our way to her garden cottage. In the inexpressible, irresistible force of this spellbinding moment, I realized firsthand the sublime mathematics of life—that the nominal unit of love is a pair.

We literally danced across the threshold of the charming poolside cottage, with its fashionable stained-glass windows, its oaken floors, and its Mission-style furniture. We swept through the living room on Persian carpets, passing by a tasteful seating of rattan chairs and into the bedroom of this attractive lady in black, which was truly a sight to behold. The room was illuminated indirectly with light that passed dimly through a stained-glass window. I could make out the forms of a dark, sculpted object that stood on a table beside the bed. It was a black-onyx leopard that appeared to complement the leopard-print bedspread that beckoned us into the wild. Isadora spun out of my arms as she unclipped her skirt and laid herself down obliquely on the deep plush of the bed. I watched the skirt drop casually to the floor as she held out her hand to be taken, caressed, and conjoined with mine.

I undressed as quickly as humanly possible and took hold of all she was offering. In the welcoming arms of the beauteous Isadora Vanderbilt, I would find the strength, the daring, and the passion to reach for the distant stars.

In the eagerness and ecstasy of rising and falling in love again, Isadora spoke to me softly in French.

"*Il y a des spiritueux dans l'obscurité,*" she whispered in my ear as we moved together as one. "*Il y a des spiritueux dans l'obscurité, équitation, équitation …*"

I struggled to make the translation from French, which was not nearly as good as my Spanish. *There are spirits in the darkness*, that much was clear, and *these spirits are riding, riding*. But why? And where? And what comes next? These questions needed to be answered.

"*Il y a des spiritueux dans l'obscurité, équitation, équitation. Il y a des spiritueux dans l'obscurité montée sur des chevaux du vent.*"

Okay, so *there are spirits in the darkness, riding, riding*. So far, so good … but what was that last refrain? *Listen carefully, it might be important … wait for it … don't lose it. Here it comes again:* "*Il y a des spiritueux dans l'obscurité montée sur des chevaux du vent.*"

There are spirits in the darkness mounted on horses of the wind.

17 Who's That Lounging in Those Chairs?

All through the early part of May, I was a busy man-about-town—a veritable juggler of unsolved agendas. I was busy chasing down leads, managing the crime lab, detecting things with my illustrious cohorts, and meeting with my ultra-provocative female client on a regular basis. I had four balls in the air, so to speak, with the LAPD. Let's see. We had the unsolved *Case of the Dangling School Children*, the unsolved *Case of the Suspended Schoolteacher*, the unsolved *Case of the Bathing Tar Babes*, and the unsolved *Case of the Dislocated Limbs*. Sure, we had made some progress, and we were beginning to point the accusatory fingers of suspicion in a certain direction, but we were still no closer to collaring the perpetrators of any one of these highly publicized, plasticized acts of human taxidermy than we were from the start.

More importantly, as a bona fide, certified, card-carrying, gun-wielding private investigator in the state of California, I was passionately enlisted and personally compelled to investigate the unsolved murder of Lauriana Noire. For the first time in a long time, I was running with healthy reserves in my bank accounts. Thanks to the encouragement and support of Dash Brogan and Isadora Vanderbilt, I was willingly propelled into each and all of these unsolved cases with a full head of steam.

In the heady thralls of my new romantic infatuation with Isadora Vanderbilt and the breathless profusion of body blessings that spoiled me for any other woman, I was encouraged by erotic gestures, sublime thoughts, and breathtaking feats of endurance to probe for a greater understanding of my seminal purpose, to intensify my undercover mission as a private detective, and to look within, beyond the apparent, in a constant striving for some hidden and elusive narrative truth. Isadora would help me to seek and find one changeless item among all items, and in the overwhelming darkness of the fathomless void, to seek and find one inseparable element that lay at the heart of the mystery. In the course of these mind-expanding sessions, I would come to realize that all descriptive phenomena are fleeting and impermanent. Call it mystical thinking, call it peripheral vision, call it divinely inspired—yet in the exquisite womb of Isadora's feminine introspection, I was encouraged as a scientist, as a realist—as a logical positivist, for goodness' sake—to at least consider, if not to embrace, the symbolic language of the visionary and the idealist. In effect, Isadora was teaching me to embrace the reality of a shimmering unity that lies at the root of any such diversity, encouraging me to aspire for one brief and shining moment to the realm of the philosopher, the poet, the artist, and to grasp and uphold a deeper meaning that was so close at hand.

On Wednesday, I met with Detective Dash Brogan at the Echo Park Lake. I found him sitting on a bench at the north end of the lake where an expansive flotilla of South Asian lotuses—*Nelumbo nucifera*, to be precise—were amassed in serene anticipation of the summer bloom of luminous pink-tipped flowers. According to local folklore, the original plantings of lotuses first appeared in Echo Park in 1889, when they were referred to as the "Egyptian lotus of the Nile." The Egyptian lotus—that is, *N. caerulea*—is an entirely different species, by the way. Legend has it that the new and dominant strain of *N. nucifera*—which is downright sacred to millions of Hindus and Buddhists all around the world—were planted by missionaries from the nearby Angeles Temple who brought the sacred seeds of *N. nucifera* back from their trips to Asia. In many ways, this mysterious folklore of the Echo Park lotus plantings serves to reflect on the ever-changing demographics of the City of Los Angeles. But I digress ...

Dash Brogan was smoking an unfiltered cigarette, as usual. He appeared to be watching the triple spouts of a water fountain surging up into a cloudless sky. Beyond the lotus pads and the spewing fountain, past the lakeside palm trees that lined the distant shore, the dull gray sentinels of the LA skyline stood calmly, quietly in the gauzy haze of the early afternoon.

Dash Brogan told me that they were able to make a positive identification of one of the Bathing Tar Babes by running Clive's photographs of the intact faces through the vast database of obituaries. He said that the young woman in question was indeed a victim of intractable cancer and that her dead body had allegedly been pilfered from a hospice outside of Cleveland, Ohio. Apparently, the thieves and the body left the premises without leaving a trace. The only clue was a curious name—*Art House Undertaking*—that was stenciled on the side of an official-looking van from what turned out to be a fictitious mortuary. By the time the designated funeral home realized that the cadaver was missing, the perpetrators and the body were long gone.

"You mean the woman's body was taken before it reached the embalmer?" I queried.

"That's right," said Brogan, looking out across the lake.

"This means that she was preserved with embalming fluid *and* plasticized after the body was snatched," I surmised.

"That's right, bright guy. And we have reason to believe that the same outfit might have snatched a number of other stiffs from a dozen funeral homes across the Midwest—snatched them from hospital morgue units, right after the official cause of death was determined, but before the dearly departed could be properly transferred to a legitimate mortuary."

"That's amazing, Dash. This means that the Art House gang we're chasing must have purchased a hefty amount of formaldehyde, methanol, and phenol, in addition to the large amounts of acetone and liquid silicone polymers needed for the plasticization process. Couldn't we just cross-match all the large industrial purchases of formaldehyde and alcohols with similar purchases of acetone and liquid polymers to help us nail down the buyer?"

"It's a good thought, Cornell. But it's not one for us to ponder. You see, the transportation of pretty ladies—dead or alive—across state lines for nefarious purposes makes a federal case out of it. The coroner has already brought in the FBI to follow up on those kinds of leads."

"You mean we're off the case of the cancer victims? You mean we're out of it?"

"Not quite," said Brogan, lighting a new cigarette from the glowing butt of the old one. "But you and Danny had better hurry and firm up your DNA linkages to those strings of dislocated limbs before the coroner and the mayor wash their hands of the whole business."

"But how can they, Dash? We know that the latest artful exhibits are all HIV positive, but we still haven't figured out exactly how, or why, or even what these people died of."

"We have a pretty good idea of what they died of, Cornell. And it doesn't look like murder. So, I've got to tell you, son, if you and Danny don't make some headway on the meaning of this extravaganza in the next week or so, the coroner and the mayor are likely to make a public announcement and call the whole thing off as a lowdown Hollywood hoax—nothing more than petty theft with some props and special effects—and that would be a tragedy."

"How can they do that without any solid proof? And why would they do that?"

"To keep the anxious inhabitants of this dark city from burning the whole damn place to the ground," said Brogan, and then he slowly rose to his feet and walked away from the lake.

• • •

Two days later, some time before sunrise, we were off to the beach again. This time it was Monarch Bay in Dana Point. Dash Brogan did the driving, and I did the sleeping, all the way to the wealthy Orange County enclave that begins at the border of Laguna Niguel and ends at the low-tide mark of the secluded park-like shoreline. We parked the Pontiac Catalina in a lot by the Ritz Carlton Hotel and made our way on foot. We hiked through a grassy picnic area to a macadam footpath that ran up high along the beach. For fishermen, it's the swarms of birds that let you know where the quarry is; but for homicide detectives and private investigators, it's the news choppers swarming in a tight circle that point the way to the scene of the crime.

We made our way along the greater curve of the bay on the jogging trail before we headed down onto the sandy beach. The early-morning surfers were sitting half-submerged on their surfboards, bobbing up and down like so many ducks, waiting for the swells to mount and curl just beyond the rock jetty. We approached a stand of beach umbrellas with a cluster of about a dozen lounge chairs filled with early-morning sunbathers. Just behind the first cluster of beach chairs was another circle of chairs with similar occupants arrayed like a large family gathering. There were blue and white balloons tied on several of the beach chairs, which made it appear like a festive occasion.

As we drew closer, I could see that Clive was already busy with his yellow crime scene tape and his camera, taking establishing shots of the beach party. Drawing closer still, it was clear to me that this particular beach party was definitely missing something—the arms and legs of the sunbathers. These early-morning sunbathers were nothing but petrified torsos with human heads, which were staged in various recumbent positions under beach towels with an assortment of straw hats, baseball caps, and sunglasses. Doing a quick head count, I confirmed my suspicion: that these were probably a rogues' gallery of the twenty-five unfortunates whose arms and legs had been surgically misappropriated.

Dash Brogan raised both his arms overhead like a referee at a football game, signaling for the helicopters to disburse in a wider perimeter. We walked up to Clive, who was busy blowing sand from the lens of his camera.

"It's about time someone shooed those pesky choppers away," said Clive. "Makes it mighty difficult to take a decent picture."

"I'll bet it does," said Dash.

"What took you guys so long? Did you stop for breakfast?"

"I had to pick up my young protégée in Santa Monica," said Dash, pointing to me with his thumb. He surveyed the two clusters of sunbathers for quite a while, saying, "Don't look to me like these beach boys and girls will be playing any volleyball today." Then he turned to me said, "What do you make of this beach party, Cornell?"

"All I can say at this point, Dash, is that the Maui Jim sunglasses are a nice touch."

It took the better part of the day for me to tag and bag the truncated amputees, with the help of the local sheriff's men. It took longer than usual because I decided to take a number of tissue specimens in situ from each of the corpses so that Danny and I could readily confirm our previous diagnosis without any administrative delays. In each case, the torsos had not only been thoroughly amputated, they had each been dispossessed of their dentition and denuded of all the recognizable skin from their faces. Beneath the Maui Jim sunglasses, there gleamed those same lifelike replica eyeballs we had seen before. Needless to say, every one of these twenty-five quadruple amputees at Monarch Bay were preserved and plasticized to perfection.

Dash stayed with me all afternoon while Clive took one more photograph of the empty lounge chairs for good measure, and then he left with the sheriff's men to direct the disposition of the bodies to the location of the missing limbs that were archived *en masse* in the Los Angeles County Morgue.

On our way back to Santa Monica, Dash filled me in on a break in the murder case of the beautiful-but-dead poet laureate. Apparently, someone in one of the hillside neighborhoods that surround Silver Lake had managed to take a picture of the sunrise at about the same time that the lifeless body of Lauirana Noire was reportedly cast into the lake. The photograph was pretty overexposed, but with digital enhancement they managed to identify the make and model of an automobile, a red Porsche Cayenne SUV, and the profiles of two shadowy men—a thin man and a fat man—standing with what looked like a bolt cutter by the reservoir gate. Dash told me that he'd let me know more, if and when they got a bead on the Porsche.

• • •

Danny and I went on a tear of scholarly investigation and document retrieval, pulling off a collegial series of all-nighters. Just as we had suspected, each of the truncated humans was confirmed to be HIV positive. Next we focused our attention on a detailed historical, scientific, and medical analysis of the origins and transmission of this virus, which has by now infected more than forty million people. What we found in the course of our intensive scholarship and electronic sleuthing would send a shiver down your spine and make your hair stand on end at the same time. We spent a lot of time and effort to document the epidemiological footprints and the molecular biology of the beast. Then, as we gathered our harvest of incriminating forensic documentation, we prepared a slide presentation for the coroner's inquest that was sure to come upon us like a whirlwind with all the adversarial angst and suspense of a courtroom drama.

* * *

The anticipated inquest was held in the coroner's office to prevent any leaks to the press. After Danny and I had been officially sworn under oath to reveal the truth, the whole shocking truth, and nothing but the truth, as accurately as we had found it, Danny started off the slide presentation with a concise description of the forensics, which pointed directly to HIV/AIDS as a likely cause of death.

The two of us, along with Dash Brogan, had been formally summoned to present our testimonies of pertinent information on the probable manner of death and the conceivable motives for the string of incidents at the beaches. As Danny followed with a brief description of the various scientific theories surrounding the origin of the AIDS pandemic in modern times, I watched the assemblage taking in what he was saying. The coroner and his minion, Philiac, whose left nostril was characteristically encrusted where a finger had recently been, looked blankly unimpressed. Clive had accompanied Dash, and two members of Danny's staff had joined us. A well-dressed representative from the mayor's office, an assistant to the district attorney, and a scruffy criminal lawyer from downtown rounded out the group.

Here I will spare you the grizzly molecular and genetic details of Danny's formal presentation and will simply state for the record that the human immunodeficiency virus (HIV) is most closely related to an indigenous simian immunodeficiency virus (SIV) that is found in African chimpanzees. It's molecular-genetic transfer to humans, along with a marked increase in virulence, was certainly *not* the result of zoonosis, that is, a natural transfer of the simian virus to humans; rather, this fateful transmission was undoubtedly punctuated by human activities that served as a bloody red carpet that leads to one inescapable conclusion—that the dreadful HIV/AIDS pandemic is profoundly iatrogenic (i.e., physician-made) in origin.

Danny waved the laser pointer like a wizard as he elucidated the major theories that were summarily proposed and officially sanctioned by the mainstream medical and pharmaceutical organizations in an effort to point the finger of suspicion away from the dangers of liability.

"Let's see," he said. "There is the Cut Hunter Theory, which doesn't fit any of the facts, the equally unlikely Heart of Darkness Theory, where treacherous colonization of French Equatorial Africa and the Belgian Congo led to unhealthy living and working conditions in disease-ridden labor camps where the possibilities of onward transmission were accelerated. We have the Contaminated Plastic Syringe Theory, which simply shifts the blame from natives to local physicians without a shred of credible scientific evidence. And finally, we have an oldie but goodie, the Tainted Oral Polio Vaccine Theory, which we already know introduced the cancer-causing SV40 virus into untold millions of humans. However, the major problem with this theory is that the tainted polio vaccines had been expanded in monkeys, which are a far cry from African chimps. And then there is the Genocidal Theory, first proposed by the Soviet Union, which implicates the devious machinations of the West, including the US government and the CIA—to depopulate the African continent— while offering about as much scientific proof as there is evidence of extraterrestrial aliens flying over Roswell, New Mexico." Danny faced the distinguished members of the coroner's inquisition with a wry smile and said, "In summary, we contend that none—and I repeat, none—of these dubious theories of the punctuated origins and evolution of HIV come anywhere close to the truth, which is readily traceable by a fine-grained genetic analysis."

The coroner did not respond well to Danny's formal conclusion. Pointing his finger directly at Danny, he said, "If none of these popular theories holds water, in your opinion, how is it that so many medical experts in the field of virology have agreed to disagree with you?"

"Agreed upon by authority or consensus is a mighty poor substitute for modern forensic pathology," said Danny, his pockmarked face beaming with visible pride. "I believe that the issue is one of true scientific integrity versus the pragmatic practicalities of official denial."

Chauncey glared at Danny with a cautionary look of disapproval, intending to stifle further criticism. "What the hell does American pragmatism have to do with the price of tea in Africa?"

But good old Danny, bless his histopathological heart, waxed majestic with the sword of forensic evidence in his hand, and he stood his ground like a matador at a Spanish bullfight. I don't know what came over Danny, who usually trembled at the mere thought of rocking the boat, but I can't help but think that Detective Dash Brogan had something to do with it.

"In my considered opinion," said Danny, "after reviewing the totality of molecular, genetic, and epidemiological evidence, I believe that these popular theories represent formalized contrivances: collective propaganda of the medical, the pharmaceutical, and the governmental authorities who have performed a disservice, to say the least, in covering up the glaring truth. When a distinguished official of the World Health Organization diplomatically insinuates the iatrogenic origin of HIV/AIDS as a 'socio-political imposition'— shortly before he is tragically killed in a plane crash enroute to a major AIDS conference—it sends a strong signal to the entire medical community to toe the party line."

"And what, in your considered position, is the glaring truth of the matter?" asked the mayor's man.

"I'll leave that to my friend and colleague, Dr. Cornell Westerly," said Danny as he stepped away from the screen.

In the glare of the slide projector and the light of day, I laid out the pertinent details of the only plausible theory that fit all the genetic, epidemiological, and medical facts of the matter. And it was not a pretty picture. In fact, the iatrogenic origin of AIDS can be proven by anyone so inclined who endeavors to seek and find the true nature of reality. Specifically, a thorough study of the dissemination of an experimental hepatitis vaccine fits all the available data like a glove. It turns out that the human hepatitis B virus (HBV) vaccine was indeed cultured in SIV-infected chimpanzees in the early 1970s, where it was passaged in a manner that is ripe for viral recombination, genetic mutation, and opportunistic changes in infectivity. Official documents prove that human hepatitis B viruses cultured in vivo in chimpanzees were returned to humans whose infected blood serum was then pooled to develop the attenuated strains of experimental HB vaccine that was tested simultaneously in New York City and Central Africa. Low and behold, when you examine the epidemiological evidence for the hepatitis B vaccine hypothesis, and you compare the sequence and timing of the hepatitis B vaccine programs— administered in both New York's gay population and sub-Saharan Africans—with the geographical onset and distribution of the first HIV/AIDS outbreaks, you get an exact match. Add a rigorous phylogenetic analysis of the humanized viral strains, in accordance with the timing of the outbreaks, and you have more than a suspicion: you have a bona fide accusation that holds muster against all the smoke screens and distractions that were promoted to obscure this simple truth. And yet, as important as this hidden truth might be to the future of medicine and humanity, it is a truth that has never been officially admitted to this day.

The scruffy criminal lawyer from downtown stood up and asked, "Just how far up the administrative food chain do you think this official cover-up goes?"

Danny chimed in and said, "Pretty darn far, Counselor. If you take the time to study the fine print on the US Homeland Security Act of 2002, you will find a highly suspicious clause: a vaccine injury indemnity clause that frees pharmaceutical companies from liabilities associated with specific vaccine ingredients. One such stated and indemnified ingredient is the human immunodeficiency virus and/ or its precursors in HBV vaccines."

"That's very interesting," said the scruffy criminal lawyer. "It sounds to me like this indemnity clause is an oblique admission of guilt. Does anyone know who is officially responsible for the contents of this Homeland Security document?"

"That would be the US Congress," said the assistant district attorney. "As I recall, the Homeland Security Act of 2002 was passed virtually unanimously by the Senate as well as the House of Representatives."

There was a distinctive moment of silence following these unsettling pronouncements.

I concluded for the record, by saying, "If the AIDS pandemic was an honest mistake, science and medicine might be forgiven. However, as they sought to bury the truth and dismiss the apparent dangers— as they clearly did in the SV40/polio vaccine debacle—they failed to learn from their mistakes. By failing to improve safety standards in vaccine production facilities, based on their knowledge and understanding of the origin of the SV40 retroviral contamination, they turned a blind eye to the possibility that the mistake would be repeated. It pains me to think that the entire AIDS pandemic could have and should have been prevented!"

The coroner pounded repeatedly on his desk like a courtroom judge, and then he rose from his king-size chair and turned off the slide projector with visible distain. "Even if this convincing accusation is correct, which it just might be, how do you link the iatrogenic origin of AIDS with the AIDS patients we have downstairs on ice? And, more importantly, Dr. Westerly, how does any of this hyperbole fit in with the cancer victims that appear to have been petrified and exhibited for public display by the same Art House Undertakings?"

I looked over to Danny, who was nervous in the service, and to Dash, who nodded his permission. I took a deep breath and let it out slowly, and then I said, "I respectively contend that the perpetrator of all these staged exhibitions is attempting to force these issues of medical misconduct and culpability into the public eye. In what I would call an exceedingly theatrical and artistic show of affectation, I believe we are witnessing the rebirth of highly original Grand Guignol, sir."

"What the hell is a Grand Guignol?" demanded several of the spectators in unison.

"A Grand Guignol is an old-fashioned horror show that was staged in Paris a long time ago. In an intimate theatrical setting, for the purposes of entertainment, firsthand performances of shocking violence—cuttings, burnings, and all sorts of horrific mayhem— were acted out theatrically for the benefit of the vicarious viewing audience. The Parisian Grand Guignol went out of favor after World War II, when vicarious experience of death and dismemberment was replaced by the real-world horrors of the Holocaust."

The coroner returned to the authority of his desk chair, and then he inquired, "And how in the world do you, a young man, know so much about this archaic Grand Guignol of horrors?"

I swallowed hard, as I checked my speech, not knowing quite how to explain. I stood there like a fool, like a deer in the headlights, when I realized that I had no practicable explanation that I could communicate to such an exacting audience. In my silent distress, I looked once again to Dash Brogan, who smiled at me with a gleam in his eyes.

"I think what Cornell is trying to say, Chauncey, is that his uncanny knowledge of this graphic spectacle and its present-day implications might be the result of his intimate association with a certain femme fatale. When it comes down to speculatin' on a man's special talents and aspirations, it is generally advisable to *cherchez la femme.*"

18 Cry Out into the Night

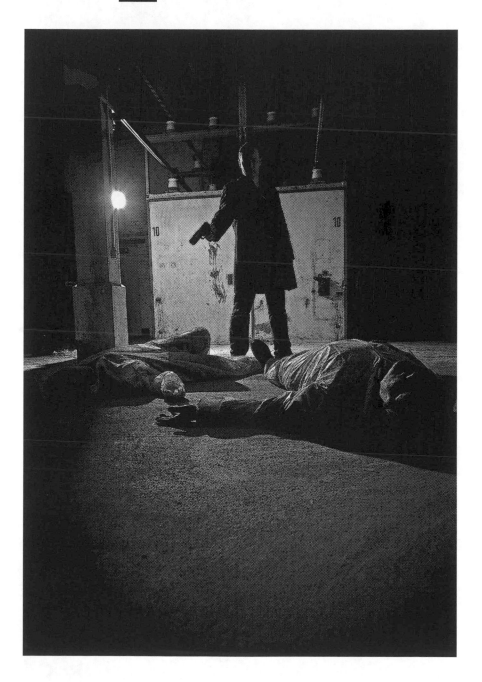

After the coroner's inquest, I met with Dash Brogan to touch base and get his read on the situation as it was or wasn't developing. It was Thursday, and Musso and Frank's was serving homemade chicken pot pie as the daily special. I parked at the Pantages lot and strolled down to the restaurant with an empty feeling and a load on my mind. Dash was sitting at a curved booth with red-leather upholstery, nursing an Old Fashioned. I couldn't tell if it was his first or second; his eyes were steady but glazed. He coughed several times into a napkin. They were hard, raspy coughs that didn't sound good.

"How are you doing, Dash?" I asked as I slid into the rounded cushion of the circular booth. "Did you catch some kind of cold from all that talk about viruses?"

At first, Dash didn't answer; he just smiled at me briefly and stared back into the contents of his glass. He coughed again, lightly this time, and put the napkin back in his lap. He raised his head and spoke to me in a cordial, fatherly tone. "I want you to know that I'm proud of you, Cornell. You've come a long way from where you started."

"It doesn't appear to me to be nearly long enough. It doesn't appear to me that the coroner or the mayor or the district attorney is going to touch this beast with a ten-foot pole."

"You're probably right about that," said Dash. "In fact, I'm pretty sure of it."

"What's going to happen now? Isn't there anything anyone can do? By following our leads and the plastic body parts, we determined the probable causes of death, and we connected the dots to a motive that merits some kind of consideration. I realize that large-scale vaccination programs are sacred cows and always have been. But don't the people have a right to know the truth? After all, it's the taxpayers who have to foot the bill. To deny the scientifically obvious seems like a gross violation of US constitutional, civil, and human rights, as millions of Americans, and more people around the world, have been forced to care for vaccine-injured family members without a shred of compensation. Are we living in the twenty-first century, for goodness' sake, because it sure feels like the Dark Age of Medicine."

"That's a nice speech, son, and I appreciate your passion. But you're preaching to the choir. By connecting the dots from a serial exhibitionist to the powers that be, you and Danny have implicated a few too many complicit officials that are pretty high up on the food chain."

"So that's it? They're going to sweep the whole thing under the rug?"

"Being good government officials, they will realize that this is way above their pay grade. So the answer to that question is yes, they're going to sweep the whole blasted theatrical occasion under the nearest rug."

The waiter came, and we both ordered the Thursday special. I was too depressed to order a drink for myself, so I settled for water and a strong cup of coffee. The meal came and went the way of all meals, and I still didn't feel any better.

Detective Dash Brogan clinked his empty glass against my raised cup of coffee, and he said the most amazing thing: "I realize you're a top-flight scientist and all that, and I'm just an old bloodhound. But I do remember reading something that Albert Einstein wrote some time ago. He said, 'The world is a dangerous place, not because of those who do evil, but because of those who look on and do nothing.'"

Dash Brogan reached into his coat pocket, pulled out a folded piece of paper, and handed it to me. "Here, take this. It's the break you've been waiting for. You still have a murder to solve."

I unfolded the paper and read the handwritten note. "I know

this place; it's a major pharmaceutical distributor just outside of Glendale. But what does this business address have to do with any of our unsolved cases, including the murder of Lauriana Noire?"

"We were able to pinpoint the location of the red Porsche. It's parked in the company lot."

I felt the west wind return to my sails, and my heart started to beat double-time. "Why didn't you tell me this right away, Dash? This is the break we've been waiting for."

"I wanted you to enjoy your dinner," was all he said.

I grabbed my hat, slid out and around, and headed for the door. I didn't have to look back to know for certain—I could feel that Dash Brogan was smiling.

• • •

The first thing I did was to log onto my computer. I had some corporate hacking to do. It didn't take me long to find something unseemly about the history and track record of this leading pharmaceutical distributer. They were indeed involved in the worldwide distribution of HIV-tainted hemophilia blood products, having emerged to prominence after an extended series of confounding mergers and acquisitions that made it difficult but not impossible to link the new corporation with the spate of lawsuits buried in the corporate records.

What I found next was quite disturbing. I found that the federal regulators and the pharmaceutical enterprisers came to an unholy alliance, of sorts. Rather than immediately barring the distribution of the pooled and unpurified blood products completely, the powers that be turned to a rather dubious form of quality assurance. While the regulators officially encouraged the actual purification of the hemophilia blood-clotting factors in time, they altered regulatory compliance to accept concentrated blood products that were determined to contain less than so-many viral particles per milliliter. In defining a practical threshold for viral contamination of pooled drug products, rather than imposing a more stringent ban, the regulators had created a convenient loophole. Considering that it takes only one live HIV particle to infect a given person, this is a loophole that should never have been opened in the first place and, if opened as it was, should have been closed long ago.

I looked into more recent corporate records, and I noticed a curious discrepancy between the distribution of blood products in the United States and the bulk of the international shipments. Is it possible that these guys are still bootlegging blood factors in this day and age? Is it possible that this is precisely what Lauriana Noire was researching undercover, right before she was strangled? I shivered violently at the thought as I headed out the door of my apartment.

It was well past midnight by the time I made it to Glendale. I bounced over a series of railroad tracks on a gravel road that led into the industrial park. I eased my beat-up Bimmer to the side of the road and turned off the engine and lights. I don't know why, but I felt more than a little uneasy as I looked around at the sinister penumbras of shadow and shade that fled from the light of the streetlamps. I reached inside the glove compartment for my .45-caliber semiautomatic and slipped it into my trench coat pocket. You never know when you're going to need your gun, but according to my mentor, Detective Dash Brogan, *when you need a gun, you usually need it bad.*

I made my way stealthily toward the designated parking lot by moving from pillar to post. I spotted the Porsche SUV; it was parked right where Dash had indicated. My anxiety rotated from curiosity to alarm, to terror, as I sensed the presence of danger. My heart beat fast, my breath rate increased, and I could feel the oxygenated blood surging into my frozen muscles. A cold, cold sweat descended upon me at a dizzying pace, and I strained to keep from fainting. Torn between the competing imperatives of fight or flight, I was clearly out of my element.

Somehow, I mustered the strength to forge ahead to the darkness and shadows. I heard the distinctive sound of a diesel engine turning over and roaring to life. The sound of the engine was coming from the rear of the pharmaceutical building. Suddenly, I heard a loud *beep, beep, beep.* It was the sound of a truck moving in reverse. The beeping sounds suddenly stopped, and then the engine stopped, and everything in the world, save my beating heart, was silent.

I made my way to the loading docks, where I spied two men—a thin man and a fat man—standing beside the truck. I stood as still as a statue, leaning against a single power pole, as I watched the two men load a pallet of cardboard boxes strapped together with metal bands into the back of the truck. There was a fog-like smoke emanating from the seams of the shipping cartons. I recognized the phenomena as the sublimation of dry ice that is used in the shipment of perishables. Without any proof, I could only imagine what these guys were shipping in the middle of the night. Whatever the medical-pharmaceutical hell of it was, I was pretty sure it wasn't ice cream.

Perhaps it was the smell of fear, perhaps it was the sounds of my enraged heart thumping against the hollow walls of my chest, perhaps it was the terror of pure foreboding and lost love that cries and screams from a wide-open mouth. Whatever it was that tipped them off, they were now running directly toward me with vigorous energy, defiance, and malice.

When, in the dark of the night, they are coming for you, to beat you, or to kill you, or take you to the gallows and throw you into the lake, you try to move, but you can't. Your body is gorged with fear and unable to budge. You try to stand your ground with dignity, but you can't. So you run, as I ran, as fast as you can, away from the danger, though the terror has made your limbs feel heavy, and you are shivering with fear and cold. You run for your life when the first bullets fly, and your wide-open mind desperately seeks to find some place to hide, some safe passage away from the terrifying here and now, some dark door of escape that you can barely make out, yet you tear it open and dash inside.

I raced into the interior of an empty warehouse, where I stopped and stood stone-cold still. The metal door slammed shut like a trap, like a cage, and I was swallowed up by the dark.

A few seconds later, it was hard to tell, the door was flung open, and two silhouettes—the thin man and the fat man—emerged before me in the spotlight. For a moment, they appeared like two paper targets at the LAPD shooting range, but a moment was all it took. I stood over the body of the fat man and fired one more time. And then, as I turned my gun to take aim at the thin man, a crystalline vision of Lauriana Noire appeared in my mind for an instant in time that was shattered by the sound of my gun.

19 Rendezvous in Shadows

Later that same night, in that quiet span of time that lies somewhere between the darkness of midnight and the dawn of a new day, Detective Dash Brogan and I walked the walk with no regrets. On a night like this, when the darkness folds around you like a blanket, and the marine layer is misty enough to be almost fog-like, you can hear the dark heart of the city beating, murmuring, gurgling in the gutters. You can hear the sound of a thousand voices whispering off in the distance. You can sense that the night has a thousand eyes. You can see Dash Brogan smoking an unfiltered cigarette. You can see him flipping the spent butt out ahead as you watch it arch to the pavement and fizzle out with one last wink. On a night like this, it's not good to be alone.

"I guess I'll have to go downtown and file a report at some point in time," I said in a rhetorical manner as we walked along the empty street.

"There will be plenty of time for you to do that tomorrow, Cornell."

"So you think there will be trouble?"

"Trouble is our business, son. But from what you tell me, and what I already know, you can be sure that your shootings were more than justified—they were inevitable."

"You know I wasn't out to hurt anybody."

"I know that, son."

"I was trying to stop more people from being hurt unnecessarily, to stop the established medical practice of disseminating live viruses to innocent folks. Dash, do you realize that the new wave of up-and-coming gene therapists are hankering to use live viruses as delivery vehicles, or vectors, vectors to deliver therapeutic genes—along with the infectious wee beasties—to unwitting recipients? Even after all we have learned about the protean nature of such resilient life forms and the dangers of such unsafe practices."

"I didn't know that," said Dash sympathetically. "Tell me, why would they do that, son, given the inherent dangers?"

"Once again, the would-be gene therapists, particularly the ones sporting medical degrees, are trying to get away with using cheap and easy manufacturing methodologies that produce high titers of live viral vectors, rather than putting in the hard work and basic research that would be needed to produce inert, synthetic vectors in ample amounts, along with the tissue-targeting components that would yield a better medicinal bang for the buck. The way they're going at it today is no different than what we saw before, and we're bound to have another breakout of something new and nasty and infectious coming down the pipes."

"That's why the world needs people like you, Cornell, people who can't be bought off the case at any price, people who are able to withstand the peer pressure and intimidation that you've endured while striving to uphold and proclaim the highest principles of forensic science. I always said you were a freak of nature, and now I know why I chose you."

"Thanks for the vote of confidence, Dash. It means a lot to me. But I really don't feel that I'm all that special. There are lots of decent scientists around the world who are equally capable but are afraid to speak up. They just—"

"They just look on and do nothing."

"Right."

"That's why the world is such a dangerous place."

We walked the walk to a darker, quieter part of town, passing by a series of brick tenement houses flanked by ominous alleyways.

"Will you be there tomorrow when I fill out the police report?"

"I'm afraid not, son. As much as I'd like to be there with you, it was always my intention to educate you sufficiently in the noble profession of private detection that you would no longer need me to hold your hand."

Dash Brogan coughed hard into his handkerchief; it was a cough that came from deep in the lungs and rumbled worrisomely through the air passages.

"You're going to have to start cutting down on the smoking, Dash. Those unfiltered cigarettes can kill you."

"Whether you realize it or not, son, these cigarettes killed me long ago," he declared unflinchingly, and then he coughed again. "You best get along now, Cornell. Your imported car is parked just over yonder."

I started walking down the street toward my car when I turned back around and said, "Where are you headed tonight, besides to bed?"

"Tonight I'm headed further down the road," he said as he raised his hand to the tip of his snap-brim fedora and bid me a fond farewell.

* * *

I didn't think too much about it at the time. But by the time I got to my car, I knew that something just didn't feel right. A man like Dash Brogan was about as intrepid as they come, and he was pretty well used to traveling alone down the shadowy streets of this aging metropolis from dusk to the dead of the night. But I couldn't help wondering if Dash was trying to tell me something as I turned his last words over in my head. I retraced my steps to the dim-lit entrance of the alley where we had just been standing; there was nothing driving on the street and no one moving on the sidewalks. I looked intently down the cobbled alleyway; it was foggy and dark in places where the feeble glimmer of the streetlamps failed to reach the pavement.

It was here at this crossroad that I suddenly felt all alone. I found myself standing very still, trembling faintly with apprehension—of what? I did not know. It felt like the first time we met, when Dash Brogan reached down and hauled me up by the collar of my trench coat, raising me physically up from the muck and mire of personal despair. I recalled the towering strength of his character in the face of appalling tragedy. It was here, in the loneliness of my life, with my lover dead, and redemption so far away, and nothing but my own tragic hands to guide me, hands that once were guided by the integrity of Dash Brogan and the poetry of Lauriana Noire in a world of common purpose, and now were left to fade and disappear into the common dark of all our deaths. I felt my heart break in general despair and the sense of all those people dreaming broken dreams, shattered dreams, and the immensity of it all—all the loving and caring for loved ones that are lost in a land where they let the children die. I was standing very still, faintly trembling, thinking of Detective Dash Brogan in his moth-eaten overcoat, eyes on the street ahead and bent to the task of uncovering the hidden truth that arises from the darkness and the elusive Art House perpetrator we never found. I was thinking of Detective Dash Brogan.

I looked up and down the block again, and again I listened in vain for the sound of the big man's footsteps. Figuring that Dash had taken a shortcut to his vintage Pontiac Catalina through the dark, cobbled alleyway, I hurried in pursuit.

The walls of the looming tenement buildings that lined the alley were stark and dense with LA graffiti, gangland graffiti in big block letters that were oversized like everything else in this dark city. It is down these mean streets that a man who aspires to the field of private detection must go, a man who is not himself mean and is neither tarnished nor afraid. Following in the unsounded footsteps of my hard-boiled mentor, I could sense the thrill of adventure that belonged to a man like Dash Brogan by right; it belonged to him because it belonged to the world he lived in.

Suddenly, I felt a wave of awareness that startled me. It stopped me in my tracks. This shadowy place that was darker than pitch was a blind alley with no exit. There was no way out, other than the way I had come. It was a dead, dead end where the backstop was painted with the same gangland graffiti, and doors and windows were all bricked up. There was no way out and nowhere to go but back to the cross street. I spun around and around like a whirling dervish trying to make sense of this amazing disappearance. It appeared to me that Detective Dash Brogan might have simply disappeared into the darkness of the night or into the vaporous night air—but that would be impossible!

20 Where Only the Mist Is Real

And that was the last time I saw Detective Dash Brogan, my mentor, my benefactor, my friend. In considering his sudden disappearance, I have to wonder if he even existed at all, if he wasn't simply a figment of my overwrought imagination. Is it possible that I, in my floundering sophomoric attempts to emerge from the dregs of my insignificant life, to learn a new trade and become a man of honor, had somehow resurrected the image and character of a modern-day "Knight-Errant"—the type of image and character that is found in romance literature of the Middle Ages—to pilot me through a particularly challenging and disappointing stage of my life?

But Detective Dash Brogan was such a far cry from the template of the chivalrous hero that tilts at dragons or windmills; Dash was a serious, lonely, hard-boiled man-about-town, a man with a rude wit, a lively sense of the grotesque, and a healthy contempt for foolishness, politeness, pettiness, and the malignant conventions of this modern day and age—give or take a fistful of decades. All I can say for certain, in the confounding high anxiety of my disconcerted mind, is that this modern world of ours—sure as hell and shooting irons—could use a few more men like him.

I know Dash Brogan was right when he reminded me, in no uncertain terms, that the world is a dangerous place in which to live—not because of the people who perpetrate the evil, but because of those who look on and do nothing. It follows that the world is in greater peril from those who tolerate and/or encourage and/or cover up the biomedical evil than those who actually commit it. While I could never pinpoint the true identity of the Art House pranksters we were chasing at the time, I couldn't help but appreciate the sublime theatrics of their artistic efforts and the pathos of the story they were trying so boldly and persistently to show and tell. When I try to point an accusing finger at the medical, pharmaceutical, and governmental officials who have allowed these dangerous practices to go unchecked for so many ears, I find that there are too many to count. There are far too many "perpetuators" of the biological dangers who have looked on and chosen to ignore the basic premises of quality control—that being, (i) to identify the problem, (ii) to earnestly, scientifically investigate and report on the problem, and (iii) to make decisive changes in methodologies and protocol allowances that would ensure and protect the public from such extensive iatrogenic harm. And who do you think is ultimately responsible for the conduct of so many "perpetuators"? If you really want to know who is to blame for looking on and doing nothing in these modern times, you might as well look in the mirror.

I never saw Isadora Vanderbilt again after that. I hear she moved back to Paris. As much as I will miss her company, her companionship, and her feminine charms, I find some pride and consolation in the strivings we once shared, those urgent, mutual strivings that served to focus my attention on the bigger picture, that awesome *thème noir*, which rises and breathes beyond the myopic purview of the written words. Sometimes I get a sinking feeling that I was used to do her dirty work, a pawn for the femme fatale. But in my heart, I know that she was truly a wonderful lover, glamorous and sincere in every way, and in my strident desire to please her, I found that my whole world was expanded. Yes, Isadora, *there are spirits in the darkness riding horses of the wind*, and in my fondest dreams of you, we're riding with them again.

Still, here in the exquisite darkness and intrigue of another night like this, when the fog rolls in heavy from the coast, when tender thoughts and memories form in the mist and drip like raindrops onto the cobbled pavements of my troubled mind, I can feel the presence of time itself moving on and on as I watch the fleeting reflections of my life turning over like the final pages of a book. I can feel myself crossing over the deserted streets of the city in a haze: I can feel myself crossing over another street, another boulevard undefined. I follow the echoes of my footsteps, and they lead me on to another crossing, another street, another *calle,* and I can feel my mind, or what's left of it, crossing over onto yet another street … where only the mist is real.